BUTTERFLY
LOST

BUTTERFLY
LOST

DAVID COLE

HarperCollins

HarperCollins

10 East 53rd Street, New York, NY 10022-5299

ISBN 0-7394-0787-2

Cover design and illustration by Peter Thorpe.

Printed in the United States of America

Visit HarperPaperbacks on the World Wide Web at
http://www.harpercollins.com

For Deborah, Rosie, and Harry

ACKNOWLEDGMENTS

All writers have patrons and angels. My special thanks to Bob Gates and Nancy Priest for continued support, including detailed critiques of earlier versions. This book wouldn't have been possible without special knowledge and encouragement by Johnstone Campbell and Caryn West. Cynthia Dagnal-Myron always kept me on track about Hopis, assisted by Thandi Myron. Thanks also to my friends and contacts in Tuba City, Tucson, and Flagstaff; to Karen Strom for her love and knowledge of native American writers; to John D. Pierce, my agent Amy Kossow, and the HarperCollins gang of Carolyn Marino, Robin Stamm, and Jessica Lichtenstein.

AT THE EDGE OF
THE FOURTH WORLD

A giant Kachina stood just inside the rusted screen door.

Head cradled in his left hand, his shoulders thrust against the beamed ceiling.

Blue prayer feathers stuck in thick, flowing black hair.

Come, Patrick, he said.

Why?

Travelers, the Kachina said.

Seeking the Home of the Dead. We must protect them from Powakas.

Two Hearts? Patrick said. *Witches?* he said.

Come.

The Kachina beckoned with his right hand. He backed outside, rusted hinges squeaking like mice in the winter corn. They left the ancient stone house and they flew over cornfields and peach trees, above and beyond ancient stone villages on the three Hopi mesas until the Kachina pointed down at hordes of travelers, gaunt, haggard with fatigue, begging for food and water. They were staggering under gigantic bales of firewood; serpents braceleted and struck their arms, scorpions thrust into their thighs, hundreds of cholla thorns pricked the soles of their feet, their armpits, their genitals. All these punishments for bad things done to others, or maybe just for speaking up against rain.

They flew until they landed upon a high desert plain.

Someone sat motionless behind the wheel of a derelict, completely stripped pickup truck. No tires or rims, no hood, no doors or tailgate, the engine throbbing at full speed, a throaty pulsation, the enormous power of a diesel semi double trailer, shifted down into crawler gear, muffler blatting as it climbed full out up a three-mile hill, the longbox pickup bed overflowing with girls and women of many ages, all bearing enormous scars or bruises or wounds or holes through their bodies, some carrying their hearts, livers, a hand, fingers, their heads.

The Kachina pointed toward the south.

Many creatures moved toward them at tremendous speed. As they drew near, Patrick saw they were young maidens with butterfly sworls of black hair braided behind both ears. Some of them were being ridden and spurred by five winged creatures with sharp beaks and enormous erections. As the women passed Patrick saw their faces clearly, and he was astonished that he knew many of them.

Four of the creatures drifted by, but the fifth circled above him, above the pickup. A woman came out of the pickup cab, her fisted right arm extending, stretching upward, striking the creature and then plucking him from the woman he rode, the arm swinging like a lasso and throwing the creature beyond the horizon.

Astonished, mute, Patrick saw the woman settle into the now empty pickup bed, and the pickup drove away. The other creatures returned in a long ellipse, and the dust of their travel rose, filled the air, swirled around until they passed, and then things

changed.

Patrick lay awake in a pool of sweat. The faces swirled through his head, and he was afraid because it was the same vision as the last three nights, and the elders had made no more meaning of it than he did, except they believed him unquestioningly and asked him to describe the girls and name those he knew.

He searched among the sheepskins for Gra and No Pictures Boy, his two great-grandchildren from Walpi on First Mesa. They came every week to hear about Kachinas, about the first four worlds and the coming fifth world after the *bahanas* destroyed civilization with their material ways.

Both children were gone.

Patrick levered his arthritic body off the sheepskins and shuffled outside. Thick, dark warrior clouds shrouded the moon. Someplace along 264 a semi downshifted before a curve, the muffler blatting until the sound faded off east toward Second Mesa.

Patrick bumped into Gra. Crouched at the edge of the house, staring around the corner into the darkness, she jerked Patrick's arm, wanting to lead him somewhere, but he told her instead to take him to the outhouse.

Once there, he decided against going inside and stood to urinate beside a rock; but he couldn't get started because Gra continued to tug at his arm, so he let her pull him toward the edge of the trail down toward the cornfields.

There, she hissed.

They walked slowly along a path that led to the shrine. Suddenly ahead of them something moved, and they saw the remaining shreds of moonlight flicker against bare skin where No Pictures Boy crouched on a large boulder. Farther down the path a light flickered.

Massau, Patrick told Gra, *guarding us this night. He carries a torch.*

No, she said, having roamed the aisles of Bashas' supermarket in Tuba City.

A flashlight.

They saw something long, flapping, maybe a wing.

Two wings.

It's a bird! she hissed. *At the shrine.*

Powaka! His heart trembled. *Two Heart.*

Head buried inside the shrine, the bird feasted on sacred food, on *talaotsumsime* and *aloosaka.*

Gra whimpered.

The giant bird pulled its head from the shrine and stood erect. It was huge, its wingspan six feet or more. Patrick fell against a rock, banging his elbow. It bled.

This is not dreaming, he said. *This is not dreaming.*

Rocks skittered against rocks. The bird twisted its head around, and the shaft of light swiveled up from the shrine and pinned No Pictures Boy against the clouds.

A sharp cry.

No Pictures Boy was airborne, arms outstretched, flying over the edge of the boulder toward the bird and

the bird jumping sideways far enough so that No Pictures Boy twisted his body sideways to catch the bird
but could not and landed upside down, bones crunching, all in one heavy thud, and from the boy's mouth an
almost indistinguishable sound, a long sigh, a light
summer breeze with no force or power beyond the sigh
of its passing.

The bird hovered over No Pictures Boy, touching
his body, lifting his head.

Gra whimpered.

The bird cocked its head at the sound.

Listen to me, Patrick told Gra. *If he sees you, he will
carry you away.*

She wrapped both arms around his legs.

*If he takes you to his kiva in the Red Rock Place, if he
asks you questions, who is your secret father?*

Taiowa, she whispered.

And your secret mother?

Corn Mother.

Now run, he commanded her, forgetting to whisper.
The bird heard them, and the light beam locked on to
Patrick's face. Gra darted off. The bird set the boy's body
down and flew up the side of the mesa.

Patrick tried to run but tripped and fell backward
heavily. Despite the darkness, and without slowing
down, the bird roared directly at him. Patrick tried to
push himself away, scrabbling backward on hands and
feet. The bird sought him out, hovered over him, wings
rising above his head, descending, encircling Patrick's
shoulders, embracing him. Patrick's heart stopped, and
he died without light or hope.

And then the bird took off its wings.

It knelt at Patrick's side.

It cradled his head.

Hoy.

Someone stepped out of a house, shouting.

The bird rose up, slowly, wings drooping to one side. Falling to the ground.

Wingless, the bird ran away into the night.

1

Two black-chinned hummingbirds swooped down from a cottonwood, the male's pendulum courtship arc bottoming out near the open kitchen window of my double-wide trailer.

It was almost seven, and the temperature was already above ninety degrees. A momentary southwest breeze rustled the cottonwood leaves, carrying an unusual promise of late morning June rain. Nearby, a dog caught the metallic smell, his bark raising a cloud of western meadowlarks whose flutelike sounds echoed as they swarmed to one and then another cottonwood. Other dogs crawled from underneath sagging trailers and partially dismantled pickups and went yipping up and down the dirt-rutted street, dust rising in sworls as they marked their territories.

I swallowed two Ritalin pills with some orange juice.

The aluminum trailer roof and side panels crackled and banged as they heated up and expanded against their corroded rivets. I closed all the windows, set my three air conditioners on high, and connected my laptop modem into a cloned digital cell phone. I punched in a number, and after the connect beep to Las Vegas I nestled laptop and phone carefully inside a cardboard box and loosely folded the tops shut. I pulled a T-shirt over my faded red X-strap sports bra and changed my running shorts for lightweight khakis.

I carried the box and my 7X50 marine binoculars outside, then settled back lazily onto one benched side of the redwood picnic table. Donna Whitehair sped by, waving hello, late as usual for the lunch shift at Kate's. I knew no other neighbor except Ella Bekaye, who lived four trailers down. I'd see Ella about five in the afternoon, on her way to the evening shift at the motel, and see her again maybe again at eleven when she walked back. I lived on a quiet street with little traffic, but just in case somebody stopped to talk, I kept the cardboard box closed.

My cloned cell phone worked illegally out of a Utah switching center. I'd rigged sniffers and data traps in a Vegas TV billing records computer network, trying to identify a bail bond fugitive who was a sports and gambling freak and had to have cable TV to figure his odds. His bond was fifty thousand. I'd been tracking him for three days and hoped my cell phone battery would last long enough to stay online until the search ended.

I'm an information midwife.

I find people who believe they'll never be found.

I never meet them. I just sell their secrets.

I don't ever *want* to meet them.

Using computers, I crack into networked databanks, gleaning unlisted phone numbers, bank accounts, credit card histories, airline travel itineraries, telephone and medical histories, records of birth and death and marriage and divorce and supermarket shopping purchases, anything to compile in electronic dossiers and hawk to those willing to pay my fee. I could find almost anybody who thought they'd skip out and remain untraceable. I never advertised, never solicited work, rarely had an unsatisfied customer.

Everybody leaves traces.

You just have to know where to look.

I stretched out flat on the table bench, the wonderful morning sun hot on my bare shoulders and legs, the sky high and clear and intensely blue like glazed ceramic. The breeze stopped for a while, and I heard the hummingbirds clicking to each other and the male swooped down. I lay motionless, following their flirtation until the breeze came up again, urging them unwillingly past the irregular line of cottonwoods marching beyond my trailer into Claude Lansa's junkyard. I rotated my head to follow their hink-jink path above clumps of larkspur, heron-bill, and red Indian paintbrush, finally losing them past some chuparosa and into the junkyard, where two people stood talking to Claude, who, at that exact moment, raised and cocked his left arm and brought it down like a hatchet chop toward my trailer.

As the two people started walking in my direction, I sat upright and focused the binoculars on them. An old Hopi and a young girl, maybe ten or eleven. I thought right then I should get up and go inside. But it was *hot*, you see, with that high, cloudless sky, so I just held them in my binoculars as they came toward me. The girl walked a foot ahead of the Hopi, his left hand resting on her right shoulder. She wore a faded flower pattern dress and what looked like plastic Spice Girls thongs. Her adolescent body, slim and brown with faint traces of developing breasts, had grown halfway between caterpillar and splendor.

Moving past the mound of tires and rusted rims, the two of them threaded their way among the maze of derelict, rusted, partially or completely wrecked pickups, cars, vans, four-by-fours, junkers of many models and years. The sun was directly behind them, and their shadows stretched out forty feet long as they walked across the junkyard, the thin, dark pointers eventually flickering across my face. Reaching the rows of purple and blue corn bordering my lot, the Hopi caressed the stalks with his fingers, nudging them aside reverently.

Weeks later I realized that that was the defining moment of the whole summer, that kind of moment when things change irrevocably, against your wishes, the memory of *before* remaining persistently invasive, no matter how hard you try to forget.

Nothing would have happened if I'd just gone inside my trailer and ignored him. But I was too satisfied with just being in the sun, too deliciously absorbing heat and color and sound, too unthinking about consequences, to bother moving. So I put down the binoculars, watching, wary but passive, as they came right up to the picnic table.

"Are you the one who finds them?" he said.

His face was creased, lined, leathered, neutral, and

expressionless. He could have been fifty or eighty years old, his breath asthmatic but steady, his body stocky and muscled. A traditional Hopi headband of faded red cloth wound around jet black hair cut at mid-ear length except in front, where short bangs hung over his forehead. He wore an old but clean long-sleeve blue cotton shirt, faded denims, and old black Nike sneakers, and he carried a plastic Bashas' Supermarket bag.

He took his hand off the girl's shoulder, and she immediately began stretching her neck and arms and legs in vague dancer's movements. Without asking, she picked up my binoculars, held them vertical with one lens to her right eye, and scanned round and round the driveway, lighting finally on a small pile of pebbles. She set the binoculars on the table and sat down to begin sorting the pebbles by size and color.

"You *are* Miss Laura Winslow?" the Hopi said politely.

"Yes," I said.

"You're the one who finds the girls?"

His wide-open eyes were as black as navy peacoat buttons.

"I only do that for the high school," I said. "And they're closed for the summer."

"Yesterday, I went over there. I talked with a Missus Tso."

"Billie Tso? The guidance counselor?"

"She said *you* would help."

I had a contract with Tuba City High School to run computer searches in an attempt to locate teenage runaway girls who fled the Rez for brighter lights and bigger cities. Girls who hated reservation life, girls who were bored or curious or in trouble or just plain bad. These girls were my soft spot, my social weakness, my one public flaw in an otherwise mostly private life. My own daughter disappeared when she was only two, taken by my ex-husband to some place where despite repeated searches I couldn't find digital tracks of their existence. She'd now be in her early twenties, but I'm still unable to grant her adulthood, having progressed only to admitting that she could be twelve or fourteen years old. By looking for other missing girls, I kept alive my hopes of finding Spider.

"Who are you trying to find?"

He frowned, not yet ready for such a direct question. Hopis' conversations are incredibly circular with people outside their families or clans, responses withheld while they explore the entrails of the stranger's words for signs and possibilities.

"What's your name?" I asked, trying to get him talking.

He pulled off his headband and wiped his neck and forehead with the left cuff of his workshirt, trying to decide how much he could reveal. After putting the headband back on, he settled the knot over his right ear and nodded.

"I am Abbott Pavatea. From Lower Moencopi. My granddaughter, she was supposed to graduate from the high school. But she left a couple of nights before graduation and hasn't been home since."

"Graduation was two weeks ago."

"I thought she'd come back," he said shortly. "She didn't."

"Okay," I said. "What's her name?"

He opened his mouth to speak, his lips moving with no sound as the unspoken name hung in the air, crackling and invisible like static electricity. I realized Abbott couldn't say the name because he believed she was dead. I stretched my arms tighter across my breasts as tears streamed down his face. For a long beat I couldn't hear the barking dogs or even the whistle of his breath, his fathomless black button eyes locked on me like those of a coyote with a lamb in sight and nothing in between them but hunger.

The young girl came up behind him and carefully wiped away his tears.

He fumbled in the plastic bag for a cheap wooden picture frame holding a faded Polaroid. He held it out toward me, but two feet off to my right, and I suddenly realized that he was blind. I cleared my throat. He moved the frame in front of me, and I took it.

A young, good-looking Hopi girl's face, powdered with sacred cornmeal. Black hair carefully done up in butterfly whorls on each side, signifying she was eligible for marriage. My hair looked like that once. Most women on the mesas called them squash blossoms.

"She looks kinda young to be graduating from high school."

"It's a few years old. Four years. Maybe five."

The girl pushed up her hair on both sides, trying to duplicate the butterfly whorls.

"Where did she live?"

"She grew up in Oraibi. A couple years before this picture was taken, she moved to my place in Lower

Moencopi. She always had a hard time with our ways. Last winter, she moved into a house here in Tuba with a bunch of other kids. Said she had to be in a place with cable TV and the like."

I nodded. *Bahana* culture was constantly available on the Rez, bombarding young reservation women and eroding clan and tribal distinctions. MTV, movies, videos, dances, drugs, magazines like *Cosmopolitan* and *Glamour* passed from girl to girl, crinkled and dog-eared articles about Madonna, the dead Diana, Janet Jackson, a hundred other young women glowing with the tides of fashions, jewelry, sex, money. *You Too Can Have Multiple Orgasms!* All these influences urging them toward Flagstaff, Las Vegas, Phoenix, LA. Anywhere. Outta the Rez.

I ran away when I was fifteen.

My father tried to stop me, but in those days I was reckless and saturated with rebellion, and one afternoon when Daddy wasn't home my boyfriend, Jonathan Begay, came by in a brand-new Dodge pickup. He stole it, he said, and I didn't think he had that much nerve, but I never found out the truth. Come on, he said, let's go see the elephant.

"How long has she been missing?"

He didn't seem sure what he could trust telling me.

"The other kids, where she lived. Did you ask them about her?"

"They don't know nothing. Nobody knows where she is."

"Do you have *any* idea where she might have gone?"

He shook his head reluctantly.

"Mr. Pavatea, it's really, really hard to find runaway teenagers. Does she have a Social Security number? Has she ever worked? Does she have an Arizona driver's license? Does she have family or friends in big cities. Phoenix? LA? Has she ever been to a doctor or clinic, someplace she'd leave medical records?"

"Why are you asking me all these things?"

"To find somebody, I need to have some personal data."

"Data?" He frowned at the alien word.

"Identification. If they leave records, I can track them through computers."

"Computers?"

He didn't know that word, either.

"I can't find anybody without personal data. Bank account records, telephone records, medical treatment, credit card activity, stuff like that is what I need to start looking. But without any data, there's not much I can do."

"All I know is that one of the elders at Oraibi had a vision last night."

Just then the Ritalin kicked in. *Jesus, I love the way it focuses me, like a magnifying glass pinpointing the sun on a dry leaf until it bursts into flame.* I fought against a smile.

"You're here because of somebody's vision?"

"Patrick Valasnuyouoma. He saw many girls in trouble."

His hand went to a small sack of corn pollen hanging around his neck.

"Girls with Powakas."

"Powakas? Are you talking about witches?"

"Two Hearts. Yes. Patrick also saw a woman in his vision. She reached out one hand and squeezed a Powaka until he was dead. The elders, they told me that one of the girls was my granddaughter, and that the killer woman was you."

I was incredulous.

"You're saying I was in an old man's vision?"

"Yes."

"And, in this vision, I killed somebody?"

"Yes."

"These witches," I said shortly. "What were they doing with the girls?"

Blood flushed quickly through his face.

"Riding them, like they were animals."

He leaned forward and grasped my hands, something so unusual for a traditional Hopi that I started with surprise. Just as quickly he released my hands and, embarrassed, stuck them underneath the table, where they touched my knees. Now he'd completely lost his composure as he worked his arms around until he felt comfortable with them extending outward, resting his palms on the table edge. I knew how difficult it was for him to have said even this much. But as much as I'd have liked to help, I could only see myself disappointing him further. I wished he and the girl would leave. He sensed my lack of enthusiasm.

"Is it money you want?" he said with some heat, his Hopi passive-aggressive nature shifting abruptly. "I hear you make a lot of money, finding people."

"That's just gossip."

"Well, that's how people tell it. That you don't work for free."

I doubted that he knew much of what I did or who I really worked for. People don't come to me off the street. I'm not in the Yellow Pages, and usually I'm contacted through e-mail or phone cutouts. So it's odd, you see, that he was talking about money, because there's always the possibility of entrapment. Law doesn't like what I do.

"The high school pays my expenses," I said finally.

"Okay. I have six hundred and fifty-three dollars."

He fumbled in his right jeans pocket for a wad of bills held together by a blue rubber band. He dealt out the bills on the table like a game of solitaire. Twenties, tens, fives, the rest ones, his fingers fluttering over the bills, urging them toward my hands reluctantly, as though they'd been in a coffee can for a year or two and he couldn't really bear to let them go. The breeze gusted and sent several bills soaring. The girl dashed after them. I watched her collect the bills, her fingers squaring them into a stack, waiting for a signal from him.

"Is that enough money?"

"Yes, that would be enough. But, tell me, how do you know she's really missing? And these other girls. Were they friends of your granddaughter?"

"No. Not friends. There's just talk about them. From other villages."

"What kind of talk? Do you know any of their names?"

"No," he said carefully, already deciding he'd told

me too much. "Others can tell you more about them.
They're waiting to tell you."

"*Who's* waiting?"

Jesus, I needed a crowbar to get anything out of
him.

"The elders."

"What elders? Where?"

"In Oraibi."

"Oraibi? On Third Mesa?"

"You can talk to them this morning."

"You want me to go out to Oraibi? I don't know
anybody there."

"Find the *kikmongwi*, Johnson Pongyayanoma.
He'll tell you what you need."

The girl rifled the bills like a deck of cards, turning
her head slowly sideways until it rested on her shoulder. She fanned the bills and then put them behind her.

"All right. Where do you live in Moencopi, in case
I need to ask more questions?"

"Just ask in the lower village for Abbott Pavatea."

"Give me a phone number. I'll go to Oraibi and call
you later if I find out anything. And where did she live
in Tuba City?"

He fumbled two folded scraps of paper from his
shirt pocket. One was a receipt from the Tuba City IHS
pharmacy with his phone number. The other was a
hand-drawn map of northern Tuba City, streets I'd not
heard of, with an X marked on one of them. The girl
tugged at his shirtsleeve, and he nodded.

"Wait," I said. "First, you have to understand that I
can't guarantee anything. Second, you have to under-

stand that I only look for information. I do *not* work
like a detective in some TV show. I'm not licensed to do
anything like that, nor do I want to. I will *try* to find
information about her, but I will give that information
to Billie Tso. Third, I want to borrow that picture. Can
you leave it with me?"

Nodding agreement, Abbott gave it to me, carefully
folded up the plastic bag, and stuffed it into the right
front pocket of his jeans. As the girl reluctantly handed
me the bills, I sat back so she'd have to get close, so that
I could touch her hand as I took the money.

"What's your name?"

I smiled into her expressionless face, watching a
small green fleck dancing in her right eye, willing her to
smile, to acknowledge me.

"I have a daughter about your age. Her name is Spider. What's yours?"

"She can't talk," he said.

I wasn't sure if he meant *can't* or *won't*.

"You still have a name," I said to her. "Can you
write it on the ground?"

She knelt to the sorted pebbles and swept her hand
across them to wipe out all trace of her presence. She
pulled at his arm to leave. He rose and stepped backward,
facing me. She spun him gently around and led him down
the street.

I picked up my laptop and the binoculars and went
inside the trailer. Propping the Polaroid against a jar of
instant coffee, I studied the young face, thinking, He's
blind, she's dumb, I'm probably a fool. Checking the
laptop, I saw the download was complete. I discon-

nected the cell phone and went to change my clothes.

The front part of my trailer included the kitchen and dining alcove and was set off from the rest of the trailer by a steel partition dressed with Sheetrock to make it look ordinary, except the single door had a key-punch combination lock above the handle. Inside the workroom, red lights glowed on opposite sides of the trailer, two long worktables holding up six computers, a laser printer, four telephones and a bank of tape recorders, two police scanners, an all-band radio, several cell phones, and a fax machine. A gun rack held a .30-30 lever-action Winchester, a twelve-gauge pump, and a scoped M-16.

Manila folders lay stacked everywhere underneath Wanted posters tacked haphazardly onto the fake walnut paneling amid a sea of color photos of dead and gutted horses, some in color, others in black and white, all of dead horses. For the past year, my primary customer was Ben Yazzie, a licensed Arizona bounty hunter. I'd find bail bond fugitives, he'd track them down, and we'd split the 10 percent finder's fees. We worked the Four Corners states, southern Utah down into Arizona all the way to the Mexican border.

It had been an extremely profitable partnership until the November before, when somebody began mutilating Rez horses and the Navajo Tribal Council eventually posted a $100,000 reward for the horse killer. We dropped everything else for seven weeks as I carefully hacked into NCIC, VICAP, and other government databases, looking for patterns. But killing horses wasn't a federal priority. Ben dreamed of claiming the high reward, but his failure to find the horse killer just drove his compulsive nature until he dropped bounty hunting; finally, when I had no money left to pay for trailer and equipment rentals, I went back to tracking fugitive locations for a Flagstaff bail bond office.

I still ran database searches for him, but he'd not called me in seven weeks.

Shrugging out of my clothes, I wet a cloth and quickly wiped my face and armpits and stepped into panties, a tube bra, and a yellow haltered sundress that hung almost to my ankles. Slipping into sandals as I moved past the open closet door, I caught sight of my mirrored image moving beside me, and I stopped and tilted my head to the left, chin down a few inches in an ancient ritual. Thousands of women tilted their heads in front of mirrors, teasing, combing, spraying their hair, and lipsticking and glossing as they caught themselves growing old in three-quarter profile.

Back in the kitchen, I saw Claude Lansa outside, waiting respectfully for me to show myself so he could talk.

"Morning," I said from inside the screen door.

Less than five and half feet tall, Claude stood so straight that you figured he was six feet tall or more. Because he worked a lot lifting junk parts and tires, his upper body was as solid as a pile of stacked concrete blocks. Thick muscles roped his neck and arms, and when he was nervous, like now, the muscles seemed as tightly wrapped as a bundle of rubber bands. Since he always wore sweatshirts with the sleeves ripped off at the shoulder, the slightest movement of any one muscle set the others in play, rippling up and down his arms so that sometimes he splayed his fingers out tight as though he could flick off the tension like drops of heavy water.

"So he hired you?"

"Yes. To find his granddaughter. I'm going out to Oraibi."

"You going out on the mesas?"

"Yeah."

"Well now," he said, cracking his knuckles. "I just don't know about that."

Claude looked down at his grease-stained junkyard hands. He wasn't a reservation Hopi, didn't completely have their aversion to talking with strangers, didn't even seem to have many limits about what he'd discuss with me. In all of Tuba City, he was my only male friend. But this morning his concern for me was out of place. He had something he wanted to *avoid* telling me and yet couldn't hold it back.

To give his conflict some working room, I stepped back to the kitchen counter and grabbed the cell phone and a bag of sugar doughnuts. Not knowing how long I'd be gone, I uncapped the Ritalin vial and popped two more into my mouth; I bent under the faucet to drink water, my head turned sideways, and as I looked at the Butterfly Maiden, I thought, No, don't do this. But I'd already taken his money, and more important, I'd given my word. Doughnuts and cell phone under my arm, I double-locked the trailer door.

"Whyever he came to see you, it ain't just for finding his granddaughter."

"Claude, what's the problem?"

"People are talking."

"Who's talking? About what?"

Unwilling to answer, he let himself get distracted by two teenage boys walked noisily down the street, hauling saddles and roping gear, both of them tall and lanky, almost indistinguishable right down to their fake pearl snap-button western shirts, except one was blond and the other a redhead.

"Claude. Is there something about Abbott Pavatea I should know about? Something about his granddaughter, is that it? Did you know her?"

"No. Didn't know them. I just don't like what I been hearing from the mesas. People from out to Oraibi and Walpi, those places, where they don't want nothing to do with the Tribal Council and the Hopi Rangers. People out there sending whispers down the lane about girls missing from their homes, their villages. Girls taken by Powakas."

"Claude, that's just gossip. Abbott told me there might be a connection between his missing granddaughter and other girls from the mesas. Have you heard *any*thing that's more than gossip?"

"Guy from Hotevilla bought four winter tires from me last Sunday. He's my mother's clan. Told me there's talk in the kivas about girls and Powakas."

"Forget about witches," I said derisively. "Did you hear anybody's name?"

"No names."

Seeing my '86 Ford step-side pickup, the boys turned exuberantly into the yard. The blond kicked the

Ford's right front tire while the redhead tried to open the hood.

"Hey!" I said. "What're you doing there?"

"We heard there was a junkyard over to here," the blond said. "Heard there was junkers for sale, and I see we found one. Our pickup broke down, axle or something, and we ain't got time nor money to fix it up. We're headed down to the Flagstaff rodeo, gotta get there and register afore ten."

"We're *bull*riders!" The redhead grinned proudly.

"You're just walking now," Claude said.

They looked at each other, and the blond reached into his jeans pocket.

"Give you fifty for this junker. Not a dime more."

The step-side's paint was faded and chipped, the body dinged and scratched everywhere, no different outwardly from a thousand other reservation pickups; but Claude had beefed up the suspension, and under the dented hood was a totally rebuilt 460-cubic-inch engine with dual carbs and a supercharger.

"Over there's the junkyard," he said, waving across the corn. "Look for an '81 Chevy longbed, rust brown."

"Whoa. This ain't the junkyard?"

"This here's this lady's pickup."

"Ma'am, excuse us, lady, ma'am. No disrespect, but"—trotting off with their gear as they burst into giggles, nudging each other—"sure looked like a junker to us."

Claude picked up several large pebbles and worked his hands together over them as I moved toward the pickup. I'd never seen him so agitated. I punched the gas pedal, revving the engine to blow out the carbure-tors. When I started to back up, he ran beside me, banging on the door metal until I stopped.

"You be careful."

"Claude," I said gently, "nothing's going to happen."

"Maybe," he replied reluctantly, disbelief hardening his gaze. "But don't let them tell you about Powakas and Two Hearts and such."

"Don't tell me that *you* believe in witches."

His knuckles whitened as he squeezed the pebbles, and I realized that he *did* believe.

"Rain coming up," he said, flinging aside the peb-bles as he pointed westward at the San Franciscos, the sacred mountains, where the sky billowed dark with bruised, heavy bands of rain streaking diagonally toward earth.

"Don't drive too fast. Them tires will skid on wet road."

I pulled out into the street, wrestling the steering wheel hard to the right until the trailer and Claude's anguished face disappeared from both side mirrors.

2

Lightning bolts flashed behind the inverted triangle atop the Hotevilla water tower.

The pickup's headlining had rotted away, and raindrops crackled like marbles on the uninsulated metal roof. Distracted by memories and by the noise just inches above my ears, I almost drove past the green sign at the Old Oraibi turnoff. I pumped the brake pedal *hard*, trying to make the right turn and skidding clockwise, the pickup floating on the slippery blacktop, right side wheels rising two inches off the pavement until I got some control just in time to get all four wheels down and stand on the brake pedal to avoid slamming into a row of fifty-gallon steel drums and a blurred, unreadable hand-lettered sign.

Shaking, I got into neutral and lifted my foot off the brake and started *rolling backward, Jesus Christ!* stopped dead and straddling the middle of 264 at right angles to the yellow line, fear rising as I popped the clutch and stalled. I cranked the starter until the engine raced, wanting *off* the blacktop before a semi broke through the curtain of rain.

Inching up snug against the sign, I checked the

misted side mirrors to make sure my rear bumper was completely off the blacktop. My headlights parted the rain curtain just enough to illuminate a plywood signboard propped against one of the drums.

WARNING!! WARNING!! WARNING!!
NO VISITORS!! NO OUTSIDERS!!
YOU HAVE FAILED TO OBEY OUR LAWS AND YOURS!
THIS VILLAGE IS CLOSED!!!!

After pulling my sundress up over my knees into my lap, I yanked on the hand brake, my left foot heavy on the brake pedal as I sat there listening to the rain, lightning veins threading all around the truck. The Ritalin revving my blood, my heart pounding, I punched the gas pedal all the way to the floor, the engine screaming louder than the noise from the raindrops, and I screamed right along until my fear finally subsided, steam rising from under the hood and the oil pressure gauge going crazy. I eased my foot off the gas pedal and sat quietly for five minutes, listening to the rain until the lightning moved eastward and my anxiety lessened enough to slow my breathing.

It's no small thing, I tell you, to go home again after twenty years.

But in truth the memories no longer had their terrible powers, and I couldn't resist banging the horn ring, exulting that I had come back and it was okay.

Behind the seat I found my Detroit Tigers baseball hat and put it on to keep water off my head as I got out and rolled two drums aside. Raindrops slanted like bullets, exploding like shrapnel in the pooled ground water. Sopping wet, I scuttled back inside the cab. Even with both windows rolled up against the flood, water leaked in through the front vents and doors. Because the morning temperature was already in the high nineties, the inside of the pickup steamed like a sweatlodge.

Double-clutching down into first gear, I drove slowly past the drums onto the Oraibi turnoff road. The pickup slid in and out of watery ruts, which, after twenty feet, deteriorated into several wide dirt tracks fanning outward along the hardpan toward the edge of Third Mesa. I bucked and jolted across stones and through puddles, the deluge subsiding enough to let me see a concrete block building off to the left of a large sign for Old Oraibi Crafts with an arrow at the top, black quills and arrowhead pointing toward the right.

I inched past the sign and passed between the main village houses, some built from concrete block and others from centuries-old slabbed stone partially surrounding a ladder sticking out of the top of a kiva.

How old *was* that ladder's wood? How old *were* those stone slabs in houses without plumbing or electricity or TV antennas, some houses nobody knew how old except some anthropologists who measured time according to meticulous studies of cross-sections from the house's wooden beams. The rain intensified, shrouding everything beyond my windows. I flicked on the high beams, the two cones of light quickly diffusing in the heavy rain.

The only lights on Third Mesa, the only lights in the world.

I shook my head, flicking water everywhere inside the cab. Somebody was shouting, but I couldn't see anybody and barely heard the voice because of the rain, the words indistinguishable as I inched forward. Suddenly something *spang*ed noisily off the hood, and I saw a long groove, sideways left to right, paint stripped right down to metal. A young Hopi rose up suddenly, two feet in front of the pickup, rain cascading off his thick black hair onto a blanket over his shoulders. I stomped frantically on the brake pedal to avoid hitting him. He raised his left hand, palm flat against me, his right forearm swinging the blanket open and the sighted tip of a rifle tilting up, the muzzle pointing at *me*.

"Go . . ." *Furious!* A gust of wind tugged his words away.

I rolled the left window down halfway so I could hear him. A thick rope of water curled inside the cab and ran over the dashboard, cascading on my thighs. I opened my mouth to talk, but he shook his head violently, anger contorting his face.

"Village closed to you."

He stepped backward, swung the rifle to full horizontal, pointed somewhere between the headlights and my face. A gust of wind rocked the truck. I goosed the accelerator, thinking I'd get in reverse and back away, but he mistook the revving engine for a signal that I intended to move toward him, and *bam! bam!*—he shot out both headlights.

I switched off the engine.

Three men came running, and I rolled my window down all the way.

"I'm Johnson Pongyayanoma," one of them said.
"I'm the *kikmongwi*."

"She's got no call to be here," the rifleman shouted.

"It's all right," Johnson said quietly. "It's the woman
we've been waiting for."

The rifleman hesitated, came closer to stare in the
window. He was barely a teenager, anger stretching his
lips into a string-thin line. The gun muzzle dipped
inside the window, and Johnson's hand immediately
clamped on the barrel and forced it up.

"People are really angry," Johnson said to me, "and
they don't know just yet what to do. Please, forgive a
young man's anger."

He took the rifle away from the boy and walked
him ten feet away, where they talked briefly. The rainfall
slowed as the storm moved east. When Johnson refused
to hand him the rifle, the boy trudged off reluctantly
toward the highway.

"He's enchanted with a young AIM group. They
think they can move into our village, they think they
can protect us. We do not welcome them. Come with
me."

Acknowledging the apology with a nod, I climbed
out of the pickup. I didn't want to show my feelings,
but *Christ!* I was *really* angry. Lightning struck repeatedly east of the village. I lifted my face toward the rain.
Fat, warm droplets curved along my forehead, on my
arms. I palmed water in my hands and splashed it
across my face and took out a sugar doughnut just to
give me something to do.

"Why is the road blocked off?"

"All in time. Come with me."

He led me past toward a house near the edge of the mesa, motioning to the cluster of people outside to let me in. A body lay on a rough-veneered table. Several women were talking about preparing yucca suds to wash the body, but everyone quieted immediately as I appeared just inside the door. My tongue worked nervously to clear pieces of doughnut stuck inside my front teeth as we all stared at a body lying faceup on sheepskins.

"Who's that?" I said dumbly.

"His name is Patrick Valasnuyouoma."

Clad only in his rust-colored long underwear, right temple crumpled and bloody, lips drawn back in terror, eyes wide open, his skin frail and wrinkled and *gray*, Patrick Valasnuyouoma looked as old as Oraibi itself.

"Please," Johnson said. "I know how confusing this must be. You came to hear his vision, and you are shown a horrible sight. But first, there is something even worse to show you, and then I will explain everything. Come."

"Excuse me," I said quietly. "I don't think these people want me here."

"I apologize for this horrible experience. Our village is sad and anguished. But you are here for a purpose, to which we have agreed. Come, now. Please."

Outside, several dozen people had gathered, facial muscles taut, lips compressed, some quivering with anger at my presence. Johnson murmured something, and the crowd parted reluctantly to let me walk forward. We trooped along a muddy road to the edge of the mesa and started downhill past stone slab houses with huge chunks of black, shiny coal stacked along-side penned-up sheep. Beyond the houses the ground leveled out at the edge of the cornfield, where a boy's body lay doubled almost completely backward over the top of a rock, his spine snapped cleanly in two, arms and legs spread wide apart.

Thick streaks of blood coagulated on the rock, and although the rain had already washed most of the blood into the ground, I turned my face from his dreadfully mangled body because I recognized him.

During the summer tourist season, No Pictures Boy patrolled Highway 264 on his old Schwinn coaster brake bicycle, every day pedaling from Oraibi east all the way past Shungopovi to where tourists would stop and point their long lenses up toward Walpi on First Mesa, where families had been living continuously in the same stone houses for nearly a millennium. The boy harassed all tourists, shouting, "No pictures, no pic-tures!" and shaming the tourists, who'd quickly rotate their cameras toward a bush, saying they were just nature lovers, just taking pictures of creosote bush while they hastily climbed into their vans and alu-minum cocoons to get away from him.

Two men waited for word from Johnson. He nod-ded, and they stood tenderly on each side of the body, putting their hands underneath the boy's shoulders and knees. Johnson turned to me.

"Now. If you could leave us, just for a while."

"Why did you make me look at this?"

"It's all connected. I wanted you to see him, but for

now, please go back up to the village. I'll be along. Wait
for me."

He saw my hesitation, my fright, my anxiety, my
complete confusion.

"Please. Trust me."

I walked back upslope and sat down near a house,
slumping wearily against the stone wall, closing my
eyes, marveling that I was back on the mesas of my
youth.

My mother ran off with a rodeo calf roper when I
was four. Once my father learned that she wasn't just
another Vegas white *bahana* hooker, but had Hopi
blood somewhere back in her past, he brought me back
to Hotevilla to stay with my mother's clan. Accustomed
to bright lights, television, and the excitement of the
rodeo world, with lots of people at all times of the day
and night, I rebelled against the ancient village, but my
father made sure I stayed there with my mother's sister
while he was away on the rodeo circuit.

Something pricked my arm. I looked up at a young
girl, about four, a bag of piñon nuts in her left hand, her
right hand holding out a twig. She saw me watching her
and turned away, scratching her twig in the dirt. She
was like a cat that wants you to pet it, but then turns its
back to show that it knows you're there but it really
doesn't care.

"Gra," a woman called to the girl, "don't do that."

"It's okay," I said.

"She's bothering you."

"No, really," I insisted. "Please. It's okay. Let her stay
here, if she wants."

I smiled at the girl, understanding exactly what was going on. The girl had poked me with the twig to see if I was asleep or dead.

The most terrifying thing in all the world is the fragility of life as you helplessly watch it disappear. I'd learned this well, watching the Hotevilla village elders when they fell as quiet and still as the thousand-year-old stonewalled houses. Because I had a childlike confusion between the worlds of explosively sudden rodeos and the timeless Hopi villages, I found an uncertain balance by watching the elders. I wanted to be there at the exact instant when one of them died, when maybe something would spring or fly or sigh from the body, something as friendly as a passing bird, or maybe a Kachina that would appear for an instant, something grand and unimaginable and terrifyingly quick.

There were several ancient men for me to watch. I spent time outside their houses, not standing back, usually hunkered down nearby, watching them, never sure about things when they got so quiet because sometimes they just slept or, like all old men, nodded in and out or were consumed with suddenly recalled memories, about which they talked continually. All of them loved children in the way of most Hopis, and they eventually grew comfortable with my solemn, silent presence and would smilingly wave me closer.

Thomas befriended me more than the others, probably because he was nearly blind and able to distinguish only between light and dark. He had huge cataracts in both eyes. These could have easily been removed over at Tuba City. One of the elders even had some plastic lenses put in his eyeballs over at Flagstaff, and it took longer to drive over there and back from Third Mesa than to do the operation. But operations were useless for Thomas, who had been born with retinitis pigmentosa, a condition he hardly understood beyond the certain knowledge that his retinas would slowly be eaten away. So he loved to follow the after-noon sun, his face precisely and unerringly positioned toward the heat, like a stage actor seeking a single spot-light, or a mayfly hungering for the last kerosene lantern.

I marveled at how he knew I came around. Bare-foot, I hardly made a sound and attempted to muffle the slightest swish of my foot, careful to kick no pebbles. Then it got to be a game. At first I signaled him as I grew near, sometimes clicking a stone against the walls, sometimes squeaking like a mouse in the winter corn. Like most blind people, he knew the sounds of life about him, knew with certainty when I watched him, so we developed casual rituals that became daily rou-tines.

As Thomas and I became inseparable, he'd tell me about the four worlds and the different clans and Kachinas and the dances. Every day I watched and talked with him, placing food and things within his reach, even guiding him to the outhouse poised at the edge of the cliff rocks, standing outside and talking to him while he pissed and shat. But I watched him most carefully in those times of silence and stillness in his ladderback chair, when nothing moved except maybe his right arm, trembling, a palsy that came and went, unpredictable, something in his brain that wired the visions to whatever controlled the arm and hand. In these moments I studied only his head, awaited the time when he no longer swiveled his head to track the sun's passage, to keep warmth on the clouded eyes.

Footsteps clicking on stones. Johnson appeared beside me and beckoned for me to follow him into an old stone-block house. Parts of the ceiling had fallen in, there were holes in the wall, and the wooden roof timbers looked shaky. Ducking inside the low doorway, I saw smooth spots worn on the latch side, just at that place where for hundreds of years somebody's hand had reached for steadiness to open the door. Johnson pulled a candle stub from a pocket and after lighting it screwed the stub into the sand floor. The house was completely empty except for several things lying on the dirt floor in one corner of the main room. Pieces of a sandwich, an empty bottle, a crumpled paper sack. A stained yellow rain slicker. A faded brown canvas carryall.

"We found the slicker this morning," he said, starting to touch it and then pulling his hand back. "On the edge of the mesa, near Patrick's body."

"And the bag?"

"Here."

"Why would somebody leave it inside the house?"

"Somebody who hid in here until night."

"How could any stranger possibly be here without somebody from the village challenging him? And if anybody drove into the village, people would see the car."

"It was dark, it rained, people sleep. We don't know how he got here."

"What's in the bag?"

He zipped open the carryall and pulled out a long plaited rope. Part of it was knotted into a loop, with two battered cowbells threaded inside the loop. I fingered the rope. A brief spasm of raindrops hit against one of the dirty windows, and I shivered with memories from the rodeo circuit.

"My father had ropes like this," I said. "I remember playing with them, trying to jump rope, and one time . . ." He whipped my butt with the rope, I remembered, but I wasn't going to say that.

"Do you know what it's used for?" he asked.

"bullriding, calf roping, bareback bronc riding . . . I don't really know."

Inside the carryall, I saw two blunted spurs, rowels wired tight, a leather glove, and two boots that were badly creased and worn. I pulled out the boots. The insteps were taped with gray duct tape. Inside the left boot, a man's name had been burned into leather.

Albert Grody.

"Why did you keep the slicker and bag hidden in here? Why are you showing them to me now? And how did those two people die?"

"Whoever was hiding here last night, we believe, somehow, he caused their deaths. But we don't really know. We just know it is all connected with Judy Pavatea. And you."

"I don't understand how you can say that. *Why* are they connected?"

"Because of Patrick's vision."

"Ahh, well. Dreams."

I shrugged, held up my hands, palms up, waggled my fingers, wondering how to avoid getting further involved.

"Visions are not dreams. We truly believe that Patrick's vision shows that all that has happened is connected. The girls, the Powakas. You."

He told me the entire vision, word for word, just as he'd been told by Patrick two nights before, and then word for word the story from Gra about Patrick's last night. Finished, he watched me fidget.

"I don't believe it," I said finally.

"It doesn't matter what *you* believe. Will you help us?"

"I gave my word to Abbott Pavatea to come out here and try to learn something about his granddaughter's disappearance. Beyond that, well . . ."

"Miss Winslow, this *is* about Judy Pavatea. And *all* our children."

"These other girls. What are their names?"

"Since they are of other clans, other families, other villages, I cannot tell you. Others must make those decisions. If they give me permission, then I *will* tell you. But my belief is that in finding Judy, you will open the portal to finding the others."

"The high school always gave me full details. The girl's family, her relatives, her picture, *everything*. But I can't find people without even knowing their names."

He sighed and slumped on the floor.

"Most of us who believe in the traditional ways, we are getting old. We have so few children to pass our life to. Little of our life is written down. We pass it on by talking, by dancing, by Kachinas, but we don't have many children to hear about the four worlds. If we do not care for our children, no matter how wild and unbelieving they may be, if we do not care, our whole way of life will die out as surely as corn without water."

"The boy. How is his death connected?"

He hesitated for a long time, measured his secrets against my evident disbelief that any other girls were involved and against what outsiders must never know.

"Sacred things have been taken. The boy tried to protect a shrine."

"What was stolen?"

He sighed.

"Four *talaotsumsime*. Two *aloosaka*."

"What do they look like?"

"Very small, made of cottonwood. I can't describe them exactly."

"How can I find an *aloosaka* if I don't even know what it looks like?"

"I know that you don't believe me, but you *will* know them."

The slicker caught my eye. I pushed it away, and it fell flapping to the dirt floor like a yellow shadow. I picked it up again, holding it by both shoulders and shaking the sleeves before setting it on the table.

"I'd say that a short man, wearing this slicker, with these sleeves so big, they'd probably flap around if he waved his arms. If you saw them flapping from a distance, especially if your eyes were bad, you might think you were looking at a big bird."

Johnson's eyes widened.

"Go to the tribal office at Kykotsmovi. Give it to the Hopi Rangers."

"We will not deal with them. Only with you, because of Patrick's vision."

"They could send it to forensics to find out if all this blood was Patrick's or from somebody else. It might be evidence. Please. Take it to Kykotsmovi."

Unwillingly he folded the slicker, avoiding the blood spots.

"And while you're there, please try to find out if there's any reality in these stories about missing girls. I'll go ask the same thing at the Tuba City Navajo Police Station."

"Don't do that! This is none of their business."

"You have to let me do whatever I think needs doing. Work with whoever can help me. Don't involve me in tribal politics. Don't make rules about what I can and cannot do."

"Others in the kiva were against you. They said you would want to work with the BIA and the Hopi Rangers, but I said that you would work only with us. They argued with me for hours until I convinced them."

He smiled and pulled a crumpled ball of twine from his pocket.

"I told them that if they wanted to argue and grumble, only this much would get done." He held up the end of the twine, an inch of it blackened with red dye. "Then I wound the twine four times around the inside of the kiva and said if we hired you, you could do more in the outside world than any of us. So they agreed to pay, but in any case, they chose to believe you would help because you are Hopi."

"I am *not* Hopi. You don't know anything about me."

"Your father was Hopi. Your mother was Hopi. I remember you well, I remember all your family, since your mother's mother was my aunt. How could I forget? You think that with another name you can deny who you are. But you can't run from your blood."

He suddenly put a hand between our faces, peering between his fingers.

"For a moment, I saw your mother," he said, smiling at the memory. "She danced beautifully, she made the best blue corn *piki*, she helped anyone who asked. She would not have taken my money either. And then your father took her away, and she changed."

"You might have known them, but you don't know me at all," I said bitterly.

"Ah, I would astonish you with how much I know. About life with your father. About how he went on the rodeo and disgraced your mother. About how after she died he brought you back to live in Hotevilla, but you ran away with Jonathan Begay and had a baby girl. About how Begay got mixed up with AIM, then got into more trouble, took your baby and disappeared, and that for many years you've had visions of finding your daughter, and that to keep that vision alive you help find other missing girls."

"I do hope to find her, but that's not a vision."

"Do you see her face before you? Can you deny believing that your daughter is still alive, still healthy and wonderful, still waiting to be with her mother?"

Yes, I thought, and he read the affirmation in my face.

"So you also follow a vision."

"Not like you mean. Listen. You know too much about me. I don't like people talking about my private life, so please don't say these things to others."

"You cannot run from your family, from your clan, your blood. You are named Kauwanyauma. Butterfly Revealing Wings Of Beauty."

"Don't *ever* call me that name. I didn't believe in Hopi ways then, I don't now."

He recoiled in shock.

"As you wish," he said finally. "Wait here."

He returned with a faded Bass shoebox bound by a wide rubber band. He opened the box, then removed and held out a stack of bills.

"Abbott gave you enough money to get you here, but we agreed to pay you more."

"This is way too much," I protested. It was almost $3,000. "You don't seem to understand that I can only find information. Whatever I might learn, somebody else must go looking for her. I don't do that kind of thing."

"Yes," he said. "I know that is what *you* believe. Take the money. We only hope that you become the woman *we* believe you to be."

"I won't take it unless I earn it."

After shutting the money away in the box, he led me outside into a burst of sunshine.

"So how is it? Coming home?"

"Please," I said. "Don't do that. You have a way of insisting that the past is the present. This isn't home to me. I spent ten years of my life over there in Hotevilla, but it was a *bad* ten years, and I ran away from it."

"Then why did you move back among us?"

"Money. Nothing else but that. I know how to find out things that people down here want to buy."

"As you wish."

"Yes! That's all I wish, that you see my being here as nothing more than business. I know how to do something. You're paying me to do it. Are we clear about that?"

"As you wish," he said again without defiance or sadness.

He walked toward the house where the women washed the bodies with yucca suds. Carryall heavy in my hand, I hesitated and then went to the edge of Third Mesa, where I stood on a rock ledge with a two-hundred-foot drop below me. I looked westward toward the Hotevilla water tower, and without warning my body began to quiver. I felt dizzy, my thighs wobbling uncontrollably, my knees knocking together as my ancient anxieties returned. Almost hysterical, I wanted to jump so badly that I could hardly restrain myself in my frantic desire to fly away, to escape, to be free.

Then the most amazingly unpredictable thing happened. My thighs stopped shaking, and my confidence returned. For years I'd had to force myself not to go near a balcony, a railing, a precipice, willing myself not to rush to the edge and jump and *fly!* And now I stood deliberately and provocatively on the absolute edge of the rock, my toes extending into space, staring at the high desert floor hundreds of feet below me with no apparent panic, no apprehension, no fear. Exhilarated, I thought I'd finally convinced myself that height no longer terrified me, that I was free of tradition and memory.

And so we deceive ourselves, the better to keep our beasts in their cages.

3

After driving past the Navajo Nation Tribal Police substation for the third time, I finally pulled into the parking lot and sat there, switching the engine off and on, off
and on.

I'd spent twenty minutes looking for digital information about Judy Pavatea. Aside from an Arizona driver's license, there were no records of any kind about
her. Although I could tap into a wide variety of illegal
data pools, I doubted any of them would give me something useful. Billie Tso wouldn't answer her phone, and
the Tribal Police were the only other local resource.

I'd never been inside their substation, but what
worried me was that I had no idea what they might
know about me because of my computer hacking,
which always skated back and forth across the edge of
what is legal and what is not.

I'd not told Johnson the whole truth about moving
to Tuba City.

The year before, in Yakima, somebody discovered
my hacks into Washington State bank accounts, and I
left at three in the morning when I came back from an
all-night bar and saw the unmarked van with unmis-

takable tracking antennas on the roof. I abandoned
everything I owned. Clothing, computers, identity.

I knew how to change who I was, and I did.

I backed out of the parking lot. Mistake to go in
there.

Still uncertain what to do, I drove past the high
school stadium and up through the streets lined with
HUD houses toward Billie's place. But at the intersection before her street I remembered that I'd put the
small map Abbott had given me in the glove compartment and pulled it out. None of the streets were named,
but Tuba City wasn't all that big, and I worked my way
past a boarded-up concrete block building on the last
paved street to a dead-ended dirt road and a line of six
connected single-level row houses, all of them unnum-
bered, their front yards marked off by three-foot-high
chain-link fences.

Abandoned pickups lay haphazardly outside the
fences, propped up with jacks or concrete blocks where
the wheels had been removed. An old Chevy Citation
rested on a makeshift trailer next to a heap of different-
size tires, some still on their rims. I parked beside a cor-
rugated tin workshed and walked along the chain-link
fence toward the end house. The chain-link gates for
the last three houses were either locked or rusted shut,
and the windows in all three units had the front curtains drawn. Climbing over the fence at the end house,
I went up to the door and knocked, expecting an echo
from a cheap hollow core door, and was surprised by a
solid *thunk*.

Nobody came to the door after I knocked several times. I jumped over the fence to the next house and looked closely through a small crack in one set of curtains, which were backed by unfinished plywood. Deciding I'd misread Abbott's map, I started to leave when a door opened at the other end of the row and a young Navajo woman came out, cradling and breast-feeding a baby in one arm as she lit a cigarette.

"Hey there," I said.

She jerked her head toward me and fumbled with her screen door, dropping the cigarette in her haste to get back inside. By the time I got to the house she'd already shut the inner door, but I banged on it until it opened and a Navajo biker stood silently inside the screen. He was small and solid, wearing only yellow running shorts. Alligator tattoos ran up and down his arms and chest, and his stomach was covered with nested tropical birds and what looked like Zuni fetish animals.

"I'm looking for a girl. Used to live here, her father said."

He stroked his long black hair, pulling it around his neck as a woman might so that it lay against his chest.

"Judy Pavatea. That's her name."

"She don't live here no more," the woman said from inside.

"No," he said quietly without turning his head. "You're wrong about that."

He pushed open the screen, came outside, and closed the main door behind him. "I been here eight months," he said. "There've been some girls, stayed overnight at a party, but that's all. Coulda been her, but nobody named Judy ever lived here."

"How about her, inside? Would she remember?"

"No."

His eyes roamed all over my face and nowhere else, not threatening, but intensely probing, as though he wanted to peel back my face to get at why I was asking questions.

"Okay."

I backed off to the gate, keeping him on the outer edge of my vision as I got into my pickup and drove to the corner and turned right, went up the block a hundred yards, turned around, and came back down to the corner. He was still there. I stopped dead in the middle of the intersection, marking the street and the houses. On the roof of the very end house a tall ventilator stack rose alongside a cottonwood. I'd never cooked metham-phetamines, but I'd seen enough labs to know a fume exhaust stack.

I drove directly to the police substation.

A silver Lincoln Navigator, bristling with antennas, pulled up beside me, but the woman driver stayed behind her heavily tinted windows, a cell phone clamped against her left ear. Switching off the engine again to get out of the pickup, I decided that I'd treat them as a data resource that might possibly have some leads. My hand near the doorknob, I hesitated again, drumming my fingers against my thigh, uncertain, con-flicted. Finally I blocked off my paranoia and opened the door quickly.

Inside, the worn linoleum floor smelled of industrial cleaner, and I skidded on a wet spot before catching my balance. A policeman sat behind a wooden desk, reading the *Navajo Times*. He was unusually tall and lanky, and his uniform shirt hung loosely around his too thin and rounded shoulders, as though he'd spent his youth hunched against December winds, watching the family's sheep. A metallic tag over his left pocket read WILLIAM BENALLY.

"Excuse me," I said politely.

His eyes came up to me from the newspaper, and his body froze, his anger vibrating in the room like swarming bees, like August lightning. People aren't rude in Tuba City. They may not talk much, or may talk a lot without revealing anything, but Benally's rudeness was a red caution flag.

"I'm here about a missing girl."

Benally reluctantly picked up a ballpoint pen, peeled a yellow sticker from a pad, and stuck it on the desk in front of him.

"What's her name?"

"Judy Pavatea."

"Pavatea. That's the Hopi girl."

He crumpled the yellow sticker and dropped it into a trash can.

"Can't help you."

"You said, 'That's the Hopi girl.' What did you mean?"

The back office door opened, and a lieutenant came out with another Navajo.

"So there's nothing you can do?" he said to the lieutenant.

The Navajo was big boned and big chested, his black hair cut short, back and sides cropped close to the skull. His khaki pants were frayed around the pockets, but pressed and clean. He wore a white shirt with a blue-and-red Saveway patch sewn on the left pocket.

"Kimo, I'm really sorry that my closing down the Saveway store is gonna cost you your job. Nothing personal in this. I just do what the Tribal Council tells me."

"Sure."

He walked past me, his head swiveling so that he kept looking at me until he almost bumped into the door and reached out to steady himself. His left hand was misshapen, two fingers bent in different directions and covered with scar tissue.

"I know you from somewhere," he said.

His right eye was black, but the left eye was flecked with greenish spots that danced as he blinked, the flecks astonishingly alive, like a kid's marble, like a fortune-teller's crystal ball. Like the eye of the young girl who came with Abbott.

"Not likely," I said.

"Was a long time ago."

Shrugging, he left the door open for the Navigator driver. In spite of the heat she wore a long-sleeved beige silk blouse, a yellow scarf, and dark brown silk slacks. Hooking her right index finger on the bridge of her sunglasses, she pulled them down just enough to peer inside the room, and I recognized her face from one of the Flagstaff TV news programs. She looked different off camera. Something about the perfection of her cheekbones, her nose too straight, too cosmetically perfect.

"Lieutenant Yellowhouse?" she said.

"Yes."

"I'm Shiyoma Lakon. Channel Thirteen, Flagstaff."

"No statement," he said.

"I haven't asked anything yet."

"I know who you are," he said neutrally.

"Any statement about what happened last night in Kayenta?"

"What *did* happen?" he said.

"Forgive me, Lieutenant." All those wonderful, straight, smiling, and beguiling white teeth. "I don't believe you. I've got press releases from Window Rock."

"Then don't bother us."

"Okay, but maybe I'll be back."

"My pleasure, ma'am."

She left. Yellowhouse, shaking his head in disgust, stared at me.

"You another reporter?"

"No," Benally said before I could speak. "This is Yazzie's partner."

"*Ben* Yazzie?"

Yellowhouse focused directly on me, not smiling now. He was shortish, barrel-chested without any gut, nose like a hatchet blade in an expressionless face drawn so tight, you could strike a kitchen match into flame.

"We're not partners," I said. "I'm not a bounty hunter."

"She feeds him information," Bennaly said to Yellowhouse. "They do work for Marvin's Bail Bonds, down in Flag."

"What's your name?" Yellowhouse asked.

"Winslow. Laura Winslow."

"Is that true, what he says? You work with Ben Yazzie? What do you do, if you're not a bounty hunter?"

"I look up records and things."

"Computers," Benally said. "I hear that's what she does for him."

"We don't even have a computer," Yellowhouse said. "Tell me, did you help Yazzie find the Tso brothers last March?"

"No," I said, trying to remember that name.

"After that freak snowstorm, Yazzie found them up near Kayenta and took them to the Flagstaff jail. I said we had jurisdiction, but he took them anyway, and they wound up down in Florence prison. Did you get a percentage of his fee?"

"No."

"Don't get me wrong. The Tso brothers had three felony convictions staring them right in the eyeballs. They deserved prison time. Quite a coincidence, you being here today. Did Yazzie send you over here so he wouldn't have to come in himself?"

"I only came to report a missing girl."

"That so?" he asked Benally, who nodded, clearly wanting to say more. "I know that you help Billie Tso, over at the high school, looking for this girl or that one. I like Billie. Our mothers are both Turning Mountain People. That's a good thing you do for her, and we're all grateful. Guess I didn't really know that you used computers to do that. Normally, I'd help you any way I could, but you coming in here today, that's some wild coincidence. Where's Ben Yazzie?"

"He's in Phoenix," I lied quickly.

His eyes widened slightly and his nostrils flared, just for an instant.

"You sure about that? He wasn't here last night?"

"No. He doesn't live at my trailer, you know."

"Where *does* he live?"

"Somewhere in Phoenix."

"Then give Officer Benally whatever details you've got about this missing girl."

"Lieutenant," Benally said impatiently, "she's asking about Judy Pavatea."

Yellowhouse had his left arm halfway to his head, and it froze there, hand open and extended to me as though in welcome, like a plastic Colonel Sanders. He removed a folder from Benally's desk drawer and shuffled through the papers. One fell to the floor, and as he picked it up I saw front and sideways police photos on an arrest record.

"Well now. You'd better tell me, what's your *real* interest here about Judy?"

"Her grandfather, Abbott Pavatea, hired me to look for her."

"Why didn't he come in here himself?"

All three of us knew Abbott would never go to a Navajo police station.

"Do you know Judy personally?"

"Never met her."

"Did Abbott say anything to you about Judy about her lifestyle?"

Lifestyle?

"About selling drugs?" he added.

Where was this going?

I immediately thought of the exhaust vent stack in the row houses, and my eyes must have flickered because he noticed my reaction and cocked his head.

"Gang involvement?"

"Gangs? In Tuba City? Why are you asking me these things?"

"'Cause you look like you've got something you want to tell me."

"Not at all."

"Okay. Then let's leave it at that. We'll deal with Judy and you just go on home."

"No. Wait a minute. Are you saying Judy was involved with gangs and drugs?"

"I will tell you there's an APB out for Judy, issued by the Flagstaff Sheriff's Office. Now you tell me something. Was Yazzie anywhere on the Rez last night?"

"No. He wasn't. Why do you keep asking me about him?"

"Thank you for your time," Yellowhouse said, not unkindly. He went inside his office. Benally picked up the newspaper, holding it up so he wouldn't have to look at me, but he snapped it open so hard that it ripped in two.

"Marvin and Albert Tso were Living Arrow People. My clan brothers," he said coldly. "Yazzie handcuffed them right in their mother's hogan. That's disrespect for my clan, disrespect for my people."

"I had nothing to do with it."

"You're his partner. That's close enough for me. And if I find out that Yazzie was up in Kayenta last night—"

He bit his lower lip, realizing he'd said too much but almost unable to be silent. Wanting *out* of there, I stepped backward without looking and slipped and fell heavily on the wet linoleum. He leapt around the desk.

"You all right?"

He knelt and duck-waddled closer to me, his body coiled like a rattlesnake on hot sand. I saw a small triangular-shaped scar in the hollow of his throat.

"You all right?" he said again, but this time it was a different question.

He put his face close to mine and looked into my eyes, and I realized he was checking my pupils for signs of drug use. His eyes followed me as I stood up and backed away from him. Reaching for the door, I spread my fingers open and saw they were shaking. I touched the door handle, and a chill ran through me because I was afraid the door was locked, that he'd never let me out. You can't know that feeling if you've never been locked inside a cell and doors won't open to your touch. I twisted the door handle and it moved freely, and I backed outside.

A long RV with Missouri plates, a Honda Civic in tow, partially blocked off my pickup. A woman climbed down from the passenger captain's chair and pointed a camera at the building, the flash winking in the bright sun.

"Excuse me," she trilled. "Is this the Jim Chee building?"

I scraped past the RV, leaving a streak of blue paint along its side as I wheeled out of the parking lot, turning left without looking at traffic, and headed toward the red light. Horns started blowing. The light had changed, and I didn't notice it until people started pulling around me, a woman throwing me the finger from a Dodge convertible. I slammed the pickup into first gear, not even looking at the light as I popped the clutch and accelerated; but the light had changed to red again, and I had to stand on the brakes to avoid a Porsche Carrera hurtling through the intersection, *fucking tourists!* With horns shrieking I popped the clutch again, the drive wheels chattering on a patch of gravel and the rear end swaying—*Christ, I was angry*—weaving through the intersection, one hand smashing the horn button *out of my way!* the seat belt biting into my left breast as I accelerated up through the gears and bulled my way through traffic, releasing pressure on the horn only when nothing was left in front of me. I was now hurtling east, but just past the road into Moencopi I swerved violently and braked hard because two bodies lay along the right-hand side of the road. I got out of the pickup and ran back to find they were just drunks, Tokay bottles littered beside them, one man's arm lying in friendship around the other's. I sat beside them and sobbed until one of them sat bolt upright and vomited, and then I went back to my pickup and stared at the Moencopi cornfields a hundred feet below without actually seeing anything; my gaze moved over cornstalks, vegetable plants, and fruit trees in irregularly shaped family plots, with cottonwoods lining the damp soil along Moencopi Wash, none of it registering as I worked through what I should do with my promise to Abbott Pavatea.

Overhead, a red-tailed hawk dipped toward the

two drunks in a lazy spiral. I shrank back against the pickup, feeling suddenly vulnerable.

Your father was Hopi. You are his blood.

My father was trash, and yes, I'm of his blood, but I'm not trash anymore.

Have you ever felt that you've finally put the miserable bits of your life behind you and started happy all over? And if not happy, at least satisfied, with pockets of joy most days to get you past those patches where memory leaks through?

If we do not care for our children, no matter how wild and unbelieving they may be, if we do not care, our whole way of life will die out as surely as corn without water.

Gra poking me with a stick.

"This is *not* helping me."

Take too much Ritalin and, without realizing it, you start talking out loud, the words always a surprise when you catch yourself. Don't worry about talking out loud, a therapist once told me, unless you start *answering* yourself out loud.

I twisted my head back sideways, sun heating my closed eyelids, counting to myself. *One Mississippi, two Mississippi,* and as high as you can go without losing track of counting. An old trick a rodeo bullrider once taught me, back when nobody knew how to make me concentrate and I'd spurt from one thing to another, sometimes fidgeting in midsentence or halfway home in hopscotch and wandering off to skoosh bugs or, later, to find whatever boy wanted to poke at me. Restless, impulsive, impatient, quickly bored, quickly stimulated, according to one doctor. Low self-esteem,

underachievement, difficulty getting organized, no fol-
low-through, attention deficit disorder, *Jesus*, those
doctors, until one started me on Ritalin and I found
focus and life slowed down to something manage-
able—no, not just managing but enjoying as I survived
all those transient years, transient rooms, transient
lovers.

I admit I abuse it sometimes.

But dex, speed, crank, meth, those are abusive *illegal* drugs. I have a prescription for methylphenidate,
another name for Ritalin. It's a controlled substance,
entirely legal and proper and doesn't cloud the senso-
rium. There's always another tiny white pill and then
another, but too much Ritalin is like fifty cups of coffee.
Your mind stutters, repeats things, your fingers tremble
at the keyboard, veins throb in your temple, you're
fucking *invincible*. Too many Ritalin bring hallucinations, like a hot wind, a Santa Ana, a ghibli, the hottest
wind you've ever felt blowing inside your veins, the
wind of hummingbirds' wings in fall-yellowed cottonwood leaves, the wind of every man I've ever known
exploding inside me, their suddenly old memories
falling away like dead leaves.

To get Ritalin in Tuba City, I had to see an IHS therapist, and after I ran through twelve refills she made
further prescriptions dependent on my joining a support group. Don't *ever* let somebody tell you that therapy is a con, a ruse, an expensive path to avoid reality.
Ultimately you know that therapy works when you're
able to channel your anger into something useful, even
something just diverting for the moment, to defuse the

anger. You never *never* lose your memories, you just learn how to deal with them.

"Yoooooooooo, sweet mama!"

Horn blaring, a Ford supercab flew by. In the pickup bed, stretched among three saddles, the young cowboy called, his voice trailing behind with the dust as he waved his right arm lazily, twirling a loop and flinging it out past the tailgate toward me, his carefree exhilaration unexpectedly flooding my spirit. I stood in the middle of the road until the driver noticed me and braked hard over to the shoulder.

Standing on top of his saddle, the cowboy waved for me to get in, and I actually took several steps toward him as I'd done many times in those early years, when I all wanted was food and a ride somewhere else and a night inside somebody's sleeping bag.

The downside of Ritalin comes when you're tightly focused, *really* focused, but when you take another and another your blood roars way too fast and you hallucinate and you get, well, I tell you, it's like watching the sun set over blue water, but as the sun gets lower to the horizon the water changes color, blue maybe purple maybe green, and you can't *name* the color, you only feel it; there's no word, just a feeling, and if there're no clouds and you stare stare stare *one Mississippi two Mississippi* at the red sun at the exact moment it plunges below the horizon, there's this green flash, just for an instant, and your bones shiver. You can't give it a name because there's no real words, no words at all to tell what it's like to be ferociously *alive* as you channel all your purposes, hopes, ambitions, dreams, everything channeled into that green flash.

I counted and counted and narrowed down my purpose to one thing.

Find Judy Pavatea.

"Come on, mama."

The pickup had stopped on the shoulder. He beckoned me toward him.

"Flagstaff rodeo's calling. Let's ride 'em, mama, let's ride."

I shook my head with a smile, waved at him, and started back to my own pickup to go visit Billie Tso.

4

"Why are you asking me about Judy Pavatea?"

Billie Tso's exquisite silver squash blossom necklace lay over a full-sleeve green velveteen blouse. We sat at a round patio table behind her concrete-block HUD house, moving our rusted steel chairs into shadows from time to time to escape the late afternoon heat. My pitcher of iced tea sat on the table next to her bottle of bourbon. We drank from tall squarish glasses while eating a pepperoni pizza.

"Her grandfather Abbott says she's missing."

"*Missing*. I don't *think* so."

Something glowed in her face, a momentary pulse of color that subsided as an unwanted thought came and went. She poured more bourbon into her glass and watched as I fumbled some Ritalin out of the vial in my purse and washed it down with iced tea.

"You still using that shit?"

"You still drinking that shit?"

It was an old ritual from our support group, but today's sarcasm had no bite. A wasp circled the uneaten pizza, its buzz, buzz the only sound for several minutes. You get used to silence on the Rez. Nobody chatters just to escape silence, the way they do in cities or on TV. Silence is okay, silence is a way of life.

She set down her glass, carefully, so that the moisture ring on the bottom fit exactly into the ring left when she'd first picked up the glass. She slid the glass sideways, left and right, inch by inch.

"God, I'm near falling-down drunk. Today is Huskie's birthday and I wanted to celebrate, to dress like when he was courting me over in Chinle."

He'd been dead nine years. She'd probably started drinking yesterday afternoon, but aside from slightly puffy eyes, she was doing okay. During the school year, when she didn't drink at all, Billie tightly wrapped her emotions within off-the-rack blouses and skirts, panty hose and leather shoes. Outsider's clothes, she called them. Once school ended and she was alone for the summer, she turned Huskie's picture to the wall at night and drank enough bourbon so she could fall asleep.

"Okay," she said, standing up abruptly. "I don't know where we're going with this. But I'll listen. Let me get something inside."

She brought a bowl of ice cubes and a book with thick, imitation leather covers.

TUBA CITY HIGH SCHOOL
1999 YEARBOOK

She found a page and reversed the book so I could see.

"Judy's senior picture."

The same young, good-looking Hopi face as in

Abbott's Polaroid, although this one was at least two years later. Short hair, plenty of lipstick and white teeth in a posed smile, bangs in front, and no squash blossom hair.

Her senior motto read BORN TO RUN (AWAY).

"That picture's a few years old. Maybe three. She couldn't be bothered with graduation activities, didn't care about having a senior picture."

"What did she do when she wasn't at school?"

"We'd hear stories, like she'd get some man to pay for a night or a week at one of those run-down motels along old Sixty-six in Flagstaff. And at rodeo time, Judy Pavatea was one dedicated buckle bunny."

"What's that?"

"You know the girls that hang around rock bands, looking to get laid?"

"Groupies?"

"Yeah. Well, a buckle bunny, that's a rodeo groupie. Go down to the Flagstaff rodeo this weekend, you'll see buckle bunnies everywhere."

I studied the yearbook photograph again.

"So if this is a few years old, what does she look like now?"

"Slim, tall, more than just good-looking. A knockout, really. Finger and toenails painted with Carmine's Secret polish, usually shoplifted from Basha's. Hair twisted or swirled or teased or streaked with different colors of Kool-Aid. Decal tattoos on her shoulders, usually bare. Usually a *lot* of her bare. She was the first girl to start wearing her bra straps deliberately showing. That was after we sent her home because she wore a red bra underneath a see-through blouse."

"Sexy?"

"In a word, ripe."

"What about her girlfriends?"

"I only heard stories. Like Judy and a bunch of girls getting wrecked on pitchers of something she called 'strip and go naked.' A quart of vodka and a six-pack of Corona mixed into pink lemonade. Kids out here never used to drink so regularly, at least not until they left high school."

I flicked through the yearbook section of senior pictures.

"Any of these kids hang with her?"

"Most school girls avoided her. Except . . "

She fumbled slowly through the pages, finally put her fingers on a picture of a Navajo girl, head cocked down and sideways, almost hiding a shy smile.

"A quiet one," Billie said sadly. "It wrecked my heart, seeing her with Judy."

Mary Nataanie. A Navajo.

"Mary lives down at Sand Springs. Her family lost their land because of the partition. Mary won an Honor Society certificate at graduation. I can't imagine her with Judy, and hate to think about what Judy could teach her about life. Anyway, two weeks before graduation, Judy and Mary were together at the Saturday night dance. Later, one of the mothers told me she saw the two of them hitch a ride east."

"Did anybody say they *went* there together?"

"No. But I saw them talking at the dance, and it surprised me. Later, they both went outside. Somebody told me they saw Judy later, huffing nail polish remover and drinking wine. When she didn't show up for school Monday, nobody thought it unusual or even much cared because Judy hadn't been at school that often. Listen. Can I give you some advice?"

"Sure."

"Forget about Judy. She's just not worth the trouble."

"What if . . . what if Judy wasn't the only missing girl?"

"On any school day, five percent of the students aren't there. What do you mean by that, anyway? Who else is missing?"

"Other Hopi girls."

"Well, not many Hopis come all the way to Tuba City from the Mesas. Most of our students are Navajo. Tops, only fifteen percent are Hopi."

She tucked in her chin, eyes down and to the left, where you always look when you're trying to remember something.

"What?" I said.

"Last year, I got a call from a parent over in Shongopavi. She wanted to know when her daughter was coming back from the three-day trip to Phoenix. When I told her there was no such trip, she got very quiet and then hung up the phone."

"Do you think that girl is missing?"

"I called the Hopi Rangers, asked if they could send somebody over to talk to the parent. But I heard nothing, don't even remember her name. Later, though, there were three others."

She leafed through the yearbook. "The first was

Minnie Solema from Walpi. Thirteen, in the ninth grade. She disappeared from school in early February, and nobody's seen her since."

"Did you talk to her parents?"

"Yup. They just said Minnie wasn't coming back to school."

She turned the page to another group picture. "Sophie Tuvenga, also from Walpi. Fourteen. Gone since last April. And here's Jennie Coochongva, thirteen years old. From Kykotsmovi."

"Could you talk to their families?"

"Laura, I'm Navajo. No Hopi family would say anything to me. Besides, how serious is this? School's not in session, the students are scattered everywhere. I'm telling you, just forget about Judy. She'll turn up, or she won't. What do you care?"

"I've been paid to look for her."

"Paid! Let me guess. Ben's been on his own so long the bills are piling up, and he's not sending you a dime. Listen. If you need money, I'll loan you some."

"No. I gave Abbott my word."

"Okay, that's important. But you spend all your time hunched in front of computers. Even when you help the school locate girls, it's mostly through what you can dig up on computers. You go looking for Judy, you're gonna be out in the world."

"It's scary, thinking about that. But I'm ready to do it."

"Tell you what. I'll call a friend of mine who's a reporter for *Tutuveni*, the Hopi tribal newspaper. I'll give her those three names, see what she can find out.

And I'll call somebody I know at the Hopi high school, and the school over at Keams Canyon."

"Can you talk to any of the girls living here in Tuba City?"

"A year ago, sure. Our girls trusted me. Being a guidance counselor used to mean being involved with their whole lives. Now it's . . . different. Things are changing around here. Let me show you something you *don't* know about Judy."

She returned with a shoebox and dumped the contents on the table. Knives, the pointed half of a pair of scissors, and a dozen box cutters. She picked out one with a five-inch aluminum handle, a single-edged razor blade jutting out from one end.

"We took this away from Judy this year."

"Does anybody use these things?"

"That's the *good* part. So far, at least inside the school, nothing."

"And outside?"

Billie cocked her head.

"You don't know about gangs at the high school?"

"Gangs? You mean like in Phoenix? LA?"

"Yeah. From what we hear, there are over a thousand gang members on Arizona reservations. My sister-in-law, down in Tucson, she says gang bangers are all over her neighborhood. But it's getting serious up here on the Rez."

"You know," I said, "last week at *To Naneesdizi* plaza, there were these guys outside Bashas'. Indian, for sure, but they weren't *dressed* Indian."

"Baggy pants, tattoos?"

"I wasn't close enough to see tattoos, but their clothes were just . . . different. And now that I think about it, one of them flashed a sign toward me. Paid no attention to it then, but I can see him now, right hand across his chest, middle two fingers and thumb into the palm, the other two fingers out."

"Vice Lords. Our first serious gang. One of the young ones flashed this box cutter. We called in two deputy chiefs of criminal investigations for the Navajo Nation. They asked this kid, maybe fifteen, why he'd want to cut somebody. He said cutting was nothing. He said, If we have to, killing is the end of the line for the Tribal Police, for the BIAs. If they want war, he said, we'll fight back. That's when we started searching students for weapons. We're not dumb about gangs, you know, especially offshoots of big gangs like Crips and Bloods. It's really bad over near Window Rock. We hear that prospective girl members have to cut somebody, as an initiation rite."

"Cut somebody?"

"Slashing their face." She grimaced.

"That's not Indian."

"Yeah. That's what one kid said when they asked him what gangs had to do with being Navajo. He told them that being Indian was nothing but name and color. He couldn't do anything about the color, but he said his name was now Dinoraptor."

"He's seen too many movies."

"I wish it was a movie. But they're real. I hear they hang at a place south of Tuba City. You can see their spray-paint tagging down near Black Knob."

"Is there any connection between the gang and drugs?"

"Oh, we've had a few drug problems at the school this year. Usually methamphetamines. No crack, no heroin, if that's what you mean. Nobody can much afford that around here, not with meth and booze being so much cheaper."

"Any connection between drugs and Judy?"

She weighed this for at least five minutes before answering.

"There was a buzz that Judy peddled meth at the high school."

I wanted to tell her about the row houses but kept quiet.

"And last month, down in Flagstaff, police raided a meth cooking lab. Kids running every which way but up, the police grabbing whoever they could. Judy wound up in the Flagstaff jail overnight because she had traces of meth crystals in her jeans."

"Was she charged?"

"Nope. We kept it confidential. All the records are sealed. I could be fired for just telling you."

"Is there any possible connection between her peddling drugs and the gangs here? Could she have pissed somebody off to the point of trouble?"

"I don't know."

"The Flagstaff police are looking for her."

As I told Billie about talking to Yellowhouse, she shook her head firmly.

"Listen, this is making me very nervous."

She rose to her feet, steadied herself with a hand on

the table, standing rigid, straight, cheeks flushed, forehead veins throbbing with uncertainty.

"When you helped us before, the high school
approved it, the principal approved it, the board
approved it. But school's out. Here's my advice. You've
got to forget about this girl. She's just not worth it."

"But you will check with this reporter?"

"Sure. What are friends for? But that's all I'll do.
And I don't want to talk about this anymore today. I'm
going to get my hair done, just like when Huskie first
saw me."

At the front door, she pulled me beside her in front
of the hall mirror.

"Ever think about covering up your gray hair?" she
said.

"What?"

She held a few strands of my hair out straight.

"Tell you what. We'll *both* get a haircut. And Friday
night, we'll both show up in Flagstaff, check out the
rodeo, and then hit some bars and check out the cowboys."

"I don't want a haircut," I protested just as her
doorbell rang. Billie hesitantly opened the front door.
Julia Crow Dog stood there.

"I told you not to call the support group," I said
angrily to Billie.

"What group?" Julia said bitterly. "Jesus *Christ*,
Laura. You do nothing for a hundred years, you never
call, never write anything, you have no idea what I'm
doing or anything, and you think I showed up here just
for you?"

She shouted the last few words just a few inches from my face. Her dress was spotted, and part of the hem had come unstitched and hung down. Her hair was died an obvious coal black, and she'd gained at least thirty pounds since I'd last seen her. I could smell vodka on her breath. She carried a plastic quart Sprite bottle without the screwtop and drank what was left, then flung the bottle onto the living room carpet. We stood apart uneasily, silently, nobody quite knowing what to do, all of us with our own problems of abuse. We used to meet weekly, but not for the last two months.

Julia burst into tears.

"I'm sorry," she said, "I'm really sorry. I didn't mean to do this."

"What's happened to you?" Billie asked.

"Didn't get tenure."

Julia taught anthropology at Northern Arizona University in Flagstaff.

"How long have you known?"

"A month. A lifetime. All of this . . ." She gestured vaguely at her dress, her hair, at the Sprite bottle. "I sure know how to make a mess of myself."

"What didn't you call me?"

Julia staggered, leaned back against the wall, and slid down to the carpet.

"I can't deal with this," I said, hearing the shrillness in my voice.

"Wait," Billie said. "I seem to be the best off of the three of us. Help me get her into my bedroom. She can sleep it off while you and I get haircuts."

"I don't want a fucking haircut," I protested.

But I helped her with Julia, then followed dumbly behind her Toyota to the Tuba City beauty parlor; and two hours later, parking at my trailer, I bent over for my purse and started at the sudden reflection of my new haircut in the rearview mirror. I turned my head sideways one way and then the other, assessing the haircut. Once black and long and streaked with gray, it was now short and shaved a bit on the sides like Flagstaff teenagers, really comfortable in summer heat and needing no care at all. I even smiled at myself in the mirror. Not doing too badly, I thought, unlocking the trailer door and pushing it shut behind me without looking, thinking it felt heavier, hearing a strange whirring sound.

It was a rattlesnake.

Hands to my chest in horror, I jumped backward, trying to see where the snake had coiled, saw it climbing up the back of the door. I reached for a heavy skillet to *smash* it but saw that the snake couldn't move up or down because somebody had driven two roofing nails through its body and into the door. Still alive, at least five feet long, it flicked back and forth, diamond figures black against brown scales, rattles whirring. I rammed the skillet against its head, mashing it flat, hitting again and again until the body finally stopped wriggling. The rattles flicked weakly, no longer a whirr, but still clicking with life.

The workroom phone rang, and I heard the answering machine click on.

"Hey, baby."

A man's low, throaty voice.

"Did you like your present?"

I fumbled at the combination lock, fingers trembling so I got it wrong three times before before I could get to the phone.

"Who *is* this?"

"A good friend, who likes to leave you presents for when you come home."

"This is an office," I said. "Nobody lives here."

"Baby, I know who you are. And I know when you're there."

He vibrated his tongue in his mouth, first like a cat purring, and then ululating in a falsetto. *How did he know I'd just come home?*

"And if you don't stop looking into things, I'll just come by where you live, I'll just find you and fuck you and then decide what else needs doing."

I hung up, and the phone immediately rang again. The answering machine clicked on, and Ben started talking.

"Ben!" I shrieked, picking up the phone. "Where are you?"

"North of Flagstaff, headed your way. Laura, you're hyperventilating. Calm down, tell me what's wrong."

"Ben, oh God, Ben, please come help me."

I started explaining, but his voice faded in and out.

"Say what?" he shouted.

"Somebody broke into the trailer and nailed a rattlesnake to the door."

The line crackled and snapped, and for a moment we were disconnected; but then I heard him again, breathing in silence while he figured a way to deal with me.

"I just passed Cameron," he said finally. "Be there in twenty minutes."

He faded out again, and I hung up in frustration and heard the rattles clicking. I ran into the bedroom, slammed the door shut, and turned on the TV. On the bed, my back against the wall, I watched a shopping channel with the TV volume set as high as it would go, feeling caged, unable to move.

Every few minutes I'd mute the TV, listening for the rattles.

It was still alive.

5

Footsteps in the kitchen. Without thinking, I rushed through the workroom. Ben dropped a duffel bag and swung his SIG Sauer at me in a shooter's stance.

"Jesus Christ!" he said angrily. "Don't *ever* run at me without calling out."

He started to set his SIG down the countertop just as the rattles clicked again, and without hesitation he whirled and fired twice, severing the snake's head. Blood spurted everywhere as the head skittered across the floor, the body sagging down in two strands from the other nail. He put down the SIG, set our garbage bucket underneath the snake, took out our meat cleaver, and chunked through the body. Both sections fell into the bucket, and in one motion he scooped up the remains of the head and tossed it into the bucket and twisted the garbage bag shut, then threw it outside.

He stood briefly on the wooden porch to look everywhere. Nobody came out of their trailers, nobody spoke up, nobody was at home. You hear gunshots infrequently in Tuba City. On a residential street it seemed odd that nobody came asking, and I wondered if Claude heard them over at the junkyard. Ben came back inside, looking at the two bulletholes through the door before shutting it firmly and flipping both locks.

"Diamondback. Biggest I've seen in some years."

"Who'd do a thing like this?"

"Don't know," he said in that cautiously neutral tone of voice that told me he had several ideas but no certain knowledge.

"Do you think he's outside somewhere?"

"Didn't see anybody when I came in through Claude's junkyard. I've got a buddy's pickup parked over there."

He closed the slat blinds over the kitchen window and, picking up his duffel bag along the way, went into the bedroom, moving with a banty, bowlegged strut, not a big man but heavy in the shoulders, muscled, barrel-chested. Most people came away with the impression he was tougher, taller, and ten years younger than forty. After stripping out of his shoulder rig and clothes, he closed the window blinds and then stripped out of his clothes without caring that I saw him naked. I tried talking to him through the shower stall door, but he wouldn't answer, the blurred edges of his body showing that he had his back to me as water rattled against the cheap shower walls.

"Ben, you haven't called in days. I haven't seen you in seven weeks."

"Yeah, I know. I'm sorry."

"Marvin's Bonds, down in Flagstaff, they said you hadn't checked in with them in weeks and they'd started assigning skip tracing to somebody else."

"Yeah, well, I never much liked Marvin anyway."

"You liked his money well enough. Ben, we're partners, but I'm not the one who actually collects the money. Friday I went to Flagstaff to pay some bills, and there's almost nothing left in our account. We owe almost two thousand dollars. I've got enough money to pay off the land-line phone bill. The computer lease payments are weeks late, the trailer rent's overdue, and I don't know why the electricity doesn't get shut off."

After toweling off quickly, he upended the duffel on the bed and rooted through the dirty clothes, found some clean jeans, and pulled them on without bothering to look for underwear, hopping on one leg to settle the jeans. He held up a plastic evidence bag and four packets of hundred-dollar bills, which he tossed on the bed.

"Four thousand. All I've got right now."

In the workroom, he took down the M-16 and began collecting ammo and clips.

"Where you going? You just got here."

"Up north."

He held the evidence bag up to the window, some light coming through the drawn blinds. Inside I saw what looked like a horse bit, the leathers worn and abraded.

"What's that?"

"A Spanish bit. There's an ATF guy down in Phoenix. Mister Goodwrench when it comes to lifting prints from old surfaces. To see what *might* be on the shank here, he's gonna try the Krazy Glue test for fingerprints. This could be worth one hundred thousand dollars, if I'm right, and I *know* I'm right."

"Where did you get it?"

He sniffed twice and ducked his face away from me, always a signal he didn't want to tell me something. Ben's face could never hide his emotions. Whoever thought Indians were stoic didn't know Ben. Anything he wasn't prepared to deal with revealed itself like tossing an emotion into a pond and watching reactions rippling outward. Holding up the TV remote, he switched from one channel to the next, finally just holding down the button. Channels kept clicking by until he stopped at a basketball game.

"Whatever's in that evidence bag, does it have anything to do with the hose killer reward?"

"It belongs to the guy in Kayenta whose mare was gutted last February. He saved it, got to talking about it, word got back to me."

"Oh, Ben. Don't tell me you were in Kayenta last night."

"Why did you ask me that?" Flicking the mute button on and off, on and off.

"Lieutenant Yellowhouse wanted to know if you were here yesterday."

"Yellowhouse? That Navajo cop? What did you tell him?"

"Nothing. I said you weren't here. Ben, what's happening to you?"

"Man. Look at that," he said, staring at the silent TV. Two basketball players faced each other nose to nose, their faces contorted, their mouths open, teeth bared, shouting at each other as they ran downcourt.

"Check this out," he said. "That guy in blue, he just

blocked a shot from the guy in yellow. So the blue guy, he's in the yellow guy's face, saying, I just spanked you once. I'm gonna spank you again and again. Yellow guy saying, Hey, when I see you coming up to defend, I holler at whoever's got the ball, gimme that ball, I got a shrimp on me."

"What aren't you telling me?"

"Man, ya gotta love that in-your-face, fuck-you trash talking."

I picked up a shoe and slammed the heel against the power button, shutting off the TV. He raised his hands, and I slapped him. Startled, he rubbed his knuckles on his head, hard, as though trying to clear out bits of broken glass from inside his brain. Slumping on a chair, he worked his lower jaw from side to side, chunks of cartilage shifting around.

"Ben. What's *happening* to you?"

"I'm working on something for major money. I'm also in some trouble."

"What have you done?"

"Been working with the wrong crews, down in Phoenix and Tucson. Smash-and-grab crews. Three survivalist guys, you know the kind, no laws but their own. Anyway, a month ago, we smashed down the wrong door. Three people got beat up pretty bad by another guy in the crew before we understood it was the wrong address, but this Garcia, he kept banging the woman's head against the wall heater. The Phoenix police put out an APB for our crew, but Garcia kept saying, Just one more score until we find a big one. And then we went last night to Kayenta."

"What were you doing in Kayenta?"

"You haven't heard about Wilson Tsosie? Man, it's all over the news."

He picked up the remote, and I struck it from his hands.

"Garcia somehow heard about this Spanish bit, that Tsosie kept it to remember his mare. Garcia thought there might be some evidence trace that we could use. We just wanted to ask Tsosie some questions, but when we busted down his door Tsosie went into the bedroom and levered up his .30-30, and one of these assholes I was with started popping away and killed Tsosie. The whole fucking neighborhood came outside and turned their pickup lights onto Tsosie's trailer, and I ripped off my ski mask, grabbed the bit and headed into the bedroom, busted out one of the windows, and crawled through."

"When did you start wearing a ski mask?"

"Yeah, well, that's how it's been with this crew."

"And where are they now?"

"Headed toward the Four Corners area, going to hole up in some canyon. They've got stashes of food, weapons. It's how they live. Don't worry about them."

He fingered the bit through the plastic evidence bag.

"Way I figure it, last October Tsosie's mare let a stranger come right up to him, hold him alongside his head. Look at this bit."

"I don't care about that," I said, but he wasn't listening.

"It's a mule bit. A lip getter. Horse wearing this

thing doesn't want to deal with strangers, doesn't want to deal with *any*body. That horse wasn't broken, wasn't riding the way the owner wanted, so when the rider works the reins, this little thing saws inside the horse, gets his attention real quick. So it took a special person to gentle him and come up alongside his head. Hell. It's all guesswork, anyway. And I don't really much care about the why until I find out if I've got a fingerprint. And I know it's the same person. He only guts mares, and he's gotten better at cutting out their organs."

He ran his fingers lightly across photos on his bulletin board showing a pinto mare gutted from withers to rump, the intestines spilled out between her legs. Two Septembers earlier, a series of Navajo-owned horse mutilations had begun in the Four Corners area. Many of them suffered deep genital gashes and rents, and the mares had their ovaries cut out with an amazing surgical precision. Some of the Navajos blamed skinwalkers. Others blamed the Hopis, who occasionally butchered a lone sheep or cow.

"I'm going to the airport and overnight this evidence bag down to Phoenix."

"And leave me here after somebody breaks into my home and threatens me on the phone after leaving a rattlesnake?"

"Laura, I don't have time to deal with that. Nobody in that crew knows about this place, nobody knew I worked with a partner in Tuba City. Now, if you still want to work with me, I'm on to major reward money. Do you want to hear about it?"

His mistook my silence for acquiescence.

"I called in a favor last week, had a friend search VICAP for violent crimes against animals. He tells me there's no recognizable pattern, but he has data that somebody has been killing horses all over the country. I called the head of the American Horse Shows Association last week. She says that in the past four years, nineteen show horses have been killed, probably for the insurance money. I told her I've got my own theory about who's doing it and what would that be worth to her. Mid- to high-six-figure reward, she says. The Kentucky show horse people have tons of money. So if I find this guy and bring him in for the reward, I'll quit Arizona and go somewhere else."

He took several maps from his travel case and spread out a U.S. map.

"The red marks show where the horses were killed. You can see there's three groupings. Kentucky, Missouri, and the Four Corners. These green marks, that's my hunch. Every place a horse gets butchered, within the next day or so, there's a rodeo nearby. Guys are coming into Flagstaff for the rodeo this weekend. The last two nights I've been out on horseback, watching the Rez for somebody that's in the wrong place. People are watching their horses so tight, nobody could much get at them. But I've found two places where nobody's home, so I'm going back out there."

He shrugged into his shoulder rig and seated the SIG home.

"Ben. None of this makes any sense. I work on computers at home, I don't go after people. Unlike you, nobody knows what I do. But somehow, in spite of all

I've done to protect my privacy, you've drawn attention to me. And I'm being threatened."

"Laura, you got two choices. You can stay here, or just leave this place. Take all the equipment, go and settle somewhere else, and work with me from there."

"I can't do that again," I protested. "I'm tired of leaving places."

"Then stay here. I need help processing this map information. You've got software that can analyze patterns, times, whatever. Do you want to work with me?"

"Ben, Ben. I don't care about horses. I need somebody here to protect me."

"I'll be gone for at least three days. If you want protection, have Claude show you how to use my twelve-gauge shotgun. Or if you want a handgun, go into Flagstaff to Freddy Awl's gunshop. Tell Freddy, you say to him, 'Painted Butte.' He'll sell you whatever you need. But I'm not staying in Tuba City. I'm just outta here, and if I hear what you're saying, I guess I'm out of our partnership."

My heart plummeted. I felt as if I'd been sucker-punched in the stomach, like a cottonwood bent against a gale, fighting bursts of wind. I backed against the wall to steady myself, pressing my palms against the wall to stop my hands from trembling.

"Ben, somebody's *threatening* me!"

"If you're really freaked out, you should leave. Tonight. Find another place, become somebody else again. You know how to buy another name, another identity."

"No. I've been Laura Winslow for over a year. I

don't want to be somebody else. I don't want to start that all over again."

"Then you've got a problem."

"You sonofabitch!"

"Yeah. I am that. Always have been since Vietnam. I'm sorry. I'll call you. That's the best I can do for you right now. I have my own problems."

Trying to avoid looking at me, he hesitated at the kitchen door, flexing his fingers, trying to say good-bye without having to say it. And then he was gone. I veed the kitchen blinds, watching him move carefully alongside the trailer. I ran into the workroom, saw him briefly through the blinds there, and ran into the bedroom so I could watch out the back window until he disappeared through the corn.

To avoid having to think about what to do, I spent an hour cleaning up blood in the kitchen. After stretching duct tape over the bulletholes, inside and out, I gingerly lifted the trash bag and slammed it into our garbage can. I looked up and down the dusty street, seeing nothing but dogs. Inside the bedroom, I started tossing clothes onto the bed, wanting to pack up and just drive somewhere, anywhere, out of the trailer, out of Tuba City. For a few wild moments I thought of having Claude load all the computer equipment into the pickup, but I couldn't bring myself to that decision.

Stay or leave. Fight or flight.

I took some more Ritalin, aware I was taking way too much, unable to help it. No, I told myself, I'm not out of control here, it's just temporary. I unpackaged and counted the $4,000 Ben had left me, all of it in hundred-dollar bills. I stuffed some of the bills into my jeans pocket and locked the rest in a file cabinet. I took the shotgun down from the wall rack. Five shells were duct-taped to the butt, and I peeled them off but had absolutely no idea how to get them into the shotgun. I racked the slide back and forth, clicked the trigger, helplessly aware how strange I felt hefting a weapon for the first time in twenty-odd years.

When I ran away with Jonathan Begay, we wound up three weeks later at Pine Ridge during the five-hour firefight where two FBI agents and Joe Stuntz got killed. Wads of Juicy Fruit gum stuck in my ears against the constant explosions, I'd catch the rifle Jonathan would fling at me and I'd reload while he emptied another. I must have slid a dozen boxes of shells into the pipe of those two old Winchesters. After a while the barrels got so hot that I gripped them with stove pads, but I never pulled a trigger then or since.

Guns kill. That's what I'd always believed and had wanted no part of it.

I carried the shotgun outside, laid it on the picnic table.

"Ya at eeh."

An elderly Navajo spoke a soft greeting as he passed by, his eyes sweeping quickly across the shotgun as he walked away. It was the first time I could remember somebody on the street actually talking to me. Three small children chased a dog down the street, their bare heels kicking up dust that hung in the twilight, the sun far in the west, leaving long-fingered shadows streaking toward my trailer. Lights flickered on in other trailers, and several people sat outside with beer bottles, talking, laughing, escaping their stuffy overheated trailers. Two men walking by with a six-pack eyed the shotgun.

"Eh," one said, offering me a bottle of beer, "Winchester extra full choke."

"I got a Remington four-ten autoloader," the other said. "But this is neat, eh?"

They walked on without talking to me directly, but the sense of being recognized and accepted on my own street was very unusual. Several children appeared with long packets of weeds bunched in their hands. They struck matches to the ends and ran up and down the street, streaking fire loops through the dusk, sparks falling behind them. A child thrust a packet in front of me and another child handed me a lit match, and I fired up the packet and wheeled it round and round, the children laughing until it burned to embers; and while I still didn't feel safe, at least I knew I belonged to this trailer, to this life, to the growing certainty that I wasn't yet ready to leave Tuba City.

At some level, I knew it was just the Ritalin talking, but I didn't care.

Back in the workroom, I erased the blackboard and picked up a sliver of chalk to start outlining what I'd learned about Judy. But after an hour I had written very little.

Drugs? Using? Selling?

Meth labs in Tuba and Flagstaff? Arrest? Sheriff's Office?

Judy—gang connections?

Find Judy's friends. Find Mary Nataanie.

Who is Albert Grody?

I started as somebody knocked softly on the un-locked screen door.

"Hey in there."

It was Claude, frowning at the way I clutched the empty shotgun.

"Heard a couple of shots over here a few hours ago. You okay?"

I shook my head from side to side.

"Saw Yazzie come and go. He the problem?"

"No. But I need to trust somebody right now," I said. "I need some help."

"Whoa," he said. "What's going on?"

"Can you show me how to use this thing?"

I thrust the shotgun out in front of me.

"Yeah," he said without hesitation. "I can do that. Anything else?"

"Weren't you on the rodeo circuit?" He nodded. "Did you ever hear of somebody named Albert Grody?"

He suddenly picked up a stick and traced lines in the dirt.

"You know him, don't you."

"He the reason you're loading up with double-aught buckshot?"

"I brought back some rodeo gear from Oraibi that may belong to Grody. Maybe you can tell me something about it."

"I said to you, Don't go out there. I said, Don't get mixed in their business."

"It's too late for that. Will you still help me?"

He threw down the stick with a snort.

"Come over to my place. People will just think I'm shooting at rats."

I got the carryall and locked the trailer. We walked silently toward the junkyard, the shotgun cradled securely in my right arm, already growing familiar and comfortable.

And so I began traveling down the rapids of my future life.

What I would become began that moment.

6

Claude slid two shells into the shotgun, showing me how to nose the paper end in first and push down on the firing cap. Handing it to me carefully, unspoken questions in his eyes, he watched as I put in five more and pumped the slide.

"Chambered," he said. "Fire one off."

"No, thanks. How do I get the shells out?"

"You got to shoot it at least once," he insisted. "I'm not asking why you're carrying it, but I need to know that you can use it if you have to."

I tucked the butt hesitantly under my arm, and he came quickly alongside me, repositioning the gun against my shoulder.

"When you shoot, it's gonna hurt you. And it's gonna make a lot of noise. Be ready for that. That tractor tire over there. Twenty feet away. Do it."

I pulled the trigger. The explosion was deafening, the butt rammed my shoulder hard, and the pain made me dizzy. He took the shotgun as I massaged my shoulder.

"Try another one."

I pulled the trigger, tried to ignore my shoulder, pumped, and fired again.

"Not bad. You hit the tire all three times."

"Show me how to unload."

"Keep pumping the slide, but don't go anywhere near the trigger."

I racked the pump. The shells ejected into a patch of oily dirt and sawdust.

He picked up the shells, frowning as he wiped them off carefully on his shirttail as I upended the carryall, dumping everything on the ground. I handed him the rope.

"What can you tell me about this?"

"bullrider's rope. It's old, it's cheap. Guy who owned this is down-and-out, flat busted, and can't place in the money, so he's got to keep using a cheap five-plait rope. Had he the money, he'd get a nine-plait, a much better rope. These days, the young guys go in for colored ropes. Pretied nylon. Don't cost that much different, but what with a red or green or purple rope and your riding chaps with stars on 'em or 'Jesus Saves' in leather letters, buckskin fringes hanging all over, well, you got the ladies' attention. Not that you think of that while you're riding the bull, but after you stay on the full eight seconds people are hollering because maybe the ride is eighty points or better, and then, well, those ladies remember who had the good ride."

"How does this work?"

"You take the belled end of the rope." He showed me the small loop on which the two cowbells were strung. "Wait a minute. We need some light, we need a bull."

He flicked on a high-power security spotlight and

rolled over an empty fifty-gallon drum from his junkpile into the pool of light. He tipped it sideways, the open end on a rusted transaxle.

"You sling the rope underneath the bull's belly, like this. Well, *you* don't do it. There's guys standing on either side of the chute. One guy reaches through the bars of the chute, they pass the rope under the bull, the second guy grabs it and hands it to you on top of the bull."

Straddling the drum, he tucked the fingers of his gloved hand between the rope and the barrel, lacing the loose end of the rope around and around his fingers, pulling it as tight as he could get it.

"Last thing in the world you want, being tied on top of a wild bull. What if you was bucked off, and he dragged you until all your bones broke to pieces? bull-rider, he rosins up the rope where it winds around the glove. The whole idea is to make it so tight the bull don't shake you loose, but when you're ready to get off, you don't get hung up. Guys that can't let go, the bull drags them across the arena."

He pounded on the rope with his left fist.

"Open the chute and let 'er rip, boys."

He rocked back and forth, his left hand flailing in a horizontal plane in front of him as he bucked, slicing back and forth like a windshield wiper, like a scythe. I had a sudden memory of my father in an old picture, on top of a horse with his hand out like Claude's, and I realized I'd always thought he was just waving people away from him. That was my father. *Get out of my way!*

"Whoa," he said, climbing off the drum. "That's too close to memory."

He coiled the rope loosely and draped it over the carryall. I picked up one of the boots and handed it to him. He turned it over and over and snorted.

"Heels worn down. Rope's old. This stuff belongs to somebody who doesn't place too often, doesn't have enough cash to get new gear. Okay, you've not said what all this has got to do with Albert Grody."

I showed him the name burned inside the other boot.

"What you want with a man like that?"

"How do I find him?"

"Why bother? That's what I'm having trouble with. Albert Grody, he's the worst part of rodeoing. Had no more respect for women then the animals he rode."

"Did he fool around with young girls?"

"Always."

"So. If I did want to find him, where would I look?"

A long beat while he thought on it.

"After he quit riding full-time, I heard he hooked up with a local guy named Kimo Biakeddy. Folks said they were pot hunters, but that was a few years ago."

"Biakeddy lives in Tuba City?"

"Works at the Saveway. Big guy. Busted left hand. But if you're thinking of going over to the Saveway to talk to Biakeddy, better do it tonight."

"What do you mean?"

"The Navajo Tribal Council, they cut off the Saveway place when the lease expired. Wouldn't renew it cuz the owner negotiated it with the old tribal chairman."

"I thought you stayed out of tribal politics."

"That guy stayed open twenty-four hours, seven days a week. He hired ten people, not just Navajo, either. I say, what the hell. Guy's got a business, he's got the right to *do* business. Closing him down, that's not right."

I was surprised he defended the Saveway owner. Like many Hopis, Claude believed that Navajos were talky, arbitrary, arrogant, and pushy. A Navajo finds an old bottle, Claude would say. He rubs dirt off the bottle to see if there's anything left inside to drink, and the rubbing calls up a magic genie. You have three wishes, my master, the genie says, so the Navajo first wishes that all his problems will go away, and no sooner wished than, hey, they do. Second, he wishes that he'd look prosperous. *Whop!* he's got a brand-new three-quarter-ton supercab pickup, a house with running water, a flush toilet, a working refrigerator, and electricity. For his third wish, he wants a guarantee that he'll never have to work again.

Poof! He becomes the same Navajo he was before he found the bottle.

Claude laid one hand on the shotgun.

"Listen. Whatever's going on with you, if you need help fast and you're at your trailer, you just fire this thing off and I'll come quick. Any time, day or night."

"Thanks." I touched his arm, and he was immediately embarrassed.

"How late is the Saveway open tonight?"

"Midnight. If you're gonna carry that thing around town, just keep it unloaded."

He stood in the pool of light, one foot on the oil

drum, watching me head off toward Main Street. I passed the old hospital grounds and walked across Cedar, feeling uncomfortable and foolish. The shotgun was heavy, and I wound up hugging it to my chest, uncertain whether to hide it down to one side whenever a car drove past.

Biakeddy was alone in the Saveway, and I stepped inside. He was the Navajo from the police station.

"This a holdup?" he said, casually eyeing the shotgun as he swung a case of beer onto a dolly, wiping sweat off his forehead.

I carefully laid the shotgun against a counter and stepped away from it.

"Sorry about that," I said. "I don't like walking alone at night."

"Ah, everybody's got some kind of gun or other around here."

"It's not loaded anyway."

"Gun's not much good without being loaded."

His white Saveway shirt, drenched in sweat, clung tightly to his powerful shoulders and arms, muscles rippling as he stacked a case of beer. He wore dark blue dress pants with a knife-edge crease, clean and polished boots with little wear in the heels, a silver-and-turquoise bowstring guard on his left forearm, and long, black hair bound neatly into a Navajo *tsiyeel* bun. He cut his eyes to me, saw me looking him over. Headlights swung across the Saveway front window as a pickup drove up. Kimo went outside to pump gas. I could hear the pump dinging with each gallon, the driver fingering an old wallet and finally nodding once.

Watching the pickup drive away, Kimo wiped both hands on his jeans, cocked fists on his hips, and looked sadly at all the pumps, the signs, the parking lot, as though seeing it for the last time. He came back inside.

"You oughta fill up," he said. "Storage tanks are almost empty."

"Claude Lansa has an old pump in his junkyard. I fill up there."

"You live over near him?"

"He's just a friend," I said carefully.

"You really don't remember me, do you," he said.

"Not at all."

"People once called you Butterfly."

"Winslow," I said firmly, but a little too loud. "My name's Laura Winslow."

"Well, that may be. But back then, you were Butterfly, hanging around with some AIM dude. And you had a butterfly tattoo, high up on one of your shoulders."

He smiled at my surprise.

"I wouldn't forget something that beautiful. Well. I got to get back to work."

After wheeling the loaded dolly out the back door, he returned and began taping empty cardboard boxes on the bottom, loading them with potato-chip bags from the Saveway shelves. He filled seven boxes without once looking at me, cramming the bags so tightly that I could hear the chips breaking, and I realized he was smashing them deliberately. Set bags on top of the pile, *wham*, palm flattening them.

"Pine Ridge," he said finally.

"What about it?"

"That's where I remember seeing you, where I remember seeing that tattoo. Was twenty years ago. The exact day those FBI snipers murdered Joe Stuntz."

Sideswiped by the sudden memory, I felt my knees grow wobbly and I had to steady myself with a hand on the glass countertop. Locked into the past, he didn't notice.

"You were up in the main house. I was thirty yards away, behind a rain barrel. We all stood around afterward, revved up, totally wanting to destroy the FBI, really angry they'd killed Joe. I play those memory tapes back all the time."

"I don't think about it anymore."

"Must be nice, being able to forget chunks of your life."

"Listen," I said. "That was over twenty years ago."

"Hey. Sorry I brought it up."

He wiped his forehead again, then stretched his arms up straight, and the white shirt ripped his right armpit. Exasperated, he stripped off the shirt and used it to wipe sweat from his body. Prison tattoos ran across his shoulders, a rattlesnake winding down his left arm. He stood there, absentmindedly brushing a finger across his elbow until he saw me looking at the tattoos.

"So what do you want? I'm kinda busy here."

"I heard you might know a guy named Albert Grody?"

His eyes flickered with surprise.

"Talk about wanting to forget the past. You're a strange mix, lady."

"So you do know him?"

"Did."

"How long ago? Do you know where he is now?"

"That's a lot of questions."

"I'm trying to find him."

"Time I knew him, folks mostly tried to forget him."

"Do you know where he is?"

He looked me up and down again, trying to guess who I was, why I was there.

"You aiming to use that shotgun on Grody?"

"No. It's mostly for snakes."

"Grody and me," he said deliberately, "we was both rattlesnakes once. Hell, I've been a lot of things once, but I'm not in that life anymore. What are you on?"

"Excuse me?"

"You're talking fast. Your face is so tense I could bounce something off it. If I was to guess, I'd say you're using speed, meth, crank, diet pills, whatever you call it."

"I'm just tired."

"Hey, I see it in your face. But I don't care. I'm no judge. You name it, I've used it. Swallowed, snorted, injected, whatever it took to get up or down. But now I'm clean. I don't use anymore. And the only things I sell are gasoline and this fast-food crap in here, and after tonight, this store is history. I've got to pack up everything into that U-Haul out back. Guy who owns this place, he's so pissed off that the Tribal Council closed him down, he's taking everything over to Vegas to his other store. Soon as I'm finished, I'm leaving, too. Since we're both tired, just leave me to finish this up."

"Look," I said, "I'm sorry. It's been a weird day. Can you tell me about Grody?"

"You don't give up, do you, lady."

"Please," I said. "I'll even pay you."

"Pay?"

I fumbled for the money Ben had left me and took out one of the bills, dropping it on the counter. He stretched it flat, shaking his head in disbelief.

"You're giving me a hundred dollars to talk about shit like Al Grody?"

"Tell me anything you can. I don't care about the money."

"What if I made up stories, some shit just to keep this money, which I seriously need? You know nothing about me, lady. Whatever you call yourself now."

"Please. I need to find him. I heard you two were pot hunters once."

"That's old news. But, yeah, if it seemed valuable, we'd dig it up, steal it, whatever, and then we'd look for buyers. Never did make a big score. Never saw Grody after I was sentenced. Been straight now for three years, two months, nineteen days."

He folded the bill in half, creased it tightly with his thumbnail, folded it again, creased the second fold, and stuffed it inside his left shoe.

"Do you know where I can find him?"

"Nope. But his ex-wife lives down near Flagstaff. Cristina Carnoy. Used to be a rodeo barrel rider. Placed third at the national finals one year. Now she's got this school, charges a ton for girls to spend a week learning about barrel-riding tricks."

"How can I find her place?"

"Just look for the llamas. She raises them along in that flat country east of Flagstaff, past the shopping center."

In one corner of the display room, he flung aside flattened boxes, opened a faded leather suitcase, and removed a carefully folded Navajo Powwow Days T-shirt. Before he closed the suitcase I saw everything neatly arranged in squared piles. Pulling on the tee, he saw I was looking at the rattlesnake.

"Got that one when I was down in Florence for most of two years. . . . That don't seem to shock you much, me being in the can."

"I was in jail seven times," I said. "From Yakima to Sonora."

"Well, now."

He smoothed the tee and went back to taping boxes. I couldn't tell if he was disappointed that I hadn't asked why he was in Florence or whether he wanted to find out why I'd done jail time. But he was thinking of Grody.

"He might still be registered with the PRCA."

"What's that?"

"Professional Rodeo Cowboys Association. Most everybody that rides belongs to the PRCA. Call them up, ask if Grody's still registered, although I doubt they'd have any address other than General Delivery, Nowhere City."

"How up-to-date do they keep records?"

"All of it's on a computer, I hear. Go to the Flagstaff rodeo this weekend, talk to some cowboys about how they register for their next rodeos. Grody might even show up at the Flagstaff rodeo this weekend."

"Does he still work rodeos?"

"Unlikely. But those old-timers, they got no other life."

"Well. Thanks. And I'm sorry about being pushy. I'm kinda strung out."

"Hey. Been there. Listen, I don't think I much earned that hundred dollars. I could go along with you to the rodeo, see if he's there."

"I don't think so."

"Anything else you want to know?"

"You get much teenage traffic in here?" I said on a hunch.

"Sure. Not that many places to hang out in Tuba City."

"Gang kids?"

"Some. Pretty tame, though. Nothing like the gang bangers in Florence."

"Ever hear of a girl named Judy Pavatea?"

"Judy?" He laughed. "Offered me a blow job one night if I'd drop two cases of beer out the back door. Turned her down, though. Not my style. She had this old woven Apache satchel, full of drugs. Meth, crank, speed, whatever. Tried to sell it here, but I threw her out. That what this is about? You want to score drugs from Judy?"

"Her grandfather thinks she's run off with Grody."

"Albert Grody and Judy Pavatea? Not a chance."

"He also told me she spent a lot of time with gang kids, selling drugs."

"Our local gangbangers? I don't think so. They'd hang, drink, party. But she had to be connected with a meth lab doing heavy business, and while I don't know for a fact there's a lab here in Tuba City, nothing would surprise me."

"Okay. Thanks."

"That's your final story? Judy ran off with Albert?" I nodded. "You lie real good, lady. There's no tell in your face, nothing gives you away. But your story just doesn't make any sense. Whatever. Thanks for the money."

He moved his hand gently toward me and laid it on my right shoulder.

"If I remember, that butterfly was on the right side."

I sighed and lowered my head, turning my body far enough so he could see my bare shoulder underneath the tank top. His mouth tightened at seeing the rough, reddish patch high up near the shoulder blade where I'd obliterated the tattoo.

"See?" I said. "I'm really not that person anymore."

"But you had a tattoo there, right?"

"Once."

"A butterfly, right?"

"Once."

"How can you just sling off what you were?" he said with some bitterness. "You want to tell me the secret about forgetting the past?"

"It's just gone."

"Not for most of us, Butterfly. Not for me."

Another pickup swung into the parking lot, along-side the gas pumps, the headlights briefly illuminating his sadness. He went outside without seeing me leave.

Nobody's lights were on, nobody was left on the streets, nothing moved except me, thinking about my lie, that the past was just gone. Spooked by uncertain night noises, leveling the shotgun toward one sound and then another, I finally cut around the rear of my trailer, got as far as the picnic table, when headlights flicked onto my face.

"Put the shotgun down, miss!"

I froze.

"Lay it down! On the ground! *Now!*"

7

A uniformed officer stepped into headlight glare, a handgun in front of him.

"I live here!" I shouted. "This is my trailer, I live here."

He picked up the shotgun, shoving it aside, uncertain what to do.

"Keys. In my purse."

I started to grope for the keys, and he put the handgun against my forehead.

"Please," I said, dumping the purse upside down. "My name is Laura Winslow. I live here. Just let me open the door with these keys."

"You really are Miss Winslow?"

"Yes."

But he checked the picture on my driver's license before holstering the handgun.

"Ma'am, I apologize. I'm Captain Floyd Seumptewa? Hopi Rangers? There's some serious business out in Hopi, and I know it's very late, but I need to ask you a few questions? Maybe I could come inside your house? If that's okay?"

He stood well away from me, not satisfied until I'd

unlocked the door. After shutting off his headlights, he came inside carrying the shotgun and something wrapped loosely in brown paper. He was in full uniform. Scalloped shirt pockets, sleeve patches, long black tie, a Smokey hat with braid against the flat rim and tassels in front, and seven-pointed stars on both shirt and hat. We stood awkwardly apart from each other in the tiny kitchen, assessing each other. He laid the shotgun on the floor.

"I do apologize, pulling my gun on you."

"It's okay," I said quietly, taking out the orange juice bottle, shaking some Ritalin into my palm, trying not to show him the pills as I swallowed.

"Never come that close before. These guns are scary things."

"What do you want?"

"Well, first, I'd like to show you something?"

He moved just close enough to get inside my personal space, one of those confrontational things that policemen learn to throw you off balance, like his way of ending everything he said with his voice rising so it seemed to be a question, inviting a response you might not otherwise think to give. I'd thought he was as frightened as me, but he clearly wasn't. Unwrapping his package, holding the bloody slicker in front of him, his round, gentle, smiley face hovering over a sea of yellow.

"You seen this?"

"No," the lie so automatic I cautioned myself to think before saying anything.

"Johnson Pongyayanoma gave it to me yesterday. We've got no real forensic capability out on Hopi, so I'm running this down to Flagstaff. There's some question about how Patrick Valasnuyouoma died, whether somebody actually killed him, somebody wearing this slicker. Johnson is his usual quiet self, but I figure with Patrick's death turning up the same day as another problem, maybe there's some connection?"

"I was out there, but Johnson didn't show me the raincoat."

He rewrapped it, set it on the counter. And what about No Picture's Boy? I thought. Why hadn't he said two deaths?

"If you don't mind telling me, what *were* you doing in Oraibi?"

"Abbott Pavatea hired me yesterday to look for his granddaughter. I said I'd do that, but Abbott insisted that I go see Johnson."

"Abbott's granddaughter? Are we talking about Judy Pavatea?"

His nostrils flared, his eyes narrowed, and frown lines wrinkled his forehead.

"She's a wild one. I personally went looking for her three times before she moved over to Moencopi to live with Abbott. Found her once down in a Sedona motel with a fertilizer salesman. She's wild, but I always liked her spirit."

"I'm glad somebody cares about Judy Pavatea."

"Miss Winslow, I've been on the police for twenty-three years. I care about everything that happens in Hopi, no matter what village or family or clan. It's awful hard sometimes, being on the police when some folks don't believe I want to help them, but they complain

anyway. Like today. The Hopi Tribal Council got a slew
of complaints about this woman Billie Tso asking
around about missing Hopi teenage girls? She only
called a reporter, but the Tribal Office is a small place.
Friend of yours, this Billie Tso?"

"She's a friend, yes."

"Tso being Navajo, you can imagine how some
folks got powerful worked up, her asking about family
things that shouldn't be her business at all?"

"Maybe you should talk to Billie."

"She's not answering her door. No lights on. So I
came over here. Now, these girls' families that are being
called? Problem is, all of them are from villages where,
like I said, people don't want anything to do with Tribal
Council folks or Hopi Rangers?"

"You're making everything you say into a question,
and it confuses the hell out of me. Am I being accused
of something here?"

"No, Miss Winslow. I'm just trying to figure some
things out."

His attitude changed smoothly, dropping the question marks, slowing his words.

"Being Hopi, I don't much like answering questions.
Being a Ranger, I've got to ask them. Maybe I've been a
Ranger too long, maybe I even talk too much. Everybody
at the Tribal Office, they're just mad at Billie Tso, instead
of showing concern for missing teenage girls whose families aren't even willing to acknowledge that they might
be missing. But me, I'm an uncle to Sophie Tuvenga. And
I know, flat out, she'd never leave from her family without them know exactly where she was going."

"What did her parents tell you?"

"Down in Polacca, I'm told. No reason not to believe them, but I'll go calling down there to check things out."

"And Minnie Solema? Jennie Coochongva?"

"Their families aren't talking, either. Reason I'm concerned about this, some people are saying that Powakas took the girls."

"I don't believe in witches," I said angrily.

"You don't live out there," he replied intensely. "With all my police training, I'd have to be against witches, but people believe in them. There's no sense going against that belief. You got anything else you might want to tell me?"

"No."

"May I see your ID, please? Something other than the driver's license."

He carefully studied my Social Security card, credit card, and bank ATM card. I watched calmly, knowing they were excellent fakes that would stand any reasonable test.

"What exactly do you do?"

"I'm a computer consultant. I work out of this trailer."

"Hey. Lots of people need you, I'll bet. We've just wired up the Tribal Office, but I haven't had much time to figure them out yet. Got a girl for that. We're not dumb out there, Miss Winslow, just because we're hanging off a rock plateau in the middle of the high desert. I've got police contacts all over the state. I work with BIA officers, FBI when I have to, anybody that helps me get my job done. And I'll be straight out here about something. Your identification is just a little too good to be true to me. How long have you lived here?"

"About a year. Are we done here?"

"Uh-huh. You don't much trust us policemen, do you."

"I never said that."

"Uh-huh," he said again. He took out a business card and placed it carefully in front of me.

"Here's my personal phone number. If there's even just one girl missing, I want to find her. And if it's more than one girl missing, I want to find them all. You've got to understand, I just think it's a misunderstanding. They'll all turn up."

"Thank you. But you will ask about Sophie?"

"Yes, ma'am." He studied me for several minutes. "Look. Everything I do as a Ranger, it's all small stuff. Guy cuts wood without a permit, I write up a fine. Somebody throws a stone through a store window in Kykotsmovi, I find the guy. People smash up their pickups, I help get them to the hospital. New agers come here selling fake Kachinas, I confiscate their stuff and escort them off the reservation. Everything from too many stray dogs to bodies in accidents, I know exactly what to do. But missing girls whose families won't talk to me? I'm stuck, going nowhere. Nothing like this has ever happened. So I'll go notify the BIA, the FBI, but nobody trusts those people, and they have their own priorities anyway. Miss Billie Tso, she's probably a good person, but she's a Navajo. Nobody trusts her, either."

"Nobody trusts anybody anymore," I said bitterly, mostly to myself.

"Well, Miss Winslow, since we're dealing with trust, let me be right honest with you. I don't know much about you, but seeing you with that shotgun, knowing you're afraid of something, I gotta believe you've got something more to tell me. I'm not asking you to trust all policemen, but I sure do wish you'd put a little more trust in me. And remember. You don't live in Hopi. If we can't work out some position of mutual trust, of sharing information, then you just let us handle our own business. Clear?"

"Clear," I said.

He got into his dirty white Caprice, and as I nervously watched his taillights bounce up and down in the ruts as he drove away, I thought about how much more public my life was getting, how two police agencies now had an active interest in me, and that I could no longer count on Ben to go out into the world and let me be private.

I locked the door, checked the window locks, closed all the blinds, and sat down to look for the official Web site of the Professional Rodeo Cowboys Association. It had minimal information, some of it outdated, with no public listings of active cowboys. My heart sank when I saw that the United States was divided into twelve rodeo circuits, so whatever databases existed were probably organized accordingly.

The first step was getting past security firewalls.

The PRCA Web site was connected to a UNIX server farm, the size of which I couldn't yet determine. Somebody had installed a router-based firewall, and I began running Jakal, a stealth scanner that looks behind firewalls without leaving traces. The network administrator had set up a decoy, a sacrificial host computer, so he was no dummy. I needed to figure how to get root control so I could set up sniffers, which would let me monitor packet traffic, from which I could retrieve password strings. Then I'd start my attack scripts.

Cracking is far easier than you know. If the main computer runs on UNIX, I'd grab root access and set RootKit sniffing e-mail while erasing traces of my cracker entry from the network log files. The trick is to get Trojans running so the network system administrator can't find altered files, which give you away. The truth is that most system administrators, or sysadmins, are sloppy, leave entry holes, and don't check for crackers.

Hours passed. My only sense of time came when I checked the answering machine, saw the time readout, realized that hours had passed. I get like that when I'm zoned into a hack. Nothing else matters. Some dark nights and bright days with drawn shades, I huddled at the computers for hours and hours, eating and going to the bathroom when needed. Cracking's not glamorous. It's grunt work. It's laborious. It's dull, endlessly dull, searching for the right combinations, finding the hole, probing deeper. Day or night, it didn't seem to matter what time network sysadmins worked, I'd crack in with impunity. Once in a while I'd get bounced when they found my tracks, using tricks of their own to trap intruders, zap the damage, plug a hole. But there are always new holes, and I was trying to crack a system that used both e-mail and Web activities on a 7/24 basis. We never close.

At 3:27 the next morning, I could see that some SQL databases were set up on an AS-400, networked with the Web server, but behind incredibly imaginative firewalls. I suddenly gained access to another, carefully hidden computer, hosting a large secured database, holding what was probably the names of all PRCA cowboys. After triple-checking my backtrail, I started running searches for several strings. Albert Grody. ALBERT GRODY. AGrody. Case sensitive and so forth, it's nothing exciting, just crunching strings until something comes back. With luck I'd find some relational record linking, so that anybody doing private queries could come up with a complete history of names, performances, dates, events, and rodeo sites.

But it was boring work because I thought it was a waste of time. I quickly wrote a script that would autosearch through the database, then at four I went outside. Still dark, with another hour or so until false dawn. On an impulse I gathered the shotgun, locked the trailer, and drove back to the row house street. As I turned the corner I could see two lights flickering in an empty lot across from the row houses. They bobbed sideways and up and down with no pattern at all, moving constantly in the dark. I turned off my headlights and drove alongside the left curb, my eyes adjusting to night vision, and I saw it was two young boys passing a football back and forth, each with flashlights rubber-banded on top of gimme hats that read ARIZONA CARDINALS.

They stopped as I pulled up, both lights pointed at my window.

"It's okay," I said. "I'm just lost. Can you help me? I'll give you some money."

They ran up beside my door.

"How much money?" one said without shame or guile. He looked about twelve, a few years older than the other one.

"Depends," I said. "What's the name of this street?"

"You're kidding, right? You lost, or just drunk or something?"

They both laughed. Across the street, another light came on as the biker opened his door. The kids both shrank back and turned off their flashlights. The man stood behind his screen door, suddenly silhouetted in black as the inside light went off.

"Who is that guy?" I asked.

"Mike Kiyonnie," the older boy said hesitantly. "You don't want to fuck with him, lady. Where's our money? I get five, my brother gets three."

"What's the name of this street?"

"Dilkon," the younger boy said. "It's called Dilkon Street."

"Do those houses over there have numbers?"

"We don't got numbers on this street."

Kiyonnie opened his screen door and came out into his yard. The brothers didn't wait for their money as they ran across the lot. I backed out of the street without my headlights, Kiyonnie watching me all the way to the corner.

I hoped he didn't recognize my pickup.

Back home, I spent almost an hour hacking into an Arizona State database containing criminal records and another half an hour running through their files. But there was nothing under the name Kiyonnie. I backed out of the database and switched to a federal system that tracked purchases of known chemicals used by clandestine drug labs. Not knowing what I was looking for, I set my search scripts to flag and save anything on the "Controlled Substances" list that had been shipped to northern Arizona. If that produced no results, I'd check for sales of "Watched Laboratory Equipment." I was sure that Kiyonnie was running some kind of drug processing lab, but it could be nothing more exotic than extracting meth from diet pills or nasal decongestants.

I stretched and saw it was almost eight. I took some coffee out to the picnic table and had barely set the cup down before I fell asleep, one hand across the shotgun. An hour later I awoke with a jolt of panic and vulnerability, feeling dazed, my senses shut down and in a vacuum, like being in the middle of a desert where it's so quiet you can hear your heartbeat.

I showered and dressed, looked for orange juice, and found a totally empty refrigerator; but I wasn't hungry anyway and was distinctly on edge. I'd always felt safe when I was hacking, and people like Ben went out to bust down doors for bail jumpers. Now I was out on the streets and didn't like it at all.

More Ritalin, mouth under the tap, greedy for lots of water, and then I left for Flagstaff to find Cristina Carnoy. No farther than that, I promised myself. If I got any information about Grody, I'd find myself another door-bashing partner.

8

"Don't lean inside, Mary Ellen."

But she did, the horse drifting in a wide, lazy turn around the first barrel.

"Goddammit, don't lean *toward* the barrel. Lean *away!*"

Approaching the second barrel, Mary Ellen pulled back on the reins, and I saw the horse slow down to and lean into the turn, Mary Ellen leaning the other way, the horse slipping closer to the barrel and clearing it by only two feet.

"Fan*tas*tic. Now. On the next barrel, sit back just before your whoa."

Seven feet from the third barrel Mary Ellen sat farther back in the saddle, the horse slowing noticeably. She rounded inches close to the barrel, gathering speed in the straightaway, whipping her hand against the horse's flanks, urging it toward the gate.

Cristina Carnoy clicked her stopwatch.

"Sixteen point three," she said to me, shaking her head.

Mary Ellen came back toward us at a slow trot.

"You're too slow, toots," Cristina barked.

"It felt like a good ride."

"Shit, Mary Ellen. You're half a second away from tenth place. You want to be at the national finals, you've got a long, long way to go."

"I keep forgetting not to lean into the barrel."

"Yeah, well, you forget more than that."

"I'm ready to try again."

"You might be, but that horse isn't. Let him rest half an hour and you go eat some lunch. We've already done five runs. Always give your horse a rest, Mary Ellen. He's what'll get you to the NFR, if you ever shave off a second."

"Okay, Miss Carnoy. Should I unsaddle him?"

"Just walk him around a bit, sitting in the saddle."

"That last turn felt really good. I think I've really got it now."

"Yeah, sure," Cristina muttered to me as the girl kneed her horse away.

"I can come back later if this is a bad time."

"Nah. Just hold on, I'll be with you in a minute. Neil!" She yelled at a man sitting on the railed fence across the field. "Come over here." He jumped down and ambled across the dirt arena, carrying a small videocamera.

"She's never going to make the national finals, you know," he said.

"Nope, she isn't. But don't you go telling her that."

"I don't tell her anything she doesn't want to hear. And who are you?"

He smiled at me. Clean, perfect white teeth, clean and pressed stone-washed jeans, an immaculately pressed blue-and-white-striped cowboy shirt.

"Neil Blackgoat," he said, extending a hand to me.

"Jane Fonda," I said without hesitation, grinning when I saw the smile slip for a moment and then reemerge, wider and more brilliant than before.

"Jane. Caught some of your movies."

"Neil," Cristina said not unkindly. "This woman is here for a short talk and then you'll never see her again."

"I liked *Klute*," he said. "Watched it nine times."

"One of my favorites," I said, thinking he looked barely twenty, maybe twenty-two, and had more poise than I'd ever seen in someone that age.

"Your body, in *Klute*, I mean. Had that solid look. Like a green apple."

"Get out of here," Cristina said.

"Okay if Mary Ellen and I get something to eat?"

"Help yourselves. While you're in the house, play back the video for her. Get her to notice what happens when she comes up to the barrels, for God's sake."

"Want me to bring you ladies some coffee?"

"Sure," Cristina said, leading me to a table and chairs underneath a canvas awning. "And bring some sandwiches. This lady looks awfully hungry. Now. Let's talk about what kind of TV piece you're looking for."

"TV?"

"Aren't you the TV reporter from Flagstaff?"

"Not me." I laughed.

"She was supposed to be here at one, and when you showed up I just figured you were the one. Well, set a while anyway, and have some coffee with me."

"Who *is* that hunk?" I asked as we sat down.

We watched him stand next to Mary Ellen's horse while she slipped her off leg across the saddle. He put his hands around her waist and, taking her full weight in his arms, lowered her slowly to the ground, turning her body at the last moment so her pelvis rubbed against his. They went inside the house.

"You don't follow rodeo, that's one thing for sure."

"People have been saying that to me lately."

"Neil rides bulls better than anybody on the planet. He's way ahead of all the competition for the Dodge Trucks money."

"Likes the ladies, doesn't he."

"Oh, yeah. Came on to me last December at the NFR finals in Vegas. I don't mind getting hit on by a hunk, but I knew he just wanted to get through me to some of my girls. You handled him pretty good. I'll have to remember that movie star routine. It's *very* hard to throw Neil off. He's got this control thing, it rarely slips."

"Does he work for you?"

Cristina laughed. "Neil makes so much money bullriding that he's got people working for him. He just comes around here once in a while, helps out when it's some girl he's screwing. I like him, though. He'll work all day if he has to and then party all night. Lord, I remember when I could do that."

"He seems small to be a bullrider."

"That's why he's the best."

"Small is good?"

"Bull can't whip them around."

"But if he doesn't weigh much, seems like the bull would throw him off."

Neil came outside, holding a silver tray aloft on one hand like a waiter.

"Hello. I'm Neil, and I'll be your waiter."

He rotated his arm so that the tray, starting at chin level, suddenly emerged in front of us. With his other hand he set two octagonal coffee cups on the table, laid paper napkins beside us, and began to pour from a silver coffeepot. He'd arranged slices of turkey, Swiss cheese, lettuce, jalapeño peppers, and three kinds of bread, plus two kinds of mustard and mayonnaise.

"And what did you say your name really was?" he asked me.

"I didn't. But it's Laura."

"Mmm. I've never known a Laura. And what was your phone number again?"

"Never mind, Neil," Cristina said.

"Ladies." He went back inside.

"He's a kick."

"You feel a hand on your ass, chances are it's him. I'll bet he's got her half-undressed already. Now, honey, you're not a TV reporter, and you don't know hoohaw about rodeo. You mind telling what you *are* doing here?"

"I'm looking for your ex-husband."

Caught with a mouthful of coffee, Cristina sputtered.

"Well, shit. It's too fine a day to talk about Albert." She wiped her mouth, shaking her head in disbelief. "You actually want to find Albert Grody?"

"Yes."

"He didn't come on to you somewhere, leave you with a week's motel bills, and you want to find him and get even?"

"I've never met him."

"Then why in creation are you looking for him?"

I'd figured she'd ask me that eventually, and the lie came out readily.

"I've been thinking of my father a lot lately, and I have so few memories of him, I thought I'd look up people who knew him on the rodeo circuit."

"What was his name?"

"George Loma."

"I saw you once," Cristina said with amazement. "Reno, I think. You must've been all of two, three years old, and that bastard had you sitting at a poker table with a whore on each side of him."

"You knew my father?"

"He and Albert were a pair. More like father and son. No offense intended, honey, but your dad was one worthless sonofabitch."

"That's how I remember him, too."

"Lord, honey. Then why do you want to find out anything about Albert?"

"Just do."

"Mmmm. I only saw George that once. I'd just met Albert, actually, and I told him he had a quick choice. Either me or the whores. He chose me, but kept on seeing those whores for years until I had enough of it."

"Do you know where he is now?"

"Haven't a clue. Don't want one. Don't be disappointed, honey. You're better off. I could call around, but I doubt I'd find out anything. Albert's an old man now."

"He doesn't still work the rodeo circuit?"

"I can't say, for sure. After he got busted up one too many times, he swore off the rough stock, but kept his hand in at calf roping."

"Does he still do that?"

"Lord, girl, I have no idea and care even less. He'd be fifty-two this year, if he's still alive, and I don't even know that. But still riding? I doubt it. My best guess is that he stopped riding eight, ten years ago."

I wrote my land-line phone number on a napkin.

"If you find out *anything*, please call me here."

Neil returned to pick up our plates.

"You haven't eaten anything," he said to me. "Here. Let me fix you something."

He quickly put together two sandwiches and wrapped them in paper napkins, after which he put all the dishes on the silver tray and carefully wiped off the table, using the rest of the napkins, including the one with my phone number.

"He's very clean, that boy, very well trained, very controlled. Always a touch too controlled for me, but we all have our style. Here. Write in this."

She handed me a small address book. I wrote down my name and phone number.

"Thanks again," I said, looking at the neatly wrapped sandwiches. I realized I'd not eaten anything in almost fifteen hours. That worried me, because one of the very first signs of Ritalin abuse is loss of appetite. I smiled and tucked them into my purse.

"You will call," I said, "if you find out anything about where he might be."

"Yes. I will. Because you're George's daughter, not because I think you should have anything to do with Albert. So don't say you're not warned about him."

"One thing more. I'd like to find out if he's still involved with pot hunters."

"This isn't about your father at all, is it? Or are you even who you say you are?"

"I am George Loma's daughter, but I don't want anybody to know that, and it's not relevant anyway. Will you still help me?"

She reached for the eyeglasses that had hung unused from a cord around her neck, put them on, stared intently at my face with disgust and disappointment.

"You conned me, missy," she said coldly. "Neil I can take, but I don't like that in a woman. I gave you my word, so I'll call around, but I doubt I'll find out anything. My best advice? Albert is ten miles of ugly road. Whatever you want, stop looking for it."

"Well. Thanks for warning me. But I have to keep looking for him."

"Then go right down to Fort Tuthill and ask the rodeo people there. You might find some old-timer who'd know where Albert can be found. Not that I think he's worth finding. He's a parasite, honey. And you surely do understand about parasites."

I drove slowly back to the main road, stung by her calling me a parasite and asking if I was the person I said I was. Computer hacking always involves faking your digital identity, but with people, my main defense was just not talking too much, as opposed to deliberately deceiving. I didn't like this part of the business, having to see people, to lie to them, to parry their questions while digging for information.

Am I who I say I am? I suppressed the conflict and headed to the rodeo grounds.

9

"If it's all gray, it's prolly all Brahma. If it's all Brahma, it's prolly one rank, mean, son of a bitch of a bull."

"I thought all rodeo bulls were Brahmas."

"Hell no," he said, cackling.

Turning to look at me, he swiveled his whole torso and head to the side as if they were welded together and his neck didn't work anymore. Almost bald, he had individual strands floating off his head, so few I thought I could probably count them by number. He swiveled to his left, squirted a brown stream off to the side away from me, and twisted so he could face me directly, his eyes crinkling with a smile and no apology.

"Looky over there, that black un with the white leg markings, white face. That's a Hereford. One over there, that un's an Angus. Then you got your breeds, cross between, say, Brahma and Angus. Call 'em suckers Brangus. Cross between Brahma and Hereford, call 'em Branford, some say Braford."

Another quick stream.

"What's your name, honey? Whatcha doing here at the rodeo grounds?"

"Just a tourist," I said. "I don't know much about

rodeos or bulls or bullriding. My name is Laura. What's yours?"

"Jason. First time at a rodeo?"

"Yes."

"Decidedly un-American. Hey. You interested in a beer or sumthin'?"

"No." I smiled at being hit on. "But maybe you can tell me where I could find some of the bullriders."

"The big-name riders, they'll all be here tomorrow."

"I thought the rodeo started today."

"Just for small-timers. Younguns. Wannabe champions, hoping they'll catch a ninety-point ride on one of these uglies here."

"Ninety points?"

"Do you know *anything* about rodeos and bullriding?"

"You try to stay on for eight seconds. If you do, you get points."

"So does the bull."

"I don't understand."

"They give as many points to the bull as to the rider. Fifty points each. So you can ride your heart out, but if the bull just piddles and struts, it's a no-count embarrassing stroll in the park. Most usually the judges offer the cowboy a reride if the bull is lousy."

"Do many riders get near a hundred points?"

He cackled. "Hardly. At a rodeo this size, score in the eighties, that's a money ride. Into the nineties, top money for sure. No matter how good you ride, you don't get into the nineties without a pure rank bull. You truly never seen a rodeo?"

"Never. What's a rank bull?"

"Well, without you go watch bullriding, they ain't no way I can describe about being rank. They're just . . . hell, ma'am, they're the meanest, contrariest, most unpredictable bastards in the whole show. You take this Brangus here, name of Manhunter Mountain. He was at the national finals last December, over to Las Vegas. He just ain't been rode yet. Over two hundred tries, but he's flung 'em all off."

"That must be a record."

"Hell, now I know for sure you know nothing about nothing. Record was Red Rock, three hundred nine straight rides to hell, then Lane Frost stayed on him."

"When does the bullriding start tomorrow?"

"First go-round could be any time, usually the last event. Keeps people in their seats, waiting for those mean bulls like this sucker."

He spat at a bull's tail, catching it in midflick. I leaned on the rails, looking at their horns. Some curved up, others curving down, some long, some short, some quite ugly, others flowing in gentle, perfect arcs, and one with none at all.

"How come there's no horns on that bull?"

"Some don't have no horns at birth. Most had 'em to start with, that's for sure, that's guaranteed. Others get 'em hacked off. Mulies, we call 'em. Crowd's never real excited about a mulie, though. They like to think somebody might get hooked."

"Where do they come from?"

"Stock contractors, mostly. Want to see something special?"

No, I thought. Looking for Grody was a waste of time. All I'd find here were old men, dumb animals, and heaps of cowshit. He motioned for me join him at one of the smaller pens. A yellowish bull wandered near the fence and came right up to us. I stepped back instinctively, but the bull flopped down in the dirt and half closed its eyes.

"No need to be skittish." Jason reached over the top fence rail, stroked his withered hand over the bull's hump. "Will Gates, he's a strong believer in gentling these suckers down, letting 'em save their contrariness for just about a hair of second after that chute opens, and then, oh my, they got one thing on their minds. Getting rid of their load, which is to say, bucking like crazy to get the man off their backs."

"You ever ride them?"

"Ride them." He laughed so hard that he choked on the tobacco. "Hell, that's a young fool's errand, to be sure. Ain't *if* you're gonna get hurt, just *when*. But, yeah, I rode when I was some younger. Cracked my neck after seven years. You mighta noticed, I can't move it too good. Got three vertebrae fused."

"I'm sorry."

"Hell. Years ago." He looked me up and down. "The rest of me works just fine."

"Sounds like you've been on the rodeo circuit a long time."

"Can still crack an egg, honey, should you want some breakfast. We could talk about rodeos, whatever else pleased you."

"Well, I wonder, do you know an old rodeo guy named Albert Grody?"

Clearly not expecting that question, he went shut-face for a moment, his head shrunk into his shoulders. "What you want with him?"

"I know his ex-wife, that's all."

"He's trash. I see him coming, I move along."

"Where might I find him?"

"If he's here, any of the rough stock pens like these. He mucks out, just like me. Not much work for old-timers except shit work. There's another bunch of muck-ers, due here in a few minutes. You wanna wait around, he might show up."

It seemed more likely that he was just saying that to keep me with him, but I didn't want to take the chance.

"Okay. I'll wait. How much do these bulls weigh?"

"About a ton, tops. Some less. This fellow, I figure he'll go fifteen hundred. Ain't the size, it's the meanness that makes 'em rank."

"What's in the hump?"

"Here, give it a feel."

"I don't want to put my hand in here."

"He don't mind. Go ahead. Touch him, stroke his hump."

I reached in warily, touched the yellowed skin. The hump jiggled slightly from side to side as I stroked it.

"Like five-year-old jelly, I always say. Or when you get ahold of it solid, feels as wonderful as holding a woman's breast."

Ignoring his comment, I spotted a pen containing only one bull.

"Why's that one all alone?"

"He's one rank bastard, that's why."

"What does that mean, rank? I mean, do some of them smell bad?"

That set him into a fit of cackling, and he swallowed some tobacco juice.

"Smell like shit, you don't keep mucking around 'em. Mucking out, that's my job here. But being smelly, that's not nowhere near describing a rank bull."

"Are they ranked by how many riders they throw off?"

"Well, they's lots of rankings like that. Dodge Trucks, say, they got this list, says this here's your top bull, this here's your number two. But your top bull, that's the rankest, meanest sombitch bull around. Rank bulls are just mean. You sure don't know much of anything about this, begging your pardon."

"No."

"Don't you read *Pro Rodeo News*?"

"I don't get into Flagstaff that often."

"Flagstaff. That's a good un. *Pro Rodeo News*, that's a national paper, lady."

"Oh. Is it connected with the PRCA?"

"Well, you do know *something*, at least. Don't meet many rodeo virgins anymore. Begging your pardon, nothing personal, I mean. The virgin part."

"No problem. My father used to be in rodeos."

"What events?"

"I don't know."

"What's his name?"

"Doesn't matter. You'd never have heard of him."

"He rode any bulls the last thirty-odd years, I'd know him."

"George," I said shortly. "George Loma."

"No shit?"

"You actually knew him?"

"From a distance," he said warily, studying me anew. "Where's he now?"

"Dead."

"Uh-uh." He squinted into the past. "You don't mind my saying so, that George Loma was one gawd-awful mean rank son of a bitch."

"So I heard."

"He could ride, though. Both bulls and women. Beggin' your pardon."

"Look," I said irritatedly, "let's just forget him. Okay?"

"Him and Grody, they were a pair. Just hang on here another five minutes, the other guys'll be here, you can talk to Grody about your dad. Or whatever."

A horn sounded somewhere in the arena.

"Pardon, ma'am. Gotta move on. That's the horn for slack."

By this time he was used to my puzzled looks.

"Slack. They got more bullriders than they got room for in the main program. Somebody screwed up, let too many preregister, and they gotta have an elimination tomorrow afternoon. You want to see bullriding, come see these kids ride. You want to see the best, come Friday and Saturday nights. You wanna spend some time with me, I'll give you a real good tour." He swiveled, spat, hoisted his jeans. "Hell, I ain't but fifty-two." He looked seventy.

"Thanks anyway. But I'll find my way around."

"Always figure, if I don't ask, they can't say yes."

I spent another hour wandering the Fort Tuthill fairgrounds, but feeling increasingly that I had no real idea what I was doing there, why I was trying to force a connection between a bag of worn-out rodeo gear and Judy Pavatea. And then I saw a cowboy with a cell phone, a laptop computer propped up beside him as he plugged a modem line into the phone, and I knew he was dialing up the PRCA.

"I've used a lot of computers," I said with a smile as I stood behind his left shoulder, "but I don't think I've ever dialed up from a cell phone."

"Gotta be up-to-date," he said. "Gotta ride whatever horse wins you money."

"Are you by any chance dialing up PRCA?"

"Bingo. That wins you a beer. You on for that?"

"Maybe."

"Great. What I'm doing, I'm registering for the Prescott rodeo."

I put my hand on his shoulder, just a touch, to keep him talking.

"I'll do this later. Let's start off with that beer."

He started to unplug the modem.

"No. Show me. Like I said, I work in computers, but I've never seen this."

He punched in numbers on the cell phone, and we watched the modem connect and a login box come up on his screen. He typed in his ID, cwcooper, all lower-case. I tried to watch him typing the password, but his finger covered the keys and I couldn't see the password, only the seven asterisks on the screen. He flexed his fingers and grinned. I realized he'd deliberately hid the password from me.

"No offense," he said. "Cost me too much money to let anybody know how to get to my records and maybe screw them up. Some cowboys, they get computer smarts, they know how to go into somebody who's riding against them, screw up their entries. Me, I barely make enough to keep my ranch going, keep my wife paying the bills."

He quickly worked through several screens, entering information for different events. Finished, he logged out and turned off his cell phone and computer.

"Now. How about that beer?"

"Another time."

"How about watching me ride tomorrow?"

"I don't think so."

His smile faded, and he looked me up and down.

"Then how about a quick fuck?"

I stepped backward in alarm at the hard edge in his voice. He put phone and computer in a carryall and pulled out a spur, running his fingers over the rowel for a moment before he walked off. Over the next ten minutes, one cowboy after another hit on me, one offering me $50 for a ride. Hating the feeling of being insecure, I decided to leave the fairgrounds, leave the rodeo, leave Albert Grody, wherever and whoever he was, and start looking for Judy Pavatea's friend, Mary Nataanie.

Back at my computers by midnight, I pulled up the results of my searches for drug information and started slogging away at the keyboard in spite of the heat that had built up in the trailer because I'd forgotten to turn on the air conditioners. I discovered that a breeze ran from the open bedroom window, through the connecting doors, and out the open trailer front door. I latched the screen door, carefully jacked a shell into the shotgun, and laid it against the work counter beside the keyboard.

At two o'clock I had nothing. I started probing the PRCA site again, this time setting script hacks in place to search for cwcooper. I worked with my usual enthusiasm, but I no longer had my usual energy despite a pot of coffee and a half-quart bottle of Mountain Dew. Despite all the caffeine, I fell asleep sometime around four.

10

Sunrise.

I'm standing on a four-hundred-foot tower, standing on Spider rock, waiting for a goddess to appear with
a message for the entire world. I've been chosen to write
down the message. I've got a lined yellow tablet, a black
Pilot fine-line pen.

And there's the goddess!

Streaking toward me like a comet.

I uncap the pen, eager to write. The goddess slows,
hovers twenty feet away and above me. She opens her
mouth, but instead of words out comes little . . . clouds.
No. More like stars. Starbursts, fireworks, exploding in
three-dimensional streaks toward me. No, not fireworks. Chunks of color. Raw, vivid, puffy like clouds.
Brilliant and shiny, like stars. Explosive and demanding
immediate attention.

Entranced, eager, I lean toward the first cloud, star,
color, whatever. They might even be musical notes, but
I can see they're going to pass over my head, and I *levi-
tate* above the tower, effortlessly weightless in the air,
ready to hear see feel the message, not knowing what
I'm supposed to do, feeling nervous, anxious. I breathe

deep, ten heavy, lung-expanding breaths because of too full of wanting to get things *right*. But just as the first cloudstarcolor . . . when the first *thing* is inches away, it looms a thousand times larger than the second before, and I'm so *terrified* that I backpedal in midair, trying to maintain a safe distance from the *thing*, which begins to lose substance as it nears me. It shimmers. It disappears. Just like that.

The goddess smiles at me and slowly evanesces as the *things* keep coming. I've got to overcome my anxiety, I've got to move *into* them, get completely *inside* them, or I'm not going to understand the message. But my anxiety drags me down like gravity, and the *things* keep dissolving just above my face until they start ringing—

And the answering machine came on beside me as I fought to wake up.

"I woke up, on the road again," the voice said quietly, confidently, almost matter-of-factly, "and I had to call to say I dreamed I was fucking you."

It was morning. I looked at the kitchen wall clock, saw I'd slept until eight.

"Your body's really quite delicious."

I came fully alert because it wasn't the same man who'd called before.

"Well, gotta stop for gas. But I'm on the road a lot, I travel someplace different every week, so I'll call you again. Next time, pick up the phone. I *want* you."

And he hung up.

I stuck my head under the kitchen faucet and drank and drank. I swallowed a Ritalin, and then I

swallowed another and then another. I fought off an
incredible desire to clean up the trailer, to dust and vacuum and mop. I started a pot of coffee and couldn't wait
for all the water to drip through, snatching the pot to fill
a water glass, scalding my mouth, holding the pot as
coffee sizzled on the hot plate.

Chill down here, I told myself.

Think, don't panic. Be cool, be calm. Think.

I carefully, deliberately, set down the coffeepot. I
took out the answering machine tape and duped it on
my small stereo deck. Jittery from the combination of
Ritalin and caffeine, I walked from one end of the trailer
to the other, back and forth, playing the tape over and
over, trying to recognize a phrasing, a tone, *anything*
that might give me a clue about these two men.

Part of me believed the calls were not really for me
at all, but a way of threatening me to get at Ben. Another
part believed it could be somebody who knew that I
was looking for Albert Grody, for missing girls, for
aloosaka. Or was it somebody I'd met during the past
two days, Kimo Biakeddy, one of the Navajo policemen,
or the Hopi Ranger? They seemed unlikely candidates,
which left the biker Kiyonnie.

But there were *two* voices. Distinctly different, both
threatening. Both of the voices sounded familiar, yet
unfamiliar, perhaps altered because the phone lines cut
off some of the frequencies or because the men deliberately disguised their voices.

Why were they calling me?

My dream came back vividly. Who was the goddess, what was her message? Part of me felt it was a

warning to do as Ben said, just pack up and leave. Another part of me felt that it offered some clue about finding Judy Pavatea.

But nothing made sense. I shut down all my computers, wanting to end the data searches and concentrate instead on finding Mary Nataanie. I had no idea where she lived but figured I could go to the Tuba City Chapter House and explain that I worked with Billie Tso and that Mary was a key to finding another runaway girl.

"Yo. Hello. Yazzie, you in there?"

A man's voice, determined, knocking on the aluminum siding of the trailer.

I realized with shock that the main front door was still open, and I couldn't remember if I'd latched shut the screen.

Peeking out the workroom window, I first saw a Chevy Blazer in the drive and then saw a man staring inside the front door, both hands raised to shield his eyes, his face pressed directly against the screen. I could make out only the outline of his body, a gun holstered on his left hip. He was wearing sunglasses. And he was huge, easily six feet two and over 250 pounds.

"Anybody home?"

He fiddled with the door handle, idly whistling an old Beatles tune. I started to cross to the kitchen counter where I'd laid the shotgun, but the door opened suddenly and he stepped confidently inside.

"Where is it?" he said.

He was young, barely mid-twenties, blond, clean shaven, with a very precise, almost military haircut. He removed his sunglasses and shut the screen behind him, leaving the main door open. I could see into the street, but nobody was there.

"Just give it to me."

"Give *what* to you?"

He held his hands out to his side, *what's a guy to do?* I backed up a few steps, trying to move toward the shotgun. He saw it and moved quickly to snatch it up, racking the slide until the last cartridge ejected onto the floor. After he'd laid the shotgun behind him, he wagged a finger at me.

"Where is it?"

"I don't know what you're talking about."

He considered that a long time, as though my defiance were something so alien, he couldn't quite find its spoor. His right hand, fingers curling, strayed toward his revolver butt and then moved past it, down the side of the holster toward two grooved pockets for pens. He pulled out one of the pens and started flipping it between his fingers. He'd obviously been practicing that for a long time. The pen rose, revolved twice in the air, came down exactly right between in his fingers to be flipped again. He didn't look at it once, but stared at my body, his eyes moving from my bare thighs to my neck.

"I mean you no personal harm," he said to me. "My name's Garcia. I'm a friend of Yazzie's. You must be Yazzie's partner. Not here now, is he?"

Garcia. The bounty hunter Ben told me about, the crazy one who kept banging a woman's head against a wall heater.

"He's gone to Phoenix," I said. "He had a Spanish thing, took it with him."

"I think you're playing with me. I think you've got it in here somewhere."

His eyes gradually settled on the cleavage of my breasts.

"I don't think you were expecting me. Not that

Yazzie ever told me about this place, or that he worked with somebody here. But I knew he had somebody who ran computer stuff for him. I knew he used to work for a bail bond place in Flagstaff. They gave me this address. And here I am."

He moved sideways. My skin chilled, my stomach twisted. I pulled the tank-top straps tight, knowing this kind of man who'd drift sideways, wanting to catch you on the slant, trying to get a sightline through where a blouse buttoned, into an open armhole, trying to see your breasts. He walked to the refrigerator. I twisted with him. He understood what I was doing and smiled.

"Please."

"Ah. When people say please, touches my heart. Here. Lemme touch yours."

He stood right in front of me and cupped my right breast.

"Now. Let's go look around the rest of this trailer. It's in here somewhere."

An enormous shadow rose behind the screen door as it slammed open—*wham!*—and Kimo Biakeddy came inside and rabbit-punched Garcia once, twice. Garcia staggered, dropped to both knees in agony. Kimo reached down and pulled Garcia's revolver from its holster and stood over him, the revolver loose in his right hand, the barrel just a few inches from Garcia's neck as Kimo stuck his free hand inside Garcia's collar, choking him because the collar was buttoned and the tie pulled tight against the button. Kimo pulled him back and upward so fast that he didn't even have time to avoid getting butted in the lips by the back of Garcia's head. Kimo shoved Garcia out through the screen door and toward the Blazer. He opened the driver's-side door, threw Garcia inside, and slammed Garcia's head against the steering wheel three times, whapping the horn button. Blood spattered everywhere as Garcia's nose and upper lip split wide open. He coughed, tried to wipe up some of the blood with his hand, distract-edly wiped some more off with his tie. Garcia tried to get out of the car. Kimo slammed the door shut on his hand.

"Jesus!" Garcia shouted. "You asshole, you busted my finger."

"You ready to leave now?" Kimo said to Garcia.

Garcia nodded, once, a short jerk up and down.

"Wait," I said, standing a few feet from Garcia. "What did you want here?"

"*Puta.*"

"Lady asked what you want here," Kimo said, slap-ping him again. "Lady didn't ask you to call her a whore. And I think I'm gonna call the Navajo police and violate your ass. No. I think I'm just gonna hurt you."

Kimo took the man's hand and deliberately snapped another finger.

"Lady wants to know what you're doing here."

"Kayenta," the man shouted. "I was with Yazzie up in Kayenta."

"Get the police," Kimo said.

"You call them, I'll give up Yazzie's name."

Kimo stared at me, not sure what to do.

"Let him go," I said.

"You're kidding."

"Kimo, please. Just let him go."

"Fuck you both!" Garcia shouted as he started his engine.

Kimo lunged toward him, but Garcia held one arm against his ribs, used the other on the gearshift, spun in reverse out of the drive, shifted, and tore down the road.

"Oh, God, thank you," I said. I hugged him, I held on to him, I let him stroke my forehead, and I treasured having somebody to hold me and not let go. Blood dripped from his face onto my tank-top. He stepped back and pulled out a folded red bandanna and held it against my tank top, trying to blot up the blood. Not only folded, I thought, but ironed. This seemed incredible to me, that a man would carry an ironed bandanna. He realized he was rubbing my right breast and put the bandanna quickly on his lip.

"Come back inside. Let me get you something for your mouth."

I went inside, thinking he was right behind, but he stopped outside the screen door. I stood just on the other side of the door, separated by a few inches as we stared at each other through the rusted mesh. One of my father's riddles flashed through my head. Take a newspaper page, put it on the floor, and stand on it with the one you love. Except you can't touch each other. How is this possible? Put the paper under a closed door.

"Come inside."

"I don't quite know what's happening here," he said. "Who was that guy?"

"What are you doing?"

"You look really strung out, Miss Winslow. You look like you're abusing Ritalin. I made a note about it for Dr. Melnick."

"That's none of your business."

"This is an Abuse Recovery Clinic. I don't know your history with Dr. Melnick, but we have pharmacy rules about noting down possible substance abuse."

I ran outside the hospital and stood under a NO SKATEBOARDING sign, where three kids on skateboards wheeled up a rickety plywood ramp and flew two feet off the ground. My thighs were trembling, I felt incredibly wobbly, and I had to stand back flat against the wall, shaking my head violently from side to side just as Kimo came outside, gently licking his lip.

"Okay," he said. "I guess this is good-bye."

"Listen. What did they pay you at the Saveway?"

"Five fifty an hour."

"I'll give you two hundred dollars. I want to hire you for a week."

"Come on." He laughed. "Why would you do a thing like that?"

"Because you're the only person I feel I can trust right now."

"You don't know me at all," he said. "You don't want to trust a stranger."

"I need somebody who knows Navajos, who knows how to find people."

"Been all over the Rez, that much is true. Who you want to find?"

"I'm looking for a Nataanie family."

"Don't know."

"Well, he sure seemed to know you. What was he looking for?"

"I have no idea at all."

"And you don't want to talk about it."

"No. Look, you're bleeding. We should put something on your lip. I've got some antibiotic cream, I've got some bandages."

He stopped just over the sill, the door banging against his back.

I started rummaging through the kitchen cabinets for cream and a roll of gauze.

"Who's this Yazzie guy?"

"He was my partner."

"Oh. I didn't know you were living with some guy."

"No. A business partner. Just be quiet. How did you find out where I lived?"

As I leaned over to open a bottom cabinet, I saw him look at my breasts. He said something, and I didn't hear the words, feeling giddy, foolish, on fire.

"Not hard to do. It's a really small town."

"But I hardly know anybody."

"The Tribal Police came by this morning, ready to set up a blockade around the Saveway store. I asked them about you."

Avoiding his eyes, I found the gauze packets and ripped one open. I could see several minute scars on both lips, but the lower one had a deep crack.

"We're going over to the hospital to get your lip sewn up. Let me just put on some other clothes and I'll drive you there."

"Why would you do that for me?"

"I owe you at least that much."

In the bedroom I rummaged in the closet, finally choosing a white long-sleeved shirt and a floor-length skirt, still uneasy remembering how Garcia had looked at my body. After picking out a pair of tiny seed-pearl studs, I had some difficulty pushing the studs through the holes in my ears, and that suddenly made me wonder again how long it had been since I'd bothered with jewelry, and *that* made me wonder what I was doing, dressing up for somebody I hardly knew. I heard him walk into the workroom.

"What's all this?"

He'd picked up one of the cell phones and was tossing it between his hands, looking over the police scanners, counting the nine cell phones, assessing everything in the workroom.

"What do you do with all this stuff?"

"I'm a computer consultant," I said, taking the cell phone from him. "Come on, let's get to the hospital and fix your lip."

"It's okay. Just leave it."

"It's *not* okay. There's a flap hanging down."

I collected the shotgun and stooped to pick up the shells. He started to ask a question, but I gently pressed his hand and the bandanna to his lips, and he said nothing more as we drove to the hospital, where an intern stuck him on a gurney and put a cloth over his face, with a hole for his mouth.

"What does the other guy look like?" the intern asked.

"What is this, a movie?" Kimo answered.

"You keep wisecracking like that, I'll sew your lip to your tongue."

"You really know what you're doing?"

"Three thousand bar fights and counting. I could sew you up blindfolded and play five-card stud on the side."

"Don't leave yet," Kimo mumbled at me, crinkling his nose at the burnt-flesh smell when the intern used a tiny heat tool, like a soldering iron, to cauterize the open tear before he sewed up Kimo's lip with thirty-five stitches of ultrafine thread.

I fluttered around him for a bit, wanting to hold his hand, but the intern shooed me outside. I fumbled in my handbag for the Ritalin vial and uncapped it. Only four were left, and after swallowing two of them at the drinking fountain, I went into the pharmacy and asked for a refill.

"I can't do that, Miss Winslow."

"Look," I said, "it says two refills."

"But it's a controlled substance. See the orange warning label?"

"I can control it," I said. "Just give me a refill."

"No. I can't do that. Your prescription is a thirty-day supply, and if you come in before that time, I'm not allowed to give you a refill. Only your doctor can okay that."

"Melnick," I said. "Dr. Karen Melnick. Call her."

She checked a clipboard and shook her head.

"I'm sorry. Dr. Melnick is at a meeting in Flagstaff."

She wrote something on the clipboard.

"There are dozens of Nataanie families. Which one? Which clan?"

"They have a teenage daughter named Mary."

"That would be Charley and Leona Nataanie. Towering House People, down near Sand Springs, if they haven't been thrown off their land because of the partition."

I dug out two of the hundred-dollar bills and offered them to him.

"Take me down there."

"And use that shotgun on the next hardcase that comes after you?"

"It'll never come to anything like that."

"Yeah, sure. First there's this Garcia. Then I seem to remember you asking me about Albert Grody. How many other assholes are you dealing with?"

The biker's face suddenly popped into my head.

"Do you know somebody named Mike Kiyonnie?"

"What about him? . . . Ahhh." His eyes narrowed. "The other night, you asked me about teenagers and drugs, you asked about a girl named Judy Pavatea."

"And her grandfather told me where she'd last been living in Tuba City. I went up to the place and met this Kiyonnie, living in a line of row houses. I think there's some kind of drug processing going on, but he denied it."

"He did it for a while, but I haven't heard anything about him in weeks."

"He also denied that Judy had ever lived there."

"She sold meth, he made meth, but I never saw the two of them together."

"When we get back from Sand Springs, if you still want to work for me, I'll have to find out more about Kiyonnie. And you're right, I'd rather have you do the asking instead of me. Deal?"

I held out the money and the pickup keys. He studied me for a long time and finally shrugged and smiled and took the keys, but he folded my hand around the bills.

"For now, just keep hold of your money. And keep hold of your trust, until you know me better. Then you can decide."

12

Just across the partition line we turned south on a dirt track.

For years, Rez families had defined their land by which side of the government-enforced partition fence they were on. Most knew families who were either relocated, because of the government decree, or had sold their land to Hopis and hoped to continue renting the same space their families had owned for generations. Some Navajo families had moved out, while others signed the accommodation agreement.

"Hope you know what you're doing," Kimo said. "And where we're going. People around here aren't too friendly with strangers."

"I don't give a goddamn about partition politics."

"It's not about politics. It's about who owns the land. People out here, I mean the Navajo families, their land is their heritage, and they'll keep fighting for every inch of the Rez that the government gives to the Hopis."

"I just need to find the girl."

"Okay. But let me do the talking."

I inhaled the pungent, usually satisfying aroma of burning sweetgrass. Anxious, jittery, I found no satisfaction at all this time. Kimo slowed into crawler gear when we crossed Dinnebito Wash and moved into a tiny community of trailers and concrete-block buildings. He drove a bit farther to a scrapboard house, barely more than a shack, with a fallen-down hogan out back next to a sweatlodge. He turned off the engine and sat, waiting for them to acknowledge his arrival.

"How well do you know these people?" I asked.

"Pretty good. I spent some time out here last summer, 'cause Charley's got some real modern stuff for growing crops." He gestured at the fields on the other side of the house. "He borrowed and saved enough money to buy into an Israeli thing. Some kind of drip-irrigation system, like they use over there in the Mideast deserts. Charley started out with just blue corn, now he's got potatoes, onions, even some fruit on vines. Trouble is, he's living on borrowed time, waiting for the Hopis to throw him off their newly won partition land."

A woman came out of the house, waving.

"Stay here," he said.

He went toward the woman. They talked in Navajo for a few minutes. She shook her head, but they kept talking. A man walked around the corner of the house. The three of them talked. The man shook his head, violently. He walked away, back toward the fields. The woman watched him go, nodding her head, shaking her head, frowning, finally coming over to study me through the open window for at least five minutes before pinching Kimo's shirtsleeve to draw him aside again. She pointed to several spots around the house, nodding all the time, and finally went back into the house.

Kimo climbed into the pickup.

"She's not here. Charley didn't want to let me know where she'd gone, but Leona's decided to trust you. 'Cause of me, I guess."

"Did they say where she went?"

"Up to Leona's parents' place. Charley and Leona, they're not talking about why their daughter's away, saying she's fine, it's just a visit, she loves her grand-mother. But you can tell something's wrong, the way they cut their eyes around, duck underneath a ques-tion, instead of just gazing at you steady as though the earth's at peace. They're troubled, they're worried about their daughter, wouldn't surprise me at all if they sent her away so she'd be safe from skinwalkers."

"Why do people believe in witches?" I said.

"Don't you?"

I started a sarcastic response and then realized he was serious.

"What was she pointing at back there?"

"Leona was born and raised in that house. She was telling me where her umbilical cord is buried. Where she buried her daughter's cord. That's part of why they don't want to be pushed off their land."

"You know where these grandparents live?"

"Yeah," he said shortly, as though he'd evaluated the trust between us and found it okay. "I could drive us there, if you're up for the trip."

"Where?"

"Way up near Red Rock. Place called Cove. Lots of old widows up there. Cancer killed off their men, from years of working the uranium mines. One thing for sure. They know the U.S. government is mostly at fault, so they don't go blaming it on skinwalkers."

"You're not really telling me you believe in skinwalkers?"

"That's talk for another time," he said firmly. "You want me to take you?"

"Let's go."

He clanked into low gear, and we headed north again. He looked back and forth from me to the road as if he were thinking about asking a question he wanted to ask and wanting to use the right words so I wouldn't take offense.

"Why are you looking for Mary?" he finally asked. "And for that Judy Pavatea? I don't understand what you've got to do with two teenage girls you've never even met."

I thought about answering him in a dozen different, partially truthful ways, but as the truck bucked and jolted across the wash I felt all dissembling pass beyond me for the first time I could even remember.

"Permission," I said. "In a way, it's just permission."

"For what?"

"To keep looking for my daughter."

"What do you mean?"

His gaze was open, inviting, and I thought, What the hell?

"I was in AIM, with my husband."

"Who was that?"

"Jonathan Begay."

"Johnny Begay? Really?"

"Yes. Did you ever know him?"

"Met him, once, maybe ten years ago. He was part

of a band of renegade AIM people who tried to take over a plant in Gallup."

"That's him. In the bad days, after I left him."

"Did you have good days?"

"You ask a lot of direct questions."

"People keep telling me that. So?"

"Do you like rock music?" I asked.

"Not really."

"Well, in the old days, there was this great song 'Johnny Be Good.' Except, we'd sing it, 'Oh, oh, oh, Johnny Begay.' We had a daughter, two years before we got married. We took one look at her, right after birth, and she had these long arms, long legs, moving all around, and just like that a nurse said, 'Whoa, this one's crawling up my arm like a spider,' and so we named her Spider. After Spider Woman. When I had enough of Jonathan's going bad, I left him, but he kept Spider. I tried to take her once, but he beat me, bad. We were living up north of Kayenta, that time."

I didn't know how much to tell him.

"How long ago was that?"

"Late seventies."

"Did you ever find out anything about her?"

"No."

"Any idea what happened to her?"

"No."

"Have you let her go?"

"You mean, do I think Spider's dead?"

He frowned. "If you think she's dead, don't say her name. You can say 'the one who was my daughter' or 'the person who was once my daughter.' But since you call her by name, I have to think you believe she's out there. Why are you telling me, anyway?"

"No idea," I said. No idea at all.

"Well. Thank you," he said.

"Why?"

"I'm not used to talking about other people's . . . private things. I might be direct, but I know that around here, most people don't like that. Not even to friends. Unless maybe they're drunk, or kin, and sometimes not if they're of a different clan."

"I'm surprised I'm talking about her."

"Tell me her name again."

"Spider. Spider Begay."

He put two fingers on top of my thigh, not rubbing the skin or lingering there, just a touch and then lifting his fingers off. I held his hand. His nails were carefully manicured, the moons underneath his nails clean and perfect.

"Do it myself," he said. "An old prison habit, keeping yourself clean."

"Why were you in prison?"

He hesitated, finally shook his head.

"I don't want to talk about that yet. But I always keep my nails clean. And collect the nails and the parings and bury them deep, so nobody can have a piece of me, nobody can ever control my spirit."

"Don't give me any more bullshit about witches."

As we pulled on 264, we passed an ancient Chevy pickup, the longbox bed overloaded with hay bales and four-by-fours and three children holding two sheep between them.

"That truckload reminds me of the time when I was living in LA," he said with a smile so wide, I saw several dull silver fillings. "I really needed cash one time. Heard about this insurance scam. Some lawyers set it up, they also had a few doctors rigged at a medical clinic. We'd load up four, six inside these old junker cars and then get into a convoy on the freeways, looking for a situation."

We rounded a curve and saw a billboard, the head and tail of an arrow emerged from both sides at the top. Underneath, the sign had faded away, something about a trading post with propane, gas, and disposal spelled DIPOSAL with the first S missing. Across the sign somebody had spray-painted RELOCATION IS GENOCIDE.

"Here's how it worked. We'd look for a tractor-trailer, the long, long kind, where the driver's thinking half a mile ahead 'cause he's got so much steel moving sooooo fast. They got tremendous insurance, those semi companies. We'd only go for ones with big-time names painted on the side, so we knew they had plenty of insurance. We'd box him in, since he'd usually be in the right lane. One of our cars would get into position just ahead of him, the rest of us in the lane right alongside, and then another of our cars would pull ahead of our first car and swerve in front of it, and *pow!* everybody stands on their brakes. But that trucker's got so much steel pushing him, he always smashed into what's in front of him, and the rest of us pile on, and once they swept away all the glass and towed the junk off, we'd be filing multiple insurance claims. We'd get paid maybe thirty, fifty dollars a claim. The lawyers, the doctors, they got thousands."

"You'd get into a car wreck for thirty dollars?"

"Hey. Do you remember times when you needed thirty dollars?"

Yes, I did, and the thought drove away my euphoria. I fumbled in my handbag for the Ritalin bottle, but it was empty. I'd thought I had two left, but the vial was uncapped.

"What's wrong?" he said.

I upended my handbag on the floor, rooting through the debris and finding no pills.

"I need . . . my medicine. I take medicine, and I'm out of it."

"What medicine?"

"Ritalin. It helps me focus." He shook his head. "It's kind've like speed."

"Bad for you. Why don't we get us some coffee."

Half an hour later we stopped at the Hopi Cultural Center and I got six takeout cups. Kimo bought some fry bread, and we ate and drank until he turned north on 191.

"Tell me some more about yourself," I said.

"I need a job, need to make some money."

"Take the money I'm offering you."

"I don't mean day to day. I want enough to last years, hell, even just one year. Enough to get me straightened out so I can find a place to settle. Here on the Rez there's nothing, really. Nobody makes much of a living. And outside, you gotta have diplomas, you gotta have degrees, you gotta have training, experience. And if all you've done is one scam after another, nobody wants to talk with you about a legit job, not when you're forty-five, got no clothes good enough for an interview, got no résumé. Shit. You get into a room with one of those interviewers, one of those suits, he makes you feel like an outsider, like a bum, like a nobody, like you're the enemy, like you gotta overthrow his whole concept of you just to get a chance to ask for a job."

"That's been your life the last twenty years? One scam after another?"

"Yeah. Air bags, fake caviar up in the Northwest, snakes, rare birds . . ."

"Air bags?"

"In Las Vegas, I got hooked up between this group of junkies and an auto repair shop. Junkies would steal the bags, I'd pay them fifty, resell them for a hundred. Auto repair guy, he'd sell them for two bills up, sometimes, depending on the model car, he'd go as high as six bills."

"You're saying, when they'd strip a car, they'd sell you the air bags?"

"No. They only stole the bags. Nothing else."

"How did you end up in Tuba City?"

"I got tired of the hassles of scamming, tired of the life, tired of stealing, tired of you name it. Thought I'd do something straight. Actually, my aunt died up at Big Mountain two years ago and I came back for that and decided I wanted to stay on the Rez. Went into the Saveway for something a year ago, I don't remember what for, and saw a sign in the window for night shift. Took the job right then, worked steady, seven nights a week. I figured I'd got this life, you know, where I'd be regular, where I knew what would happen every day,

where I could save up some money. And then the guy
shuts the place down and here I am again, out of work."

"Hey," I protested. "Things aren't that bad."

He lifted his foot off the gas pedal, and the pickup
gradually slowed. Without ever touching the brake, he
shifted into neutral and straddled the yellow line as we
glided along the absolutely flat and level blacktop. The
pickup stopped in the middle of the road.

"Haven't you ever wanted to just end it all? Doing
eighty miles an hour, nowhere to go, nothing to do, no
plans, no future, you just yank the wheel sideways and
end it."

"Pull off the road," I said.

"Or you see an overpass ahead of you, and instead
of going underneath and on down the road, you head
right into the concrete."

"Please!"

"I don't know what we're doing out here, but
you've got some kind of plan."

He goosed the gas pedal but made no effort to pull
off the road. I saw nothing ahead of us, but looking out
the rear window, I saw a semi coming up from behind.

"Me, I've got no plans beyond today. Let me ask
you something else. Back at Pine Ridge, I heard you
were a Hopi girl who called herself Butterfly. Now your
name is Laura Winslow. So who are you? How can you
change like that? What keeps you moving from one
year to the next, what's your game plan for getting to
the next day, the next year?"

"Kimo. There's a semi two hundred yards behind
us. Right now, all I want is for you to get off the road."

He shifted into first gear and drove onto the shoulder.

"You still think you can trust me?"

I shook my head, shrugged my shoulders, too frightened to speak.

"So just tell me this. What happened to that butterfly girl?"

"That was yesterday," I said. "That was another life."

"There are no other lives," he said sadly. "Just this one."

13

Ella Manybeads yanked the fat goat sideways, shoving it against the ground. Some of Ella's gray-black hair hung loose from her *tsiyeel*. She undid and brushed her long hair, then carefully rewound and tied the bun with some blue yarn before asking me to move aside so she could kneel on the goat's front legs and head.

"Usually they squawk at me, but this one knew it was his time."

She whipped her knife quickly across its throat and put a chipped pottery dish underneath its neck to catch the blood. Refusing my offer to help, she laboriously stuffed the rest of the goat inside a big plastic garbage bag and laid another one on the ground. Using the same knife, she made a long cut along the goat's belly and chest, opening it up so she could start cutting out organs and intestines. She cut surely but slowly, her arthritic hands as gnarled as juniper bark.

The delicacies piled up.

Heart, liver, pancreas, different-size pieces of intestines, and all the goat's different stomachs. She hacked out and sectioned the ribs into roughly equal lengths.

"Okay," she said, "bring that meat inside for me."

She took the bowl of blood, and the three of us went into her stone house. The room we entered was essentially all kitchen, with a propane refrigerator and a fifty-gallon drum cut down to function as a wood-burning stove. Another room through an archway had sheepskins on a frame and different kinds of boxes lining the walls. Mary Nataanie was nowhere around. Neither was Ella's husband.

Ella ignored me and kept up a constant chatter in Navajo with Kimo, who apparently was the son of a woman she once knew. I could hardly follow the throaty, almost raucous Navajo language, full of glottal stops and breathy aspirated sounds. I got the sense of what they were talking about but kept silent as they discussed kinship, who knew who, and which mother's son was a cousin of somebody else's son.

"All this talking makes me hungry. Come on."

Ella had switched to English, and I realized I'd been partially accepted. Kimo had warned me it might be hours before Ella decided to trust us, might be never. I was impatient to start asking her questions, but Ella's trust still had some miles to go. She lit a fire of juniper twigs and sticks in the drum stove and talked about how much she loved goat, how she favored the heart and intestines, while her husband could never get enough ribs. And never enough blood cakes to satisfy either of them.

"Please," I whispered to Kimo. "I can't stand this. How do I get her talking about Mary?"

"You'll have to wait."

Once the juniper fire caught and steadied and the

coals were hot enough, Ella threw some of the ribs onto a flat metal grill and began cleansing the intestines. She wrapped each of them in turn around her fingers and carefully placed the coils on the grill, taking pains to position both ribs and intestines in the best cooking position.

The meat sizzled and cooked. I inhaled the smell and smiled as Ella turned the meat on the grill. She put one of the stomachs into a chipped enamel bowl and slowly peeled the muscles away from the lining. Having set aside the muscles, she arranged the lining inside the bowl and filled it with some of the blood, taking care to fold the lining and create a blood-filled sac.

"Let's talk some while this finishes cook up," she said in English. "I asked Kimo before, asked what he knew about you. You're okay, he says. But I need to ask some things for myself."

"Please. What can I tell you?"

"Why do you want to talk to Mary?"

"A friend of hers ran away. A Hopi girl named Judy. Judy Pavatea."

Ella shook her head. "Don't know that name. I'm surprised that Mary would spend much time with one of *them.*"

"They went to a dance, two weeks before graduation night. I just wanted to ask Mary if she knew where Judy went after the dance."

Ella cocked her head at me, half closed her eyes.

"I don't know what's going on," she said finally, taking the last rib. "Charley and Leona, they're worried sick, what with almost being kicked off their land. I figured they sent Mary up here just to have time for themselves. But she's not talking much. Cries a lot. Something happened. I don't know what."

Ella fiddled at the grill for a moment and then turned to me with a frown.

"Whatever questions you've got," she said, "I can't help you at all. Mary says nothing, sits around all day, staring. She used to dress up so pretty, and now, well, you can see, she just doesn't care what she looks like, doesn't care about anything. I know something bad has happened. I'm surprised Leona even told you Mary was up here."

I started to say something, but Ella cut me off short.

"Bad, bad things happening since she came here. There's talk about skinwalkers. Mind, now, I don't want you bothering the girl."

"I won't."

"Leona trusted her to me, said take good care of her."

"So where is she?"

"Walked up the road a ways. I'm gonna work on these stomachs, make some blood cakes. I think you oughta go see Lee and Mary now. That Lee, he won't be so happy with me, not if he misses out on his favorite parts."

Wrestling to keep the pickup in first gear, we wound up a rough track through one of many red rock mesas on the eastern rim of the Chuska mountains.

"If they're hiding, how will we find them?"

"Who knows?" Kimo pointed at a hawk circling far

above them. "Maybe he's bringing the news. You wanna tell me what this is about?"

"I think the girl's been raped."

His face grew almost beet red, his jaw muscles flexing.

"You know who did it?"

"No idea at all."

"How come you're so certain it happened?"

"You're probably not going to much believe this, but all I've got to go on is that an old man saw it in a vision."

"Any clues? I mean, any idea what happened?"

"My guess is that Mary and Judy Pavatea got picked up at a teenage dance, and they were both raped. Mary somehow got away."

"And Judy?"

"She's what this is all about. I was paid to find her."

He worked the pickup up a dirt track past abandoned houses, the road sometimes narrowing to a single-lane track between a sparse forest of juniper and piñon trees. As we crawled past a twenty-foot rock cliff, stems from a cliff rose brushed inside my window. Some of the petals broke off, dropped fragrantly into my lap. I pinched them together, inhaled the aroma. Kimo puckered up his nose.

"When I grew up," he said, "I always associated those roses with urine. My mother packed the petals inside her baby's diapers to soak up the urine, help stop chafing the baby's skin."

"This is beautiful country up here."

"Yeah, I suppose. But would you want to live here,

with nothing but trees and sheep and goats in your future?"

Once at the top of the mesa, he had to drive carefully between a maze of large holes toward two people sitting not far away. Seeing the pickup, both stood up as though they'd been waiting.

"Hi, Mary," Kimo said to her.

She seemed nervous, anxious, depressed, a wreck. I smiled quickly, but she avoided looking at me. She'd twisted her hair so much that some of it was still tangled. Her jeans were clean enough, but her T-shirt had wet, dirty spots on it, and the left side was tucked into her jeans while the right side wasn't.

"Who're you?" the man asked me.

"This is Laura Winslow," Kimo said. "Laura Winslow, Lee Manybeads."

Lee stood on one side of the pickup's hood and thunked down his elbow. Shaking his head in mock fear, Kimo stood on the other side of the hood, and the two of them grasped palms, ready to arm wrestle.

"Don't watch now, young lady," Lee said to me. "This pup'd died of embarrassment if you was to see me whip him. Any time you think you can do it, Kimo, just start the ball rolling."

Kimo flexed his biceps, showing off for me, and in that instant Lee slammed the back of Kimo's hand against the hood. The two of them laughed. I cut my eyes toward Mary, hoping to see at least a smile, but Mary wasn't even looking at them, just staring down. Kimo shook the banged hand and blew on his knuckles while Lee climbed into the back of the pickup. Mary wanted to sit with him, but he urged her to squeeze in between us. As Kimo drove back down the mesa, Mary Nataanie moved as far away from me as she could get, trying to keep from touching me, even pulling her skirt tight against her left thigh. At Ella's house, Mary jumped out and ran into the junipers.

"She won't talk with me around," Kimo said. "I'll leave you alone with her, give you an hour. I drive up, don't see you sitting in outside, I'll back off and wait."

"You're a very sweet man," I said, leaning in to kiss his cheek. But he turned his head and kissed me on the lips, soft at first, pressing toward me. I tasted blood.

"Yeah," he said, holding his lip, "keep this up, I'll bleed all over you."

"Another time."

"Cool," he said, driving away. I went to talk at last with Mary Nataanie.

14

Mary fiddled with the sheep's organs hanging on the rack.

"Why do they put them up so high?" I asked.

"Because animals will get them," she said finally, and burst into tears.

"Whatever happened, it's not your fault, Mary."

"You know all about it?"

"I know that something happened to you and Judy Pavatea."

"Did you talk with her? Is she all right?"

"No. I've never met her. Nobody knows where she is."

"I shouldn't have gone with them," she whispered to herself.

"Who? Did you know them?"

"No. I'm to blame, that's all I know."

"Whatever happened, Mary, it's not your fault."

"It *was* my fault. I deserved everything because I went with them when Judy said we shouldn't. She held me back, but I said it was just a ride, we'd sit in back of the pickup and jump out, nothing more than a ride."

"It's not your fault. What happened to you, what

happened to Judy, none of it is your fault. You have to start believing that. That's the first thing you have to get hold of, believing me when I say it's not your fault."

"How would you know?" Defiant about being interrogated by an adult. "It was all my fault."

"Mary, the first thing you have to keep saying to yourself is that it wasn't your fault. You're not to blame."

"For myself, maybe I could think that. But I made Judy come along. Everything that happened to her, I did make that happen, I was to blame for that."

"Why don't we talk about you?"

"I just want to forget about it, really."

"Judy's grandfather wants to find her. You might be able to tell me something that could help me. Can you talk about what happened?"

I waited for her to continue, but Mary just shook her head.

"You and Judy got into the back of their pickup, just for a ride home."

"Yes."

"Home from where?"

"You won't tell my father?"

"I promise. Whatever you tell me, I won't tell any-body."

Mary thought for a long time about how much she wanted to say.

"There were four of them. We were down at a bar in Holbrook."

She immediately looked at me, thinking she'd be condemned for going so far from home at her age. But I kept my eyes on the last of the sunset.

"We'd gotten a ride down from some guys we knew, but they got real drunk and said they were going over to Flagstaff. So me and Judy hung around outside the place, trying to see somebody we knew to catch a ride back to the Mesas. Then this truck came along."

"Wait a minute. The four men, they weren't at the bar?"

"No. They just came along in their pickup. Later I heard one say they'd come in from Gallup. Anyway, when they saw us, the driver stopped just ahead, almost like we were hitching, but we weren't, really, we didn't give them any sign. Well, we did look at them as they drove by." She sighed. "It was my fault, it was my fault."

"Tell me about the pickup."

"It was kinda new. Dirty, but new. Didn't have many scratches or dings on it. And it just looked new. I don't know what kind it was, but it had the word 'RAM' on the side. RAM something, I don't know what. Three boys sat in the cab, so we had to crawl through a door into the camper shell, where the fourth man was riding."

"Was there anything else inside the camper shell?"

"Lots of saddles. Ropes. All kinds of cowboy gear."

I got the canvas carryall and took it over to where Mary sat.

"Did any of the ropes look like this?"

I pulled out the bullrider's rope.

Mary didn't stop screaming until she was hoarse. I tried to hold her, but Mary ran back and forth around the yard. Ella came outside immediately, but I waved her away. Reluctantly she went back into the house, and

I waited for Mary to calm down. It was getting dark. I lay on the ground, held Mary in my arms. After a long time, Mary sat up again.

"Something bad's happened to Judy. I know it. I just know it."

"Talk to me about the rope."

"That's what they used when they rode us. They drove partway up Cottonwood Wash. They made Judy and me get out of the back. We thought they were just going to drop us off, maybe camp there. We could see the lights of cars on Forty, maybe a mile away. Then they made us take off our clothes. They all took off *their* clothes. One of them took Judy into the back of the pickup and another—"

"No," I protested. "I don't need to hear all of this. Not right now."

"And after a long time, after each of them did it to us at least once, one man got out a rope like the one you've got. He hung it around my chest, right underneath my breasts. And there were these bells."

"Was it like a cowbell?"

"A lot of little bells. I couldn't much tell, I was so scared he was going to kill me, there wasn't anything worse they could have done to me except kill me. He sat on me, like an animal, like he was sitting a horse or a bull, they talked about staying on us without getting thrown off, how they'd get a perfect ride. And then one of them said what a great bull I was, and then he started riding me again. I'll never forget his voice, never forget him shouting down me, how I was his perfect ride."

"Enough." I was firm. "That's enough, honey. Just

sit quiet with me, for a few more minutes. Let's just sit quiet."

"I ran away when they'd finished with me and started calling for Judy, calling her a bull, saying they'd all ride. I should have stayed to help her, but I ran away."

"You couldn't have helped her then. You could now."

"How?"

"Can you describe the men?"

"I drew pictures of two of them. I only saw two faces."

"You what?"

"I thought maybe if I drew pictures, and then burned them, I could get rid of their faces. But it didn't help."

"You burned the pictures?" I couldn't keep the disappointment from my voice.

"Yes. Was that wrong?"

"Can you describe them to me?"

"They were all young."

Except to her, most men were either young or old, and she didn't have much idea what their ages could be. It was too dark to really see what they looked like. They never turned on any lights of the truck, and while the girls rode in the back, in the camper shell, it was too dark to see any faces.

"Miss Laura?"

A very quiet voice.

"How do I forget their faces?"

"It takes time," I said. "But you can get over this.

And it has to start by you saying to yourself one thing.
It. Was. Not. My. Fault."

"But I'll always believe it was my fault, what happened to Judy. If it would help find Judy, I'll try to draw
the pictures again. Miss Laura?"

Quiet, hardly even a whisper.

"Yes?"

"What if I get AIDS?"

"You won't get AIDS," I said firmly.

"What if I get pregnant?"

"When you come back to Sand Springs, I'll go with
you to a doctor. Your father won't even have to know,
I'll just take you myself. Please, Mary, don't think about
AIDS or getting pregnant. Right now, just work on how
you're not to blame."

"Will you be my friend?"

"Yes, Mary."

"Promise?"

"Yes."

"Can I come stay with you?"

I jerked with surprise, and Mary cowered immediately.

"Your parents would never let you do that. What
you *can* do, the most important thing you can do, is try
to help me find some of these men. Besides, don't you
feel comfortable with your grandparents?"

"They're nice people, but they won't let me talk
about what happened. Grandma, she said my father
was shamed. You don't shame me, Miss Laura."

"All right," I said after a while. "Maybe you can
come visit. But you'll have to redraw those pictures. I

want to find those men, I want to punish them, so you'll have to help me know what they look like. Can you do that?"

"I'll try doing it tonight."

Frightened, she cuddled up in a ball, holding her knees, lying on my lap, and stayed that way until Kimo drove up. Mary ran quickly into the house. After ten minutes Lee Manybeads came out.

"You have a way with Mary," he said, "and whatever it is you said to her, Ella and me give you our thanks."

"Don't leave her alone," I said. "Make sure one of you is with Mary all the time."

"We been doing that," he said. "We especially been keeping her in at night. Folks up here been talking about skinwalkers lately."

"Forget about skinwalkers," I said abruptly, aware that by being direct, I might be seen as rude. "Mary might think of suicide."

"Take her own life?" Manybeads was shocked. "Not likely, I think."

"Just make sure one of you is with her. Okay?"

We drove away in silence, Kimo concentrating on the rough dirt road, hugging the steering wheel tightly as though he wanted to straighten it out.

"You meant that?" he said finally. "About suicide?"

"She feels so ashamed that anything's possible."

"And you know who made her ashamed? Who raped her?"

"No. And she didn't remember anything that could really help find the men."

"There's a lot you're not telling me."

"I don't know you well enough yet," I said. "I don't trust you. Yet."

He bristled at that. I snuggled over next to him and leaned my head against his shoulder, and he put his arm around me like Clark Gable and Marilyn Monroe in *The Misfits*, where Marilyn asks how he knows the way home at night in the desert and he says, Just follow that star and it'll lead us right back home.

15

Reaching blacktop at Rock Point, we headed north to 160 and turned west near Mexican Water. At Tes Nez Ian, he turned the radio to KTNN, the announcer speaking in Navajo until his voice finally faded out.

"Kimo," I said, and stopped talking as a flush spread from my breasts up my throat and warmed my face because it was the first time I'd called him by name. "Tell me about Albert Grody."

"Two hours without a word, and that's the first thing comes to your mind?"

"Yes."

He drove for ten miles in silence.

"One crazy fucking bad dude, that's the best I can say about him. Stole some money from me once. I never got it back. What did he steal now?"

What can I tell him? I thought. To my right, the outline of Comb Ridge lay black against the night sky, a long arrowhead protecting the northern edge of the Rez, sometimes called the Backbone of the Earth. I thought of how much had happened in two days, how much had changed, how far I'd moved from that antisocial person who spent days inside an aluminum oven, connecting to the world through telephones and computers, investing trust only in networks, systems, information, data retrieval. I looked at his face, barely lit by dashboard lights, his profile reassuring like Comb Ridge.

I am going to *trust* this man, I thought. A forgotten feeling, trust.

"He may have stolen some sacred Hopi things. Spiritual things."

"Kachinas?"

"No. Something called an *aloosaka*."

"Like a *paho*?"

"Rare. Very private. Very rare."

"*Aloosaka*." He rolled his thoughts around the word. "What is it?"

"Carved from root wood. I really don't know what they look like."

"Are we talking about something worth a lot of money?"

"I have no idea."

"Why do you think Albert was involved?"

"Something with his name on it was left in the village. A canvas bag. Had some old rodeo gear inside, and his name—"

"Burned on the inside of a boot," he interrupted. "With a fireplace poker. We were total drunk and sleeping at this rich woman's place."

"And how did you sell . . . whatever you dug up?"

"You mean what we stole. He arranged that part of things. There are networks all over the Southwest. He never told me much because I didn't want to know, but

I think he mainly dealt with somebody in Sedona. You want me to ask around?"

"Would you?"

"To be honest, I don't know. I'll have to think about it."

He hunched forward over the steering wheel. I slumped back against the seat and fell sound asleep and didn't awaken until Kimo stopped at my trailer.

"Where are we?"

"Home. Well, your home, anyway."

"When will I see you again?"

"First, I have to find a place to stay."

He saw my eyes flick from him to my trailer. He shook his head.

"No, no," he said. "I'm not asking you to put me up. I'll go to the Tuba City Chapter House. Somebody there can find me a place to stay."

"Do you need money?"

"I've still got some of your magic hundred-dollar bills. What I need most is a job. I thought I'd move to Window Rock and see what there might be in the Tribal Offices."

"Maybe you could work for me," I said tentatively.

"Doing what?"

"I have to think about that. To start, though, you could find out everything you can about Mike Kiyonnie. And ask people you know about finding Grody."

"Oh," he said, "I see. You need somebody to do some rough work."

"No. I need information. I deal in information. I buy

and sell it. But there are times when I need somebody to
help me."

"Like what this Yazzie did for you, when he was
your partner?"

"He's a bounty hunter. Have you ever thought
about doing that?"

"You mean, bring some guy back to jail, because
he's skipped his bond?"

"Yes."

"All those things in your trailer, the computers and
stuff. You use them to get this information you're talking about? Don't you need a license for that?"

"Not in Arizona. Anybody can be a bounty hunter."

"You're kidding me. What would I have to do?"

And so I wound up showing him the printout on
the bail skipper in Vegas.

"You mean, I can just bring this guy back to
Flagstaff, dump him at the jail, and collect your bail
money from Marvin's Bonds?"

"Yes. That's how I earn most of my money. This
bond is for fifty thousand dollars. If I, if *we*, bring him
in, we get ten percent. Five thousand. We'd split it."

He thought about it for a long time, then took the
printout.

"Let me chew on this tonight. I'll call you tomorrow. I could use the money, that part is clear. But bringing somebody back to jail, well, I don't know if I could
do that."

He brushed my cheek with his two bent fingers.
I felt the scar tissue and kissed it, nibbling on a fingernail. He abruptly pulled his hand away.

"Hey," he said. "Don't you go stealing my nails."

"You really believe in skinwalkers?"

"Don't kid around about witches, Laura."

He kissed me lightly and backed into the darkness, lifting a hand once to wave and then disappearing. I felt radiant, exulting in the moment of his touch, walking over the land in seven-league boots, trying to remember when I'd felt so happy.

But all my memories this night led me back to my father.

I started rooting through boxes of old junk until I finally found two pictures of him, my only evidence of his life. The first picture was what I'd remembered when Claude pretended to ride a bull. Face etched against the sky, left arm bent at the elbow, holding the reins of a bareback bronc, right arm extended in a long graceful arc, hand flat like a knife ready to slice off a large chunk of life. The picture always reminded my of one I'd seen in a magazine of an Indonesian guerrilla, his hand clutching a machetelike knife, his smile revealing an eagerness to pose. At the guerrilla's feet lay a corpse, its hands tied and its severed head lying several feet away.

The other picture showed me and my father, both smiling. I remembered the day specifically because it was my seventh birthday. I was having fun playing with a girlfriend while my father read a circular about a sale at Sears in Flagstaff. Mingled with sales notices for clothing and energy-saving air conditioners, he found one of those special picture deals, one eight-by-ten, two five-by-sevens, and four wallet-size, all for $4.95. I didn't want to go, but he carried me to the pickup. When we got to Sears and it got to be our turn in the lights, I wouldn't stop crying, twisting my face away from the camera while the photographer fidgeted and frowned, a long line of other reluctant children waiting with their beaming parents. But I stopped crying immediately and smiled for the camera when my father put his hand around behind me, as though he were holding his wonderful daughter. Missy, he said, if you don't smile quick, I'll heat things up for you when we get home.

I turned the pictures over with a sob.

That's why we guard our past, I thought, so witches can't search out clipped and discarded nails and hair and memories, so they can't yank them out of the past and use them to eat away at your joy, your heart, your spirit.

16

This time I was ready for him. I'd carefully cracked into an old Flagstaff PBX and set up a very special piece of software I'd downloaded from Osaka.

"I want you more than ever."

His soft voice came on sometime after three.

"It's late, I'm on the road again, I can't sleep."

A dog howled nearby.

"I'm lying here naked, and I want to be inside you."

On hot days, under a summer sun, trailers become ovens. With all three air conditioners working, even though it was the middle of the night, the inside temperature was still in the mid-eighties. I sat at the computer, working my way through a case of Mountain Dew for the caffeine because I'd run out of coffee and Ritalin, I wasn't eating much, and I wasn't sleeping well. Way too strung out, and I didn't like it.

The dog's yowling was suddenly interrupted by a flat *crack!* Two days ago, I'd have thought it was a firecracker, a breaking bottle, a falling stone. But now I recognized the sound as a gunshot. The dog yipped in pain, running somewhere away from my trailer, and the awful noise tailed off into silence.

"I've got my hand on my cock. But it's just not enough. I'll have to come by to see you. Soon. I'd drive straight through two whole days, just to see you."

After sleeping with many men in many places, I'd still find myself at times ambivalent when somebody hit on me. Knowing their routines, I was unable to avoid being flattered by their attention. But when he said that *he* was naked, I had to be covered up. All I could think of was my thermal underwear, top and bottom. I put it on and hugged both arms around my shoulders, shivering, anxiety coiled inside my chest until he hung up.

In fifteen minutes I'd downloaded the cracker file and begun sorting through it, using my own phone number as a search character string to separate the call from everything else handled by the PBX. There had been only forty-six calls, so it didn't take long, and sorting through the routing codes, I saw he'd used a cell phone and could be anywhere in the world.

I dialed the number, and he answered immediately.

"Monica?"

Same voice, same inflections. I sniffed into the mouthpiece.

"Who is this?"

Instantly hard edged, authoritative, demanding, no longer seductive.

I sniffed again and whistled two notes.

"Parker? That you? Parker. Don't fuck with me."

I slid my thumbnail across the mouthpiece, clicking on the four little slots over the microphone, rasping back and forth, back and forth. He hung up, and I felt an immense satisfaction. Words have such power to dehumanize, but I'd never appreciated that sounds other than speech could terrorize.

I rewound the message tape after carefully saving the message. I listened to all three messages again and again and found myself punching the answering machine buttons repeatedly. My fingers jerked and danced on the buttons. I couldn't control their twitching and had to grab them with my left hand. My heartbeat pulsed stronger, and I went to the kitchen for some water—and the snake was back on the door. I squeezed my eyes shut, shook my head violently from side to side, and looked again.

There was no snake. I was hallucinating.

The barking dog faded in and out, the telephone rang again again again, and the kitchen walls moved in and out. None of the sounds were real, I thought, and then the answering machine clicked on.

"You have two days to leave."

It was the *other* voice. What are the odds of this happening? I thought. It was crazy, totally unpredictable, one calling right after another.

"Next time, you'll find the snake inside your truck. Next time, it'll bite. Next time, you'll hurt real bad."

He stayed on the line for another minute. I turned up the volume on the answering machine and heard him breathing. He hung up. Again downloading the sniffer file, I found his number quickly and was astonished because it was in my area code. Using the cell phone, I punched in the number, and it was answered immediately.

"Navajo Police Substation. Tuba City. Officer Benally."

Disconnecting, I walked back and forth through

the trailer, kitchen to bedroom to kitchen, stripping off the soggy thermal underwear and pulling on a T-shirt and running shorts, all the while counting one Mississippi, two Mississippi, forcing myself to calm down, until I suddenly became aware that I was standing in the open doorway, the shotgun aimed at the street. Horrified, I stepped back inside and slammed the door shut, hesitating just a moment as I touched the back of the door, thinking the snake was there and forcing myself to get a grip on what was real.

It's easy to say things like that, I tell you, once you've loaded the shotgun, locked all the doors, and cranked up your entire nervous system, waiting for sunlight.

By morning I'd figured out what to do. First, I'd see Karen Melnick and get some more Ritalin. Then a lot of other things I hadn't yet worked out. Not knowing what to do about Benally, but at least I was no longer terrified by his harassment. With the phone LUDs I'd downloaded, and the recorded messages, I had power over his life.

The phone rang, and just like that I was terrified again.

"Laura?"

It was Kimo.

"Where are you?"

"Vegas. Listen, I wanted to tell you something."

"Las Vegas? What are you doing up there?"

"I hitched a ride after I left you. I decided I could do this bounty job at least once, just to see how I felt about it."

"Did you find the guy?"

"Yeah, that was easy. He didn't like it at first, but he's in the trunk of the car I rented. I wrapped him up in duct tape. I didn't know what else to do. But listen, that's not why I called. First, I want to thank you."

"Half of the money is yours."

"Forget about the money. Thank you for trusting me. But, really, I called because I just found out who sells stuff from pot hunters. There's a bunch of old rodeo hands, working with Grody, who funnel all kinds of stolen things into a place in Flagstaff, off Birch Street, called Tularosa."

The long-distance operator cut in to say he had thirty seconds left.

"And there's supposed to be a woman in Sedona who sells only the very best, the most expensive stuff. She has a store, but that's all I know. Listen, that guy's kicking the trunk lid. I gotta go. When I get back, let's go down to the rodeo and I'll ask around about Grody. It's all connected to the rodeo, Laura."

He was cut off abruptly, but my mind had already moved away from him.

Rodeo.

So many connections to rodeos and rodeo cowboys. I wondered where Ben was with his scoped M-16. I wondered if the boys who'd raped Mary were at the Flagstaff rodeo. I dug out my Nikon and my long lenses, packed my camera bag with vague possibilities of taking pictures of the cowboys and showing them to Mary.

Rodeo.

Nothing made sense.

Rodeo, rodeo, rodeo. It *had* to make sense.

Mary's anguished story flooded my head.

He sat on me, like an animal, like he was sitting a horse or a bull, they talked about staying on us without getting thrown off, how they'd get a perfect ride. And then one of them said what a great bull I was, and then he started riding me again.

I remembered the two young men from my yard, the redhead and the blond.

We're bullriders!

And the old man at the fairgrounds, telling me when they rode.

You want to see the best, come Friday and Saturday nights.

So much had happened that week, I didn't even know what day it was and had to look at my calendar. It was Friday. I left a note on the front door for Kimo. *Rodeo. Tonight.* Leaving to go see Karen, I struggled with the shotgun, the camera bag, and two large taped envelopes. Unable to manage them all, I left the shotgun behind.

Guns have their purpose, but data is the ultimate weapon.

17

"You're really strung out, Laura. Why should I give you *more* Ritalin?"

Instead of sitting in the scarred, patched-up Naugahyde chair across from Karen, I settled uncomfortably in a wobbly pink plastic chair over near the door.

"I'm not sleeping much," I said. "I've got a lot of computer work, and I'm having a hard time focusing. I was driving by, and I thought I'd just stop in to say hello, and when I walked past the pharmacy, I though I might as well get a refill."

"Bullshit. Don't *lie* to me, Laura."

She rifled through piles on her desk, flinging papers and folders onto the floor until she found what she wanted and read out loud.

"Methylphenidate is just a prescription name, but it's still methamphetamine, it's no different from meth, crystal, crank, speed, cristy, glass, whatever. Psychological dependence on more meth to avoid depression and withdrawal symptoms. Usage needs increase just to maintain the same effects. Nasal damage, itchy skin, faster heartbeat, increased body temperature, nausea, vomiting, audio and visual hallucinations."

"And acrophobia."

"Oh no." She sighed. "When did that come back?"

When I first came to Tuba City I'd avoided every-body, but met Karen Melnick one day standing in a long line at Basha's checkout counter. Three days later I wandered into the IHS therapy rooms, where Karen usually had plenty of free time. She owed the IHS two years' work in return for their helping with her residency in Brooklyn. But therapy wasn't something that Navajos normally wanted from an outsider, preferring instead to have a sing or, if they were women, sometimes just be silent and endure.

"What are you thinking about?"

"Ricardo. When I told him about my acrophobia, he asked why I wanted to take flying lessons. 'You can't fly,' he said, 'if you're afraid to get off the ground.'"

"Whoa," Karen said. "Who's Ricardo?"

"This guy I met in Yakima. He flew this rinky-dink old Piper Cub. I thought if I just took flying lessons, got up high instead of *getting* high, I could deal with my life."

"We don't have time for this old stuff," Karen said. "You're not here today for therapy, you just want me to legitimize your Ritalin abuse. Tell me about the acrophobia, tell me what happened recently that's made you afraid again. I remember you first telling me about the acrophobia, how every time you stepped out onto a open roof or balcony, you wanted to fly. Is it that bad again?"

"There's this Alfred Hitchcock film. *Vertigo.*"

"Laura! Please! This isn't therapy today."

"Three days ago. It started three days ago, and I hadn't really thought about it until I came in here. I dreamed last night about Jimmy Stewart, chasing Kim Novak up that rickety bell-tower stairway. Terrified by his vertigo, but determined he'll catch her this time. I felt like a woman doing handstands on a chair held by two women balancing on top of a platform held by three men riding bicycles on a high wire. The topmost woman tips forward and back, the chair balanced on one leg, the audience ooohs and aaahs because if she tips the chair just an inch too far either way, the entire team will wobble sideways, head and arms arched back the other way for counterbalance, until they lose it alto-gether and plummet into the nets below. I was greedy, *eager*, to jump."

"What happened three days ago?" Persistent, frowning, impatient with me.

"At Oraibi, I was standing on the edge of the mesa."

"What were you doing there?"

I wondered how much I really wanted to tell her, since my only reason for being there was to get more Ritalin.

"A Hopi hired me to find his granddaughter."

She waited, clicking her fingernails on her wrist-watch, checked the time.

Her phone rang. I squirmed in the beat-up plastic chair as she listened briefly and hung up without a word and grabbed her prescription pad.

"Laura, if the acrophobia is coming back, it's con-nected to your father, and to your daughter. I've got three families waiting to see me. I'm going to write you a onetime scrip for Ritalin, enough for two weeks. You schedule a time to see me tomorrow."

She scribbled herself a note.

"Have you talked this over with Ben?"

"He's gone. I've got a new partner."

Somebody knocked on the door and she stood up, handing me the scrip. The door opened slightly, and an elderly Navajo woman poked her head in.

"Please!" Karen said. "Just wait out there, just a few minutes more."

As the door closed, I could see her debating whether to take back the scrip.

"A new partner. What does that mean?"

"A guy I met. He's going to do what Ben did. Bounty hunting."

"Have you slept with him yet? This new . . . partner? Talk to me, Laura."

"I think we've talked enough."

"Enough? We're just getting started. You *always* connected acrophobia with bad sexual relationships. You know little about *normal* relationships, about loving, about having partners. You want somebody to take care of you. You think sex means love. You wind up lying underneath some guy, and while he's eating you out you're thinking that *this* time you've got somebody you can trust, somebody who'll never leave you."

"I gotta go," I mumbled, unable as always to confront her.

"You think all of this starts with good sex, so you never see how ridiculous these guys really are and how they're going to fuck you over again and again."

Karen grabbed my shoulders as I yanked open the door. An elderly Navajo couple stood just outside, wide-eyed and openmouthed. Karen shut the door and pushed me toward her private bathroom.

"Stop pushing me!" I shouted.

"That's why you come to see me. So somebody can push on you and make things safer. What we should *really* be talking about is why you ran away from the Rez, wandered all over the world, and then come back to the place where it all started."

"Look," I said, fucking *fed up* with this. "You want to help me so much, tell the pharmacy downstairs to give me more Ritalin so I won't be such a wreck."

"Look at yourself in the mirror! You *are* a wreck. Look!"

I raised my face to the mirror and was staggered by what I saw. Black pouches under my eyes, lips tensed, cheeks hollowed. I looked badly strung out and until that moment hadn't given it any thought because I'd not really looked at myself.

"Laura, listen to me. Health, healing, it's all an illusion when you're confronted with old problems that you've never really resolved. So when there's no visible solution, you take something instead. A drink, a pill, a man, anything to get you around the problem. And when the temporary solutions don't heal *your* pain, you get psychologically involved with somebody else's pain. We've got to stop this destructive cycle. And the first thing you have to do is stop abusing Ritalin."

"It helps me focus. It helps me get through the day without feeling wrecked."

"Don't you understand," Karen said slowly and carefully, "that you've become a wreck because you're abusing Ritalin?"

That stopped me cold.

"If you don't stop abusing yourself right now, I'll stop seeing you."

Ah.

Things change.

I knew she was right. I handed her back the scrip.

"No," she insisted, "you can't quit cold, not if you've been doubling or tripling your normal dose. Get this last prescription. One pill every twelve hours. No more."

"Okay. I'll try."

"You have to do more than just try."

I walked rapidly down the hallway. I started running, turned a corner, banged through metal doors, running to the pharmacy to hand the clerk my scrip. I stopped at a water fountain, my legs trembling, and I had to grab the metal fountain with both hands as I washed down a pill and started to swallow three more and stopped to look at them lying in my palm and realized how hard it would be to stop taking them.

One day at a time, I said to myself, capping the pills back inside the vial.

18

"Keep this for me," I said to Billie, handing her a heavily taped envelope containing copies of the phone record printout and a duplicate of the answering machine tape of Benally's voice. I had another envelope in my car for Yellowhouse.

"What is it?"

"I can't tell you."

We were standing in her kitchen, and I opened one of her drawers and crammed the envelope inside underneath some flatware and cooking tools.

"What's wrong with you, Laura?"

"Nothing."

"I don't know," she said after a long time. "You're acting just like I get after a few days of saying I'm not going to have another drink, and wanting it worse every day, then every hour, and finally I'm worse off for saying no than just opening the bottle."

She saw I was crying. Yes, I *did* want to talk, but *what* did I want to talk about? Quitting my addiction? Being stalked? Trying to find a runaway teenager? Ambivalence about Kimo? Where should I start?

We sat on her living room couch. She wanted to

hold me but couldn't, and finally she put a hand on my shoulder until I stopped crying.

"You ready to talk?"

"I don't know where to start."

"You went out to Oraibi the other day. Something happened out there, but you never really talked about it. So tell me now."

I told her everything. When I got to Patrick's vision, trying to use the exact words I'd heard from Johnson, I saw I had her complete attention.

"You should trust his vision," she said.

"Why? I don't believe in those things."

"I worry about you, Laura. You should be smart enough, you should have *sense* enough, to know that even if you don't believe in the truth of visions, some of us do. If a Hopi *kikmongwi* told you this, he's not just making it up to get your interest."

We believe that Patrick's vision shows that all that has happened is connected. The girls, the Powakas, the shrine.

"I'm *very* uncomfortable with this kind of talk," I said.

"Well. Let's forget the spiritual stuff. The white college-educated teacher part of me says, All right, let's look at it with some logic. There's three things. Girls. Witches. Sacred, religious objects. You're willing to accept the first one, right? That some girls are missing. We don't know why, but they're missing. Right?"

"I do believe that part."

"Witches."

"Pass on that one."

"Okay. The sacred things stolen from the shrine. I

wouldn't know much about them because they're Hopi. But if they're *really* sacred, chances are some pot hunter took it. Pot hunters are bottom feeders. They don't steal to possess, they steal to sell. Why don't you start looking into where people sell stolen pots or spiritual things?"

I found myself thinking of Kimo, probably in part because of Karen warning me about not starting up another relationship. I knew so little about Kimo that I wondered if he might use what I told him and start looking for the *aloosaka*. That's the trouble with involving yourself with people instead of data. With computers, you collect, verify, and trust data. With Kimo, I didn't know what to trust. No. I shook off the thought and looked up to see Billie staring at me.

"Now where have you been?" she asked.

"Remembering somebody I just met who used to be a pot hunter."

"Yeah, I heard all about you and that guy Biakeddy."

"You heard what?"

"Laura, Tuba is a small town, made even smaller by family and clan talk. I saw one of our English teachers at Bashas' last night. Word's around that you brought Biakeddy to the hospital with a split lip, then you two drove off together. There were always rumors that he was a pot hunter."

"Well, he was, or so he said. I don't care about what he used to do. But I asked him if he still had contacts with pot hunters, and if he did, to find out where stolen things wound up for sale. He called last night and said there's a place in Flagstaff. Tularosa."

"I've always wondered about that place. Maybe I can help. Come with me."

Down a hallway, she opened one of the bedroom doors. Standing aside, she waved me into a room jammed with pottery. She looked around carefully, finally pointing to three colored red on buff, one with a large spiral covering an entire side.

"These are Hohokam. Santa Cruz, colonial period."

"Where do they make that?"

"You think you could just go out, shop around, and buy something like that?"

"Billie, to me it's just a pot. Why are you showing me this stuff?"

"If something sacred is stolen, it might be old. If it's sacred, it's certainly valuable, so it can be sold. That Hohokam piece, for example."

"Where did you get it?"

"An auction. One of my best pieces. This one over here," she said, indicating a red-on-brown jug covered with diamonds within diamonds within diamonds, "that's San Francisco Mogollon. Half of these are from the Southwest. But I've got pots from five different regions. This one's probably Assiniboine blackduck. This one's Arikara; this, probably Shoshone. That hunchbacked woman over there, that's a Mississippi effigy bottle. All told, I've got over two hundred of these things."

"They must be worth a lot. Aren't you worried about them being stolen?"

"They're insured. Besides, I never show them to anybody."

"Why me?"

"Don't know." She picked up the Hohokam pot. "I collected them with Huskie. When he died, I realized I had to have them around me. I love handling them."

She drew the Hohokam pot to her face, touched it with her lips without embarrassment. She fingered a small Hopi bowl covered by graphic designs, rubbing her finger across an ear of corn and a frog while she decided what to say. Lost in thought, she stroked a black-on-white pot, swirled her finger around a hatched spiral descending from the top lip. She recovered abruptly and held the pot carefully in both hands and offered it to me.

"Tell you what. Go to that place in Flagstaff and take this with you. Say you want to sell it, but you can't offer it publicly."

"How much is this worth?"

"Just tell her you'll settle for a thousand."

She pulled some bubblewrap out of a drawer and carefully bound up the pot before handing it to me.

"Billie, I can't take this."

"Is there a chance that this might help us find Judy?"

"Maybe. Billie, I'm not going to take a thousand-dollar pot. What if I break it?"

"I'll glue the pieces together."

"Very funny. Then how much will it be worth?"

"Just take it."

"How much is it *really* worth?"

"I don't think you really want to know. But I want to help you, and right now this is the only thing I can do. Please. Take it. And besides, you're only going to show it to them and then bring it back here."

"I'll be careful with it."

"Be careful with yourself, Laura. I don't know what's happening with you, but I've got this wild feeling that you're not that quiet little girl I used to know who loved nothing more than sitting around with computers all day long."

In the living room, she stopped and poured some bourbon. About to take a sip, she cocked her head at me.

"And this is the first time in weeks I haven't seen you swallowing those pills."

"I'm trying to stop," I said. "I don't know if I can do it."

"Good luck."

She raised her bourbon glass in a toast just as we heard a distant *crump* and her whole house shivered.

19

Three row houses burned furiously. Between two of them little remained except the back wall and a blackened pickup in front, its rear axle propped on concrete blocks. The Tuba City Fire Department had only two hoses and hadn't yet checked the fire from spreading to other row houses on each side. Two men were locked in the backseat of a police car.

I stopped my car next to a man watching the fire.

"What happened?" I yelled out my window to them.

He rested one hand on my side-view mirror, a seemingly casual gesture until I saw his hands were shaking. I saw Lieutenant Yellowhouse running toward my car.

"They was cooking up some kind of drugs in there. Smelled terrible. Nobody wanted to talk to the police, nobody wanted to say something."

He stared into my face, his skin taut and eyes frantic. I saw he was in shock.

"There's four people in there. Her kids were in there. Her boy's three, the girl's just a few months old. And some teenager. They're all still in there."

"Don't talk to her." Furious, Yellowhouse pushed the man away. "Get away from here, Miss Winslow."

"What happened?"

"None of your business."

"This man just told me there are people inside. He says one of them is a teenager. Is it Judy? Do you know if it's Judy Pavatea?"

His anger struggled against his sense of responsibility.

"No," he said reluctantly. "It's Margaret Whitewater and her three children."

I saw Mike Kiyonnie's face watching me through the back of the police car. He snarled something I couldn't hear. Yellowhouse saw me looking into the police car.

"Do you know him?"

"No. Who is he? Did he set this fire?"

"He's been running a drug lab here. He must have found out we knew about it and decided to make one last batch, and it blew up. Did you know about this place?"

"No. Why should I?"

"You were asking about the Pavatea girl the other day. And you just asked me if Pavatea was inside. We knew she'd lived here, we knew she was probably selling meth and some other designer drugs."

"Too bad you didn't do something before this accident," I said bitterly.

"I'm a policeman. I have to follow rules. Damn you, how dare you accuse me of being responsible for those people dying in there."

"I'm sorry," I said, "I didn't mean it that way."

"Get out of my sight."

He kicked my front tire, furious that he'd revealed that information. He decided to take it out on me. Grasping the door frame, he stuck a fist inside.

"You're nothing but trouble. I don't need to tell you anything."

Furious, I picked up the taped envelope from the seat beside me, my heart racing, my temples ready to explode. Yellowhouse's mouth dropped open at my expression, and his hand drifted halfway to his weapon as I flung open my door, stood in front of him, and slapped him on the chest with the envelope. It surprised him so much that he stepped backward, grabbing the envelope with both hands.

"Find yourself a tape recorder and listen to what's inside."

"Are you threatening me?"

I'd thought about that for a long time. Having power wasn't something that came to me very often, and those few times I had it I guarded the power religiously, so that I'd use it only when it would do me the most good. I'd had Benally's voice on tape for only six hours, but it was time, and I had to play this card very carefully.

"No. But I'm very angry. When you hear this tape, you'll know why."

"Don't threaten me."

"No threats," I said. "Just listen to the tape."

"Who are you, really?" he said.

"Nobody."

"Is your name really Laura Winslow?"

"Yes."

"There's something about you that doesn't make sense, so I called the FBI in Flagstaff to run an ID check. You and Yazzie should both leave Tuba City."

"He's not my partner anymore. I've started working with Kimo Biakeddy."

"Biakeddy! He's an ex-con."

"And he's also the only person who's trying to help me find Judy Pavatea. All you policemen, you're so hung up with catching drug dealers, you don't listen to what's really happening in your own town."

"You give me no reason to believe anything you tell me."

"Listen to what's in that envelope," I said, "and then come say that again."

I got back in my car.

"Where's Yazzie?"

"He's gone," I said, starting to reverse out of the burning street. "He's history."

"You should leave, too," he shouted, running alongside. "Both of you, we're better off with both of you gone. Both of you should be history!"

He flung the envelope at my open window as I accelerated. It caromed off the rear bumper and fell to the street, and I saw him pick it up and throw it down angrily.

I was already history, I thought. I was a forty-year-old woman whose life was woven so full of histories that I no longer knew which threads and colors were real.

20

Carlos Nakai flute music filled the single room, and a dozen sandalwood incense sticks burned in a mound of red sand.

Tularosa.

Drums of all sizes and shapes filled the left wall, across from shelves filled with books, videotapes, audiocassettes, vials of colored fluids, perfumes, incense sticks, dreamcatchers, sand paintings, Kachina dolls, a fur-covered Navajo dancing bear, and an entire shelf of Kokopellis, painted, sculpted, inscribed in sandstone, welded in various kinds of metals, and some even hand-painted on refrigerator magnets, but all genitally neutral. None had a penis.

"Peace. Be with you in a few minutes."

She poked her head above a glass showcase and just as quickly disappeared behind it, rearranging some crystals and polished stones on a black velvet cloth. Taking her time, she adjusted them carefully and closed the sliding glass door while reflexively pulling her long whitish hair behind her left ear. She wore a peach-colored sari, a strip of tanned stomach showing. Rings fought for space on all her fingers and thumbs, rings and studs rose in layers up both ears, and her turquoise nose stud glittered.

"Almost done."

I fumbled through pamphlets for healing ceremonies, sings, weekend workshops on shamanism and sweatlodge spirituality, trips and treks to view petroglyphs. A four-color, triple-folded advertisement offered lots in the San Francisco mountains, each lot guaranteed to have an authentic Anasazi ruin.

"Okay," she said. "What's your sign?"

"I don't know. But that's not why I'm here."

"First, we have to establish harmony and peace. What's your birth date?"

"January eleventh."

"Capricorn. The goat."

"That's me. I've felt staked out all my life."

She reached into the display case and brought out a pale green stone.

"Chrysolite. From Italy. Here. Touch it."

I took the smooth stone, held it to my cheek.

"Most people think it's peridot, or even topaz. It's spiritually connected to the sun. You should hang it from a necklace short enough so that it lies just in the hollow of your throat. You'll feel less depressed, less weighed down, psychically free of negativity. And it will help your tension."

"How did you know all of that?"

She shrugged, smiled.

"Okay. How much?"

"Thirteen dollars."

"Wow. All that healing power for just thirteen dollars?"

"Don't be cynical. Why should peace and good health cost lots of money?"

"How much with tax?"

"No tax."

I laid out a ten and three ones. She carefully folded the stone in purple tissue paper and tucked it inside a small box.

"You want to score some coke?" she said.

"You're kidding me."

"You look wrecked, like you've been on meth. Ever tried coke?"

"I've tried everything. But I'm clean now."

"Oh, wow. Poor you."

She reached down behind the counter, and I saw what she'd been doing when I came in. She laid out two more lines of coke stretched across a small art deco pocket mirror. She took my ten-dollar bill, rolled it into a tube, and snorted the coke.

"God, that's good," she said, her smile like the sun. "So what do you want?"

"I hear you're interested in certain kinds of art."

Her smile tightened for a moment and then bloomed again. "I don't know what you mean."

I took Billie's pot from my purse, unwrapped it from the bubblepack, and set it on the counter. She cocked her head sideways, only an inch, but a clear measure of apprehension.

"I don't hold things for sale."

"That's odd. I'm told you can match buyers with sellers."

"I doubt it."

She touched the pottery with a black-lacquered fingernail, her eyes suddenly radiant. "Early Hohokam," she said carefully. She fingered the calculator nervously and just as quickly pushed it away. "Who sent you here?"

"I couldn't say."

I took out a pen and wrote my cell phone number on one of the land pamphlets.

"If it rings, I'll know you've found somebody who'll talk with me."

"It's unlikely, but just in case I do . . ."

She picked up a Polaroid camera. As the lens rose toward me I turned half away. She laughed and gestured at the pottery and flashed three pictures from different angles.

"Beautiful," she said as the pictures bloomed into color. She poked some calculator buttons. "Just a quick appraisal, but I'd say you'd get three, three fifty."

"Three hundred and fifty dollars?"

"Yes. Maybe up to four. That would be a nice price."

"It's worth over a thousand."

"Well. I certainly don't have money for these beautiful old pieces. But, like I said, I'll ask around. Have you got any more, or is this a onetime thing?"

"Oh, I've got a lot more," I said, retaping the bubblepack.

"All of them this quality?"

"I have thirteen items. This is the low end of what I've got."

Hoping I'd remember exactly what Billie told me.

"Are you jerking me around, or what? Describe them."

"More Hohokam. Santa Cruz, Colonial period. San Francisco Mogollon. Assiniboine blackduck. Arikara. Shoshone. Even a Mississippi effigy bottle."

Somebody stopped outside, looking at things in the window, moving on.

"If you want money right now, I might go six hundred on this one, as a show of faith in the marketplace."

"Nine," I said, totally unaware how to do this but relying on how I sold information and figuring that greedy people often lose sight of what they pay.

"Maybe," she said. "It's quality, but I'll have to make a call and get back to you."

"I'll give you a week."

"Oh, you'll hear from somebody in just a few days. Cool. But I'll lay out six, no questions, if you'll leave it with me right now."

I stuffed the bubblepack into my handbag. As I turned to leave my gaze fell on the bear.

"I never heard of a Navajo dancing bear," I said.

"It's authentic."

"What does that mean?" I asked innocently.

"Peace," she said. We understood each other perfectly.

"Yeah," I said. "Peace would be nice."

Ten yards away from the store, I heard brakes squealing. A Flagstaff sheriff's cruiser pulled up alongside me.

"Laura Winslow?" the deputy said. I nodded. "Get in, please."

"Excuse me?"

"The FBI wants to talk with you. I'm here as a courtesy, to give you a ride. Please get in the back."

"How did you know I was here? I'm not going anywhere with you."

But when he opened the door, stepping out to show me his baton and a fax replica of my Arizona driver's license, I got into his cruiser.

21

Shiyoma Lakon was doing a stand-up interview out-side the Gonzaga Land and Cattle building. When the deputy stopped in front of the building and I got out, she signaled the cameraman to start taping and rushed over.

"You here to talk to FBI agent Foxburn?"

"No. I'm getting a sandwich at the coffee shop."

"You've heard. Right?"

"About what?"

"Five Indian girls have disappeared from the reser-vation."

"Where did you hear that?" I asked in disbelief.

"We got an anonymous tip that five girls were missing."

"Nothing to do with me."

"I saw you in the Navajo police station. I heard you ask inside about a missing Hopi girl. Have you been hired to find them?"

"Turn off that camera," I said. "You're an asshole."

"I can be," she said frankly, "if that's what it takes to get stories."

I stuck up my middle finger to the cameraman. He grinned, but the red light went off when she drew a fin-ger across her throat.

"Are you here to talk with the FBI?"

"No."

"Do you know anything about the Four Corners manhunt?"

"What manhunt?"

The deputy pushed her aside, and we climbed to the second floor. The FBI office was a single room on the third floor, its double-locked glass door covered from the inside with a solid coating of brown wrapping paper. The deputy rattled his fingernails on the door, which swung wide open. An angry man stood there with his hands on his hips. Indignant, balding, wearing a ten-year-old dark blue suit and a white shirt that looked as though he'd worn it to change his car's oil. Everything in the office was dusty, with files and papers strewn around haphazardly with no visible effort at maintaining a filing system. The phone rang. An answering machine clicked on immediately, silent, the volume turned off.

"Here she is, Mister Foxburn." The deputy left.

"Look over there," Foxburn said to me without any introduction, veeing his ancient venetian blinds to point across the back parking lot at somebody on the roof of the old Hotel Monte Vista. A photographer had a long lens trained on the office window. I stepped back out of sight.

"Oh? You don't want publicity? Come across the hall."

"I've already seen her."

"Allow me," he said with sarcastic courtesy. "I want to make a point."

He led me across the hall and through the glass door of a geographical survey office. Two women were staring down at Birch Avenue, and Foxburn made a grand gesture, like a ringmaster, clearing a spot for me. Below, a second TV van jockeyed for a parking spot, the driver negotiating with somebody sitting in a parked car. He handed the driver some money, and the van slid into the quickly emptied spot. Another photographer pointed up toward the third-floor window.

"Thanks to you."

We went back into the FBI office. Foxburn sat in a rickety office chair and looked at me angrily from behind the scarred, gunmetal gray desk, empty except for a telephone and several fax sheets. He tapped one of them.

"Turns out somebody is faxing everybody about some Hopi girls. Turns out it's a Navajo cop, his family's been thrown off land they've owned since Moses. This cop's pissed, he's gonna tell the world that the Hopis have a problem 'cause he fucking hates them. Then I get another fax. Hopi tribal chairman. No truth to the story being spread by Navajos. I get a phone call from the Navajo tribal chairman. They must have more money, they don't just fax, they call. No, there are *not* twelve missing Navajo girls. We've moved back up from five. Boy. I'm starting to get impressed with my importance here. But that's nothing, 'cause inbound comes another fax from ABC Evening News, national edition. Wow. Want me to confirm reports there's a serial killer loose on the Navajo reservation. Gee. Now I'm so impressed it's going to my head, I'm going to be on national TV, talking to Tom Brokaw."

"He's NBC," I said.

"Do you fucking understand how hard the Phoenix agent in fucking charge came down on my head about this? Twelve Navajo girls missing on the reservation, but we don't much give a fuck about unconfirmed reports 'cause we're working nine days a week trying to stop methamphetamine pouring across the Mexican border 'cause we're fucking cooperating with the DEA, for Christ's sake. And there's a meth lab blows up in Tuba City, now *that* gets everybody's attention."

"They're not Navajo girls," I said. "They're Hopi."

"Navajo, Hopi, I really don't give a fuck. Nobody gives a real fuck. It's just another serial killer scare, gonna generate lots of newspaper, magazine, TV reports, which are going to generate ad revenue. It's John fucking Gacy on the Rez."

He reached into a desk drawer, and I thought he was looking for some booze, but instead he took out a bottle of Evian water and drained it without stopping.

"Finally, there's *this* fax. This one tips the scales overboard. It's from the local TV, that bitch waiting for me outside. Way, way less status, but she's sharp, this bitch, she's dug up background on when I worked up in Washington, where they found some dead women on the Yakima reservation, excuse me, some dead Native American females, in nineteen fucking ninety-three. And was I the agent who didn't show up at scheduled meetings with the tribe? Maybe, I tell her, it was because I wasn't invited, or maybe there was a blizzard, but no, she's got a slant on this already. I run a check on her and find out she's three-quarters Yavapai, so now I'm targeted by an angry Native American TV reporter who believes I no longer care about the plight of Their Women."

"You're the third policeman I've talked to this week who doesn't seem at all interested in the truth."

"Ah," he said with glee. "The truth is out there. Well, I can guarantee you, this will go directly to the X-files, because I don't see any evidence of any crime. And please, don't think I'm insensitive about gender issues. Part of a new FBI directive is that agents with a history of 'emotional background' have to seek therapy. So, I've been seeing this woman down in Sedona. I lie naked in a hot tub, I crawl into a sandbox, a huge rainbow-colored sandbox and get buried up to my head while she sits across from me, naked also. I give her credit for showing me her wrinkled forty-year-old tits, and I'm told not to hold back my anger when confronted with situations beyond my control. Which is what we got here, wouldn't you agree?"

"I'm not sitting here for this," I said. "I've got nothing else to say."

"Oh. Gee. As if I'd believe *anything* you say." He pulled a file folder from a desk drawer. "Miss Laura Winslow. Here's a copy of your Social Security card. Here's a copy of your Arizona driver's license. And guess what? I think they're phony. No. I *know* they're phony. How did you manage that, Miss Winslow? Or, is there some other name I should use? 'Cause the SS number belongs to a Hannah Marie Tryanski, born February third, 1954. Died two months later. Miss Winslow. You look shocked. I'm so sorry for your loss, you being dead and all. Here. Read all about yourself."

Handing me a fax without looking at it, he tried to read any sign in my face.

"I can explain," I said, looking at the strange name. Tryanski.

"Yeah. I'm sure you've got a completely comprehensible and coherently reasonable explanation about why you're carrying false paper. Chances are I'm going to find that Mr. Ben Yazzie bought some of that good paper for the new you. Or maybe you're the one who's clever enough to make fake ID."

He took the fax out of my hand, carefully handling it by one corner as he stuffed it back into the desk drawer.

"We'll get some fingerprints off this paper, we'll run them. But right now, I don't give a fuck about you. And when this mess clears up a little, I'll take time to look into what Mr. Yazzie might have done. There are really disturbing stories about him, about bounty hunter violations all over Arizona. Not just right now."

"If you really want to listen, I can tell you more about these girls."

"Not interested."

"One of them is named Judy Pavatea. I was hired to find her by her grandfather."

"I know that. A Lieutenant Yellowhouse called me earlier, set me to looking at your paper. And yes, I know there's actually a girl by that name. But nobody, according to Yellowhouse, has a clue that in fact she's just not off partying somewhere."

"You asshole."

"Inconclusive statement. Needs objective modifiers. Embellishment. I'm an old-school FBI asshole, left over from the glory days when they were more careful. No, let's say when they had more taste about who got to be an agent."

The phone rang again. He ripped the power cord from the answering machine and flung the phone against the wall, but because the cord connecting it to the machine was only two feet long, the answering machine flew off his desk and clanged on the floor as it broke.

"Solves that problem."

He swept the faxes into his desk drawer and slammed it shut and slumped in his chair, his anger crackling like an electrical aura; but in an instant it discharged, and suddenly he was calm, his face sagging, his body slumped wearily in his chair.

"I've known Ben Yazzie for a long time. If he were here, he'd know that I really do care about anything to do with missing girls."

"What?"

"Whoever you are, you don't know me. But Ben does. I owe Ben. I've even held back some information on Ben, about his questionable taste in bounty-hunting survivalist buddies who just killed a Navajo policeman and disappeared into the San Juan River country, where nobody'll ever find them. I know what he's been doing, Miss Winslow, and with whom, and I've kept it back because I owed him. Unfortunately, I'm off this case. On the next flight up from Phoenix there'll be this young, good-looking, new kind of agent. Really good at public relations, knows how to deal with local TV reporters, especially Native American reporters, 'cause he's part Iroquois."

He buttoned his white shirt, pulled the knot of his tie tight against the stained collar. Using an electric razor he took from his desk, he began to shave his chin.

"Look at me," he said. He pulled a tan trench coat off a chair, put it on, and started buttoning it up.

"The new FBI. A clean-cut image, from the neck up, at least. Get out of here, Miss Winslow, or whoever you really are. I'll give you five minutes, then I'm going down there to declare that Washington is extremely concerned, that a task force is being assembled, said task force in due time will talk to all families involved, but I personally have an overactive caseload, and the special agent in charge will be on the next flight from Phoenix. And then I have to drive over to some place called Teec Nos Pos, where the Navajo Nation police wants to talk to me about a shoot-out. One of their officers is dead, along with some unlucky pot hunter named Gordy."

"Was it Grody?" I said without thinking.

Motionless, Foxburn stood with one finger on a button and the other looped into the buttonhole. Old, balding, slow, out to pasture, he could still recognize a moment.

"He somehow connected with this missing girl thing?"

"No," I answered too quickly. "I don't know."

He took a fax paper from his jacket pocket, read it quickly.

"Albert Grody. How do you know that name?"

"East of Flagstaff, there's a woman named Grody who raises llamas."

"Llamas. That's all you've got to tell me? You demand that people recognize that Judy Pavatea is missing. You seem to want massive resources committed to finding a possible serial killer. But the only real thing you have to tell me is about *llamas*?"

"I never said there was a serial killer."

"And I'm not Clarice Starling. And there's no Buffalo Bill out there, mutilating Indian girls and leaving their bodies for us to find. You don't seem to understand. Without bodies, without hard evidence, we can't do anything. But. What I do know about this Pavatea comes from a DEA file on that meth lab in the house where she was arrested. Yellowhouse told me she's linked to the Tuba City drug-processing lab that blew up today. DEA has targeted Arizona because meth is big here. Cheap and plentiful. Fastest-growing drug of choice today. What do *you* know about Pavatea and meth?"

"Nothing."

"Then good-bye. My replacement, he'll be looking you up very soon."

Foxburn dismissed me abruptly. AS I left the building, the TV cameras swung toward me, red lights winking on and then off as I marched down the street and around the corner and waited until the reporter drove up beside me.

22

"We might have things to trade," I said.

She'd seen me flick a nod in her direction as I walked away from the building, and I knew she'd follow. She already had a news pad out and was fumbling for a pen.

"Okay. What've you got?"

"Not so fast. I don't have much trust in newspeople, so I need your word that what I tell you goes no further."

"I don't trust anybody, either. What do you want from me?"

"How much of northern Arizona do you cover?"

The neon hotel bar sign across the street flickered on, and she tilted her face so that even in the late afternoon sun the neon lit up her cheekbones and created dark, exotic triangles beneath them and her nose. She was really beautiful and knew it.

"Normally, Coconino County. For a good story, anything from Sedona north to the Grand Canyon, east to the Four Corners. Right now, I'm trying to tie a meth lab raid here in Flagstaff with the lab that blew up today in Tuba City."

She presented herself toward me as though she were working into a camera, the red light had just gone on, and the camera loved her. Her body moved slightly sideways, or maybe just her face, favoring her strong side; whatever she did it was just a matter of a few inches, but she had presence. In the neon, her eyes shone as though they were reflecting the light from a computer monitor. She seemed incapable of not talking, so I listened, looking for an edge of information.

"If it's meth, I'd love to tie these Flagstaff people into a Mexican Mafia connection. But I've got no hard leads. The FBI never shows you its underwear until they've cleaned off all the stains. Is the Tuba explosion related to the lab they closed down here a few weeks ago?"

"Can't help you."

"God *damn*. There's a meth story out there. I can feel it."

"What have you heard about missing teenage girls?"

"It's all rumor. Ahhh, I see. Is that why we're talking here?"

"Do you work rumors?"

"I work anything that gets my face on the air at six and eleven, and maybe gets noticed by CNN or whoever. Meth labs are hot in Arizona. Serial killers are hot nationally, so that's my main interest. What do you know about these girls?"

"Just that most of them are probably Hopi."

"I already know that. How many are missing?"

"I don't know."

"A few? Five? Ten?"

"Does it matter?" I said.

"Yes. It matters a hell of a lot, and not just because it's a story. I'm not that hard-edged that I don't care about young girls. Here. Let me show *you* something."

She fumbled in her purse and pulled out a sepia print of an Edward Curtis photograph. Sitting atop stone steps, four Hopi women looked away from the camera. Wearing black skirts and light blouses with a large dark collar turned up against their necks, they all had butterfly hair, the sworled wings outlined against a clear sky. I thought immediately of Judy Pavatea's picture with the same hair.

"Hopi butterfly maidens. Virgins. When I heard the missing girls are Hopi, I dug this up. Makes a good visual, since I've got nothing else for the six o'clock spot."

"How long have you been so cynical?"

But my sarcasm was lost because she'd noticed me staring at the picture. She moved closer to me so that our faces were just six inches apart.

"Keep that. If you find out more about these girls, I can be a big help."

I stepped back from her intensity, uncertain about her motivations.

"A big help to who, other than yourself?"

"Let me ask you something else," she said while she thought through how to say it. "Your partner in Tuba City, a guy named Ben Yazzie. He a friend? Or what?"

"He's a bounty hunter."

"What do you do for a bounty hunter?"

"He was my partner. Not anymore. Why are you asking?"

"I hear he's trying to find whoever butchered those Navajo horses. The buzz is he's sold the story to a national TV newsmagazine. He's going to say there's a connection between what happened on the Rez with all kinds of horse killings and mutilations during the past three years. But I also hear he was one of the four men who busted down a trailer door in Kayenta and killed the man who lived there. And most people are already assuming that three of those men were involved in the killing of the Navajo policeman."

"Where did you hear all that?" I was stunned, and she saw it.

"I heard from a Navajo tribal policeman."

"Benally."

"Yeah, he's creepy." She'd heard the disgust in my voice. "I wanted to pay him, but he said just having the information public was all the payment he needed."

"I wouldn't trust much of what he tells you. What do you know about the other man killed up there?"

"Albert Grody? Why are you asking?"

God, she was *sharp*, noticing something in my face, my voice, my body.

"Nothing," I said. "I just heard about it. You know anything about it?"

"Nothing. I've got researchers at the TV station trying to track down something about him, but other than a prison record for pot hunting, there's not much. Look. You're obviously interested in him. If you've got something you want to sell, I can pay."

"I'm not in this for money," I said bitterly.

"Oh, how noble. Let me give you my private phone number. And give me yours."

After scribbling down my cell phone number, she handed me one of her business cards. As I read the name Shiyoma Lakon, I remembered the Lakon Society dances, remembered gathering fall corn, remembered being one of the maidens of the Four Directions, remembered holding the yellow corn with an eagle feather. The memories staggered me, but she didn't notice how tightly I held the Curtis photo.

"Are you Hopi?" I asked.

"No. I just liked the words and needed an on-camera name. My service number is on the bottom. If I find out anything about Grody, I'll give you a call."

"What's your real name?"

"What's yours?"

Here's a copy of your Social Security card. Here's a copy of your Arizona driver's license. And guess what? I think they're phony.

But she was just joking.

"My name is Sylvia Wallace. Pure white-bread name, but I'm Yavapai. I wanted people to know I'm Indian, so I gave myself an Indian name. Look. When you decide how much you can tell me, call anytime and my service will find me."

"I'm not sure what I'll be able to tell you."

"Let's get this straight," she said, tapping a finger on my wrist. "Grody, drugs, those things might have some interest. But these missing girls, that's the real story. And maybe a serial killer on an Indian reservation. If I can lock up *that* story, I can move out of Flagstaff to a bigger market. So. If that's all you've got, let's keep in touch."

"What do you know about the black market in stolen Indian artifacts?"

"Artifacts. That's a very broad, nondefinitive word. Are we talking about pot hunters? . . . Ahhhh, Grody. You *do* have something else. Is that what this is about?"

"I want to know who in Sedona handles the top-dollar stuff."

"This isn't a big city. There aren't any police or news snitches here, so I don't know. But I'll dig, if you promise me an exclusive on whatever's connected to it."

"Deal," I lied.

She tapped the photograph in my hands.

"Meanwhile, keep looking at that. If you have something to tell me, call."

I tried to hand it back to her, but she shook her head, her smile dissolving with her interest in me as she walked away. I turned the photograph around and around, seeing Judy Pavatea's face dusted with corn-meal, studying the four maidens.

And, for the first time in a long time, not feeling ashamed of memories. It was such a startling sensation that I looked again at the photograph, trying to imagine myself with the squash blossom whorls, trying to remember the dances, trying to imagine myself again as Hopi.

But I'd been too long in the world, and still had too much to do out there.

23

Handguns were laid out like jewels in several glassed cases, and above the cash register a large hand-lettered sign defined Freddy Awl's politics: TED KENNEDY'S CAR KILLED MORE PEOPLE THAN MY GUN!!

My shoulder banged against a swivel rack lined with holsters. Double-stitched leather, nylon, with and without thumb snaps, high and low ride, chest harnesses, hip extenders, open and closed muzzle, black, tan, plain tan, dark tan.

"Something for the little lady?" Freddy said, dipping into a large pack of McDonald's Chicken McNuggets, with honey mustard sauce on his chin.

"How do I buy a gun?"

"Okay. Okay. You want a rifle? A shotgun? Assault piece?"

"Somebody's stalking me," I said, the first thing that popped into my mind. "I'm afraid to leave home, I'm afraid to walk around, I'm afraid of everything. If I had any kind of handgun, I'd feel a lot safer."

"That son of a bitch. Okay. Okay. Let's find something to blow off his balls."

He pulled a Llama M-82 from the display case,

stripped it down in less then ten seconds, and without looking at me went into hard-sell mode.

"Top-of-the-line handgun. You got your full-length guide rails on the slide. Some of these other nines here, I won't say which ones, but they allow up to two whole inches of unsupported slide movement. Check this now, okay? You got your articulated firing pin, okay? Lifetime guaranteed, it never jams, never misfires."

He reassembled it and looked up, handing it to me. Because I was not expecting something so heavy, my hand sagged and the butt cracked against the counter-top.

"Something smaller, I guess, something lightweight."

Bending underneath the glass counter, Freddy brought out a small handgun and laid it on the counter-top.

"Don't be put off because there's Spanish all over the box. This is a twenty-two-caliber Bersa pocket pistol. Ten-round magazine. First one out takes just a little more trigger pull, 'cause it's double action. But once the slide racks back, the pull is easy and smooth. Now, if you'll fill out the forms, it'll be processed by next week."

"I can't wait a week."

"There's a legal waiting period. I can sell you whatever you want today, but you have to give me ID, you have to wait a week before I can give it to you."

"Painted Butte," I blurted.

That straightened him up. He finished the last McNugget, cleaned his hands carefully, and poured himself a cup of coffee, watching me over the lip with each gulp, deciding how to deal with me.

"Ben Yazzie said you'd sell me a Painted Butte."

"Okay. Never much thought I'd ever hear that come back to bite me."

"Ben said you'd give me the gun and take care of the paperwork."

I waited. He got a McDonald's bag from below the counter and took out an order of large fries, playing with one as he thought through how to deal with me.

"Man of my word, I am, I am. But how do I know who you are?"

"I won't tell anybody where I got it, and I hope that I'll never have to use it."

"Easy for you. Maybe bad for me. I meant, how do you know Yazzie?"

"Oh. He and I worked as partners for Marvin's Bail Bonds, here in Flagstaff."

"Heard he had a partner. You work with computers, right?"

"Yes. That's me."

"Okay. A man of my word, I am. You'll still have to fill out the forms, okay? I can't stretch things that far."

He clearly didn't like it, but without comment he took some printed forms out of accordion records file and watched as I carefully printed information, line by line. His ballpoint pen ran dry halfway through the second page, and when I started using a second one, black ink instead of blue, he ripped up the form and handed me another.

"Red flag to a bull, I turn something written with two different pens."

I finished.

"You want to shoot off a magazine?"

"No."

"No offense, but have you ever fired a handgun?"

"No."

"Again, no offense, but guns kill. You don't look like you much know what to do with this piece, and I don't want any problems before this paperwork goes through. They find out I sold it to you, we've both got a problem. I suggest, no offense intended, that we just take five, ten minutes of your time, so you learn how to load it and fire it."

I nodded, and he led me to the back of the store.

"This is a shooting range," he said, handing me some yellow foam earplugs. "Stick these in your ears before we go in."

He pushed another set of plugs into his own ears. After I inserted mine, we went through double doors into the shooting range, which was divided into four sections by upright partitions. We stood at a waist-high Formica counter inside the first section. Empty cartridge brass was scattered everywhere on both sides of the counter. Freddy laid the Bersa on the counter and opened a box of shells. After showing me a small lever on the side, he flicked the lever and the magazine dropped into his other hand. He gave me the magazine, positioned it open end up, and handed me a shell.

"You've got to slide it in. Go on. Go on. Try it."

I pushed the shell into the magazine. It took more force than I'd have thought. One at a time I inserted six more, and each time it got easier as I learned to push down with my thumb on the rim of the casing and then slide the shell backward. Without thinking I swiveled toward him, and he ducked as the barrel aligned with his chest.

"Jesus, Jesus, don't *ever* point that at somebody unless you mean it."

"I'm sorry."

"Okay. You got six in the pipe. Six is enough. Six is plenty. Now. This is a semiautomatic. A lotta people think that all you gotta do is pull the trigger, but that's just TV, that's just the movies. First, you gotta get the first bullet into the gun so it will shoot. Grab the barrel with your left hand and pull it back until it clicks."

It clicked.

"Now, let the slide go back to normal."

I did. And felt a strange satisfaction at the precise mechanical movement of cocking the hammer, then a metallic *snick* as the slide racked forward.

"Feels good, doesn't it?"

"It's very strange," I said, "to be holding a gun and learning how to fire it."

"Well, it's ready to shoot. Just remember, don't point it if you don't want to shoot it. See this little button? See here? . . . See here? That's the safety. Push it to the left, it won't fire. Push it the other way, you're all set."

He punched a button on the wall. A motor hummed somewhere and a line above my head started moving, bringing a paper bull's-eye target toward me.

"Okay. That's ten feet away. Aim right at the middle."

I held the gun out in front of me, turning my face slightly away.

"Wait. Use both hands. Take your left hand, put the palm underneath the gun butt. Good. Wrap the fingers of your left hand around the right hand. Good. Look right down over the barrel. Take up the slack on the trigger. When you're ready, like they say in the movies, just squeeze slowly."

The barrel wobbled, and I tightened both hands and pulled the trigger fast, the sound incredibly loud in the small room. My ears started ringing.

"Don't I have to cock it again, or slide that thing back?"

"No. It'll just keep shooting until you run out of slugs."

I lined up on the bull's-eye and squeezed until the gun fired. Without waiting for him to say anything, I aimed carefully and fired twice more.

"There's two left. This time, as soon as you've fired, do it again. Bang bang. It's called a double tap. Most cops shoot twice. Go on."

Tap tap. Just like Ben killing the rattlesnake. The slide stayed back, and I looked at Freddy. All six holes were grouped within the second smallest ring, and two were directly within the black bull's-eye. He held the doors open for me, and as we went back into the shop I dug the plugs out of my ears, which were still ringing.

"Lady, you're a *natural*. Look at this. Group of six, two in the bull."

"Oh, come on," I said sarcastically.

"Hey. No bullshit. I'm a natural shooter myself, and I gotta tell you, almost anybody who comes in here for the first time can't even hit the target. Here. You keep this for a souvenir. And please, try not to use the gun for at least a week."

He offered me the Spanish box, but I tucked the Bersa into my handbag. He laid out three boxes of shells. My hand on my purse, he stopped me.

"Nope. Part of the deal. Cost him a lot more than this. Oh yes, cost him more."

"What does it mean? Painted Butte?"

"A horse. Santa Anita, three years ago. Yazzie said it was wired, so I bet a lot of money. He wouldn't let me pay him off. Said he might need a favor someday, said he'd call up that favor just by saying 'Painted Butte.' You tell him the favor's called home."

"Then will you throw in those fries? I want to eat while I shoot some more."

"My pleasure indeed, indeed."

I practiced loading and unloading the Bersa as I started eating the fries, cold just the way I like them. Slowly, methodically, I shot two boxes of shells, feeling uncomfortably conflicted between my longtime dislike of guns and my newly found enjoyment of the mechanically precise object in my hand as I steadily hit the bull's-eye.

At eight-thirty, I left for the rodeo.

24

The Fort Tuthill parking lots were jammed, and I had to walk nearly half a mile to get into the rodeo grounds. I might never get Mary Nataanie to draw pictures of the two men she remembered, but I was convinced they were bull riders and that she might recognize them from photographs.

As I mingled into the steady flow of people headed for their seats, somebody touched my arm from the back and I turned to see Kimo smiling at me.

"Never thought I'd see you here," he said.

"Hello."

"Came by your trailer, saw the note. That Marvin, he paid in cash, only asked if I was working with you full-time now. Let me give you your share."

"Not now, wait till later," I said, trying to resolve my ambivalence at seeing him, with wariness shifting quickly to delight as he touched my cheek.

"Still some seats left way up in the stands. What are you doing here?"

"I want to take some pictures of bullriders. Can we go wherever they gather?"

"Sure. The ready room. Come on."

I hesitated before going in, but Kimo knew the security man, who waved us inside just as another camera
flashed. I saw a young photographer wearing jeans,
leather vest, scraggly ponytail and beard, acne, with a
badge around his neck from the Flagstaff paper.

"Do they mind," I asked Kimo, "if you take their
pictures?"

"Nah," the photographer said. "Just don't ask them
anything. These riders'll take all the publicity they can
get."

One rider wound surgical tape around the palm of
his gloved left hand. Squinting through the cheap lens,
I watched their faces gradually tightening, winding up
their nerves while putting on a variety of pads, elastic
bandages, some donning flak jackets, others stuffing
chunks of tobacco between lower teeth and lip,
splotching the floor with juice ejaculated in streams
and spasms. Some wound surgical tape on their hands,
knees, legs, across the ribs. Others banged on their spur
rowels, making sure they were wired solid but still had
rough edges. I took two pictures of everybody in the
room and was ready to leave when some of them started
getting down on their knees. People stopped talking.

"It's *Jesus* time," the photographer whispered.

"What does he mean?" I asked Kimo.

"Cowboys for Christ."

A dozen riders gathered in the far corner of the
room, clutching Bibles as they knelt in group prayer. All
had religious slogans on their chaps, with JESUS IS LORD
being the favorite. A horn sounded in the arena, and the

riders trooped out in bunches toward the alleyway behind the chutes.

"Can we go in there?"

"Sure. They never really know who's who."

Kimo climbed onto railings beside the chutes where the first three bulls were gated off. The first bull entered the chute with little fuss and stood relatively quietly. The second bull was a mulie, and I couldn't see much of the third.

"Aaannnnnd now, Flagstaff. Are you ready for the bulls?"

A huge cheer went up from the stands. Three men strutted around the arena in clown outfits and painted faces. One of them rolled a barrel with both ends open and the words CLOWN LOUNGE painted on the side. All wore ragged, torn shirts tied around the waist by the sleeves. Multicolored scarves hung from their belts.

"Give a big welcome to the cowboy savers, Flagstaff. The barrel clown. The bullfighters. They may look funny, but when a cowboy is down and needs a hand, these fellows will jump right in and distract the bull. All right, Flagstaff. In chute number three, the first bull rider of the afternoon is Steve Loughlin, from El Paso, Texas. Coming out on Slamdunker. Steve's gonna have his hands full here, no easy ride guaranteed 'cause this bull's got a rep, folks, he's got a big rep for getting right smack in your face, you give him any chance at all."

Men swarmed all over the chute, hanging on the rails or standing directly on rails beside the chute as a young bullrider stepped up over the rails and sat on the

top. His chaps were bright red, with white strings coming out of silver rosettes. He put a foot down on the
bull, then rested both feet on the bull's back as though
it were a hassock. He reached down and stroked the
yellowish hump. He settled into the chute, dropping
down on top of the bull. Several people were standing
around on the rails, helping the rider get his bull rope
attached. The bull lurched sideways suddenly, and the
entire chute structure trembled. I thought the rider's leg
must have been mashed, but he'd pulled it up just in
time. He resettled on top of the bull.

In front of the chute, on the arena dirt floor, three
men stood waiting while the rider settled down. One
man had on a gray sports jacket and carried a yellow
flag. The other two were poised to open the gate, one
ready to unlatch it and the other standing at the end of
a rope, ready to pull the gate open.

Kimo boosted me up onto some rails just in time to
see the rider grip the rope with his gloved hand, then
wind the rope twice around his fist and tuck it underneath his gloved fingers, which he pounded with his
free hand, just as Claude had shown me. His glove glittered with bright red words GO FOR GOD.

One of the men on the rails reached toward the
flank strap on the back of the bull and yanked it tight.
The bull jerked sideways, smashing the rider's right
ankle against the railing. I saw him suck in his upper
lip, but he gave no other show of pain.

"God," Kimo said, "would I love to be in that
chute."

"Do you really understand why I'm here?" I asked.

"Mary was raped by one of these bullriders, and I get a picture of him, I can put him away."

"Jesus, Laura, I'm sorry. I didn't think about that at all."

Ready, the rider gave two tight nods. The gate swung open, and the bull exploded straight out of the chute with two jumps, his front legs bucking a foot off the ground and the rear legs coming up almost three feet. The rider held on to the bull rope with his gloved hand, his free arm flying back and forth like a windshield wiper. His body jerked and rolled as the bull jumped, bucked, and quickly pulled two tight circles to the left. A horn sounded, and a few seconds later the rider rolled off the left side of the bull and ran toward the fence. The bull rope fell loose in the dirt as the barrel clown distracted the bull, who grew suddenly placid and trotted easily toward the exit gate. All this took less than a minute, and the announcer was already talking about the second rider and bull. Applause and groans rippled as the score was announced at sixty-seven.

Stunned and exhilarated by the explosive ride, like a train wreck on hooves, I felt extraordinarily aggressive, alive, so focused that I was aware of blood wild in my arteries, veins, capillaries; my face and hands were flushed with the blood heat, and my head throbbed with awe at the world of my father, a world I'd never really seen.

"Goddammit!" I shouted to Kimo. "I never knew it was like this."

"Hey, come on. You have no idea how ridiculous you sound."

But I did not forget why I was there, and I framed each bullrider in my zoom lens to shoot several exposures of his face. And with each successive rider, I remembered the violent way a few of them had treated Mary.

The last bull started bucking while in the chute, rearing up almost vertically so that the rider slid off and had to climb the back gate. The bull jumped across the fence between the chute and the alleyway, and people scattered. And then the bullriding was ended.

"How about a beer?" Kimo said, not noticing that I'd stopped behind him because I'd seen Ben coming toward me through the crowd.

"Another time," I said to Kimo, and he went shut-faced.

"Whoa. What is that?"

"My old partner," I said, wanting Kimo to disappear, afraid of the two men confronting each other. "Ben Yazzie. I've got to get rid of him," I said, "and you can't get involved in this. Please. Where are you staying?"

"Here. In Flagstaff. Call Marvin's Bonds. He'll tell you."

"I'm really sorry about this, Kimo."

"Yeah."

He faded into the crowd as Ben came up beside me.

"I've got something really great," Ben said. "But I need your help."

"You can't go to Tuba City," I told him. "You'll be arrested."

"I don't think so, not after Yellowhouse hears my news. Come on."

"Not Yellowhouse. There's a manhunt for those men you worked with."

"I know, but nobody's connected me to them."

"Foxburn did."

"The FBI knows I worked with that crew?"

"Foxburn knows. But he said he owed you."

"He did. But he's still FBI, so come on, we've got to hurry. I've got a fingerprint, but it's blurred. I need you to enhance it with your computer."

Neither of us said a word as we worked our way to the far parking lot.

Because of the heavy traffic, it took half an hour just to get to Flagstaff. Ben ignored the traffic, going over and over some papers. In Flagstaff we passed a minimall with a late night camera store, and I pulled abruptly into the lot.

"Hey. What are you doing? Don't stop here."

"Wait for me," I said.

Angry and confused by his presence, I pushed my way into the camera store too boldly. The teenage clerk thought maybe I was crazy, maybe it was a holdup. I took out three rolls of film and dropped them on his counter.

"Your sign says one-hour developing. Can you do these right now?"

"Lady, I close in half an hour."

I pulled out my wallet and put a twenty-dollar bill on his counter.

"That's your bonus."

"Lady . . ."

I took out two more twenties. "All yours, plus whatever you normally charge. Can you do it?"

He looked up at a digital wall clock, pointed tongue darting out to lick the left side of his mouth as he looked from the clock to the cartridges. I laid down the two twenties, and he scooped up the bills and pocketed them.

"No time for prints. But for another twenty, I could make some contact sheets."

I laid out the money.

"Take me thirty minutes. Twenty, if you don't mind wet contacts."

"Done. Get to it."

"I'll have to close the store, turn off the front lights. But just knock on the door. Hell, let me close right now, and you just wait back here."

I sat on the floor behind the kid's counter while he worked first at one machine and then another, finally handing me a manila envelope. Impatient, Ben had moved behind the wheel and barely gave me time to shut my door before he drove away.

Forty-five minutes later, as we pulled into Tuba City and turned into our dirt street, I saw the smashed trailer door from fifty feet away. Ben stopped abruptly. Moonlight flickered through the cottonwoods, but their heavy branches moved with a breeze so that the doorway was partially lit for an instant and then slid into darkness. Leather creaked beside me, and I saw Ben pulling the SIG from his shoulder harness. The street seemed frozen in plastic, a miniature street scene in a paperweight, the way they do with coins or stamps or insects.

Everything was quiet except for metal tinking as the engine cooled.

"Open your door. Slide out and keep behind the truck."

I shoved the door open just enough for me to slip through. Ben turned sideways, keeping his eyes on the trailer all the time. Once outside he crouched and went backward, motioning me to follow. We went through the passageway between two trailers, a TV flickering through slat blinds at the back of a rusted single-wide. We moved quickly until we were across the street from our trailer.

Lit by moonlight, the front door hung crazily from the bottom hinge.

"Wait," he whispered. "Don't move, don't make a sound. Just wait."

Ten minutes.

Fifteen.

Something moved behind our trailer, somebody was coming out toward the street, hidden by the cottonwood shadows. Ben held the SIG out in front of him in a shooter's stance as the person sat at the redwood table. A small figure, nibbling the fingernails of her right hand, the other hand pulling through her hair again and again.

Mary Nataanie.

25

Ben charged across the street, moving aggressively right up to Mary. Right behind him, I pulled at his arm because he had the SIG against her forehead. Her mouth hung open, and she began to mewl with fear.

"Ben, put the gun down."

"Who *is* she?"

"Her name is Mary Nataanie. She's a friend."

Ben moved the SIG aside, and she ran into my arms.

"It's okay, it's okay," I said.

"Were you here when this happened?" Ben said to her.

She nodded her head up and down, up and down, and the mewling started again. I got out my handkerchief and wiped her face and stroked her hair while we looked at the door sagging from one hinge. The screen door was nowhere in sight. Ben went into the kitchen and hit the light switch, but nothing happened. I could hear him pushing things aside. Some glass crinkled under his shoe.

"They couldn't get into the workroom. Wait a minute."

I heard him working the combination lock, and a light went on. He came back with a six-cell flashlight and waved me inside. I saw that the kitchen had been totaled. Most of the cabinets had been ripped from the walls, and almost everything from the cabinets lay broken and trampled on the floor. The refrigerator lay on its side, the door open and all the food spilled out. Water ran from the freezer compartment. He played the flashlight around to the front wall, where three small bookshelves had been ripped off and large red letters were spray-painted on the bare wall.

WISH YOU WERE HERE

"Can you tell us what happened?" I said to Mary.

"No. I hitched a ride from Cove, but it was like this when I got here. I've been hiding behind the trailer for a long time."

"I know who it was," I said to Ben. "A Navajo cop named Benally."

"No. Benally hates me for bringing the Tso brothers to jail, but a cop would never do this. Come on, you can't stay here. I'll take you over to the motel, and you can do some online checking for me while I come back for the rest of this stuff."

"I don't want to go to a motel."

"And what if it's *not* Benally?" he said finally. "I can think of a dozen people who'd do this because of what they'd hope to find."

Where is it? Garcia had asked repeatedly. Where was *what?*

"Maybe it was Garcia. He was here yesterday, looking for the Spanish bit."

"Fuck! I *knew* he'd seen me take it."

"But Claude was here," I lied without knowing why. "So Garcia just left me alone."

"Well, we don't have to worry about him. There's over two hundred lawmen tracking him now. Let's get out of here. Now."

Taking Mary by the hand, I went back into the bedroom and stuffed things into a vinyl suitcase. I slung it over one shoulder and picked up the carryall, my laptop, and a magnifying glass. Three lights winked on the answering machine. I unplugged it and carried it outside. Ben lifted my purse to make room, then swung it, testing the weight. He pulled out the Bersa, and I thought he was going to tell me it was too small, but he nodded to himself and stuffed the Bersa back into my purse.

"We can't just leave all the equipment."

"Forget it for now. Just take your laptop. The guy in Phoenix got a fingerprint off of the bit. I'm going to call in a favor with a guy who works for NCIC, but I need you to enhance the fingerprint with one of your magic computer programs. I've got it scanned on a floppy disk for you. Come on, come on. Out of here. Now. I'll call Claude after I drop you at the motel and have him nail up the door."

We rented two rooms, and Ben waited until Mary and I settled into one of them. Mary couldn't figure out the tension between us, but she was glad when Ben left me the floppy disk and went to his own room. Mary started to lie down on one of the beds and then quickly bounced up.

"I forgot."

Digging in her backpack.

"I drew the pictures again."

"What pictures?"

Two young male faces.

"I only remember these two," she said, putting the drawings in my hand and hopping onto the bed to rock back and forth.

"Very good," I said, hugging her. "Very brave."

The faces were crudely drawn, but she'd paid attention to the details she remembered. A crooked nose, a mole on a left ear, *a scar running through an eyebrow.* I'd seen that scar through the camera lens. I started to pull out the contact sheets.

"Are you hungry?"

"No. Maybe a Coke."

"Let me go see what's in the machines."

"Don't leave me here."

We got change at the motel office, and she fed it into the machines for two cans of Coke, some cookies, some peanut-butter-and-cracker things, and a package of corn chips. Back in the room I relocked the door and she flopped onto the bed.

"Want a Coke?" she said.

"Sure."

She picked up the TV remote and started switching channels while she ate, all the time pulling at her hair, one strand a time, starting at the root and stretching it out, her fingers running all the way to the end, letting it drop, picking another hair.

I spread the contact sheets on the other bed and popped the Coke tab.

"Mary. I've got some pictures. They're kinda small, but I've got this thing."

I turned on the bedside light and stretched the cord enough so the lamp shone directly on the prints. I got the magnifying glass.

"You have to look close, but this will magnify the pictures enough so they'll be clear. Just look at all of them and see if you recognize anybody."

"I want to watch this program."

She nibbled at her fingernails, morose, apprehensive. I took the remote from her, turned off the TV. Mary hugged her legs to her body, rocking back and forth.

"Let's just do this quick," I said.

"I don't want to look."

"It won't take long, and then it'll be over."

"If I look, will you promise not to take me home?"

"But your parents, they must be worried sick, not knowing where you are."

"He won't care," Mary said sourly. "He's too busy with his water pipes."

"Okay. We'll stay one night. But then I've got to take you back to them."

I laid out the contact sheets on the bedspread and handed the magnifying glass to Mary. She fiddled with the glass for several minutes, got up to get her Coke, and finally sat still enough to look at every sheet quickly, taking only a few minutes to zip the glass over all the tiny pictures. I thought she was going to give up at that point, but she started all over again, this time looking a little longer. She finished one contact sheet and pushed it aside for the others. After ten minutes she'd narrowed it down to several pictures, then finally she put down the glass and positioned two fingers of her left hand on one sheet and three fingers on another. Two men. Two shots of one and three of the other. Mary got up, trembling, and ran into the bathroom and vomited. I followed her immediately, wetting a towel, wiping off her face, comforting her, pulling her back into the bedroom, stroking her hair until the trembling stopped.

"Okay. Thanks, honey. You've been really brave."

She sat on the bed, twisted to lie down, pulled her knees almost up to her chin, and fell asleep immediately, huddled into a ball. Switching off the bedroom lights, I went into the bathroom, shut the door, and turned on the fluorescent fixture. My mouth under the water faucet, I drank and drank and then sat on the toilet to look at the contact pictures. I recognized both of them from the rodeo. One was white, the other not distinct enough for me to be certain. Both were young, barely twenty if that. Both had cocky grins underneath their hats. The white man wore a flashy shirt, the other a shirt of solid burgundy. They were just boys, I realized, except they'd given up childish things. I stared at the pictures a long time, memorizing their faces, internalizing what I remembered of both of them from the ready room, finding absolutely nothing in the photographs that helped me separate good from evil.

Turning out the light, I continued to hold the pictures while I went to sit on the other bed, uncertain what to do next but understanding I held enormously powerful things in my hands and had absolutely no

idea what to do with that power. I got the Bersa,
thumbed cartridges into the magazine, and popped it
home. After racking back the slide and letting it go forward, I stood in front of the mirror and aimed at myself,
feeling foolish but feeling it was necessary, feeling
mostly strung out and anxious.

At four o'clock I was stretched out on the bed, wide
awake, when somebody tapped three times on the
door. I picked up the Bersa and stood next to the door.

"Laura."

I opened it. Ben started to come in, but I pushed
him backward, pointed to Mary sound asleep, and
reached behind me to unlock the knob and close the
door. Parked in front of the room next door, the pickup
was loaded with equipment.

"I took out the computers and scanners. I'll put it
all in my room for tonight. And I e-mail-attached the
fingerprint to NCIC, so I probably don't need your
help. But come on into my room, listen to something,
and tell me what the hell is going on."

The answering machine from our trailer was set up
on the dresser, red light no longer winking, and I knew
he'd already listened to the messages. Rubbing the back
of his neck, he punched the playback button.

"I saw you again today, on the TV. Now, I want you
even more."

The machine clicked off. It wasn't Benally, but the
other, unknown voice.

"You have any idea who that is?" Ben asked.

There's a moment when you're safe, when you're
comfortable, satisfied, maybe stretched in the hot sun

with some drink in your hand and smiling. And then there's a moment when you hear the wolves behind you, and for a moment you wonder *why* they're after you, and then you wonder how much longer you can run.

Some *animal* wanted me, and I'd not yet seen its face.

"No."

"And what does he mean, he saw you on TV."

"I don't know. When I was called in to talk to Foxburn, this TV reporter was outside the building. I thought they didn't get me on tape, but she was too smart for that. And she couldn't resist showing whatever she got. Must have been on the late news."

"You don't know who this guy is? Maybe the one that left the rattlesnake?"

"No. That was Benally."

"He's a cop. I just don't believe that."

"Just this once," I said bitterly, "I wish you'd believe what I tell you."

"My God, Laura. What the hell have you been doing this week?"

"Why would you care?" I said bitterly. "I asked you to stay, but you wouldn't."

"Yeah. You're right. I'm sorry."

"That's just bullshit, Ben. You wanted to do your own thing. So forget it."

"Well, anyway, I brought you something."

He emptied a heavy manila envelope on his bed. A packet of twenty-dollar bills, "$1,000" printed on the wrapper. Wyoming driver's license, Social Security card, birth date April 14, 1962. A VISA gold card, a library card, and something from a Cheyenne mailbox store. All in the name of Elizabeth Jane Henderson.

"When we bought the Laura Winslow identification, I paid for an extra one, in case you ever needed an out. I kept it in a safe-deposit box down in Phoenix."

"Now I'm totally freaked. Just, just keep this stuff, just leave me alone."

He tried to read my face like a TV screen, looking for some channel to my feelings and finding none. I went back inside my room, relocked the door, and put on the chain. Once I got my computers, I knew if I cracked into the PRCA site, their multimedia databases held digitized pictures of all current cowboys.

I lay on the bed, unable to sleep, totally wired until my cell phone went off at five. It was Shiyoma Lakon, telling me a hiker had found the mutilated body of a teenage girl in Canyonlands National Park, and if I was ready, she would pick me up in a TV helicopter at the Tuba City airport, because she'd told the national parks ranger that I could identify the body.

26

I looked down uneasily through the Plexiglas floor panels at a series of rocky spires, arches, and domes, all clumped together like a giant carnival barrel organ. The chopper twisted directly between two spires that seemed at least four hundred feet tall and leveled out nose down through a long canyon to fly even with some Anasazi stone-walled ruins tucked into a long niche along the canyon wall.

Nauseated from the vibration, I looked over Ben's shoulder at his watch.

Shiyoma handed me a sheet of fax paper from her briefcase. Albert Grody, known pot hunter, killed along with a Navajo policeman in a gun battle.

"What's that?"

Ben's voice in my headset. I shook my head and finished the short bulletin released by the FBI before handing it back to Shiyoma. It seemed very strange that Grody could be in Tuba City, but neither Kimo nor Cristina Carnoy knew about it. Shiyoma tucked it into the briefcase and said something into her microphone, but I couldn't hear. The pilot pointed at a small knob. Shiyoma clicked it to another position.

"We've got a small window before the FBI gets there," she said. "The chief park ranger is . . . how do I say it? . . . somebody from my great sex days. We have a bank of radio scanners at the TV station, and the graveyard shift operator picked up a police message. I called Dan, that's the great sex ranger, and said I wanted to come up right away. He got really excited about keeping me away, but I told him I'd bring him a thousand dollars and somebody who could possibly identify the body."

"Ten minutes," the pilot said.

God, I hate helicopters. They leap into the air like spring rams, butting the clouds, depending on raw power instead of airfoils, so that when the power stopped you went down, the rotor still windmilling as though it were holding you up, strictly an illusion as the chopper sank toward the ground like a three-ton boulder. I could see sweat on the back of Ben's neck. The pilot noticed his discomfort and grinned.

"Sorry about the vibration."

"Feels like you need some rotor tracking," Ben answered without thinking.

"One per rev, I make it. These asshole mechanics, they think once you balance the rotors, you don't need to bother with anything but ground tracking, or they keep fiddling with the blade pitch links and pay no attention to trim tabs."

"Forget it," Ben said.

"Tell me, man," the pilot said, "do you miss it?"

"Miss what?"

"Being there."

"Where?"

"'Nam, man. Do you miss it, too?"

"I never said I was there."

"You got 'Nam eyes, man, checking out the LOH when you first climbed on board. I seen right through your eyes into what you was remembering about 'Nam."

"You saw wrong," Ben said, and ripped off his headset.

"Hey, man. It ain't no embarrassment, being in 'Nam. Best time of my life."

He'd never told me about being in 'Nam. I studied every inch of his face, every hair on his head, realizing how little I really knew about him.

The pilot stroked the collective control, and the chopper bounced upward a hundred feet or so to avoid a sandstone ridge. For the next fifteen minutes we flew up and down and around isolated mesas and buttes, canyons, arches, and spires. Two major rivers channeled gorges deep within a landscape of rock, the spires casting thousand-foot elongated shadows because of the early morning sun, which was already eight diameters above the horizon. Everything was suffused with color, rock structures segregated into horizontal bands of color according to the different geological strata, looking from a distance like holiday candles of many different-colored waxes, lighter colors on the top, blending down toward centuries-old dark bedrock. Blacks and browns formed the background for striking variations of ocher and umber, blending into tones of muted red, rust, yellow, and, most of all, orange.

"What makes all those colors?" Shiyoma asked.

"Different kinds of sandstone," the pilot answered. "Shales, limestones, gypsum, jasper, siltstones, and mudstones."

"We in Utah yet?"

"Oh yeah. We came into Canyonlands ten minutes ago. Right now we're over the Needles, following the Salt Creek trail. On the ground the only way in here is on foot or heavy-duty four-wheel-drive machines. Two, three hours, at least. But with all the rain lately, even four-wheel-drive vehicles can't maneuver."

Far below, sunlight winked off glass or metal, deep in the canyon.

"Okay, folks, hang on. We're going in."

The chopper abruptly began to slip sideways and then dropped down three hundred feet between the narrow canyon walls. I opened my eyes only when the chopper settled on its skids. A Jeep with heavy off-road tires was parked in front of the entrance to a large cave, and two men in national parks uniforms stood looking at us. As we ducked out underneath the rotor blades, one man came over while the other slumped down to sit beside a tire.

"Hi, Dan."

"Shiyoma, hello."

She started to embrace him, but his face was so pale that she touched his cheek. She handed him a white envelope. He turned it over in his hands, no longer certain he wanted the money. She took the envelope and tucked it into his pocket.

"You've got to hurry," he said. "The FBI helicopter is

ten, fifteen minutes away. And the state police are really pissed off. If they were here, they'd make you people leave, even with this possibility of identifying the body."

He looked at me and then Ben. Shiyoma didn't offer introductions.

"Any idea how the body got here?"

"There's a mess of tire tracks outside, all kinds of off-road vehicles, wide-tire stuff, maybe even an ATV or two. So little wind down here, hard to tell how long any of them have been here. I had your chopper land up canyon, so the wind from the rotor blades probably didn't wipe out anything."

"Who found the body?"

Shiyoma knew exactly what she had to get done.

"Some day hikers, rock hounds, looking for old Anasazi sign. This canyon's on all the maps, no secrets, no special hiding places; there's even a book tells you exactly where to look for rock art. My partner over there, Ernie del Papa, we're national parks men, not law enforcement. We spend most of our time keeping people from prying off pieces of rock art for souvenirs, or teenagers fooling in here with their spray paint."

Del Papa stood up and walked over. All of his clothing and equipment looked nearly brand new. He was also distinctly green in the face and very nervous.

"Sorry, I'm a little shaky. I've seen my share of road wrecks, but nothing like what this girl looks like. Been puking my guts out."

"She in the cave?" Shiyoma asked.

"Yeah. But, Dan . . . these people can't go in there."

Shiyoma pointed at me.

"This woman might be able to identify your vic-
tim."

"Gee, Dan, I don't think we should do anything
until the FBI gets here."

"Laura," Ben said urgently, "what are we *doing*
here?"

"I have to know," I said.

Dan borrowed del Papa's flashlight and led us back
inside the cave, winding around several corners until
we came to the body of a young girl; in that instant my
eyes went to her face, believing I'd recognize Judy. But
it was another teenager, her face unmarked, bluish,
drained of expression, blood, life.

She lay face upward on a rock shelf about three feet
above the cave floor. Naked, arms stretched out to the
side, legs pulled slightly apart. She'd been sliced open
from her collarbone to her navel, the rib cage split
raggedly and completely apart, and parts of her intestines
and other internal organs had spilled out. Her skin was
waxy pale, almost translucent. Her eyes were open.
Bruises were scattered over her body. Her vagina appeared as normal as could be expected, given the stage of her
decomposition, but certainly not abused. Dark stains ran
down the side of the rock and into the sand.

Dan took out a pouch of Red Man tobacco, tucking
some into his left cheek to combat the body's stench.
Ben reached down to touch the sand.

"Don't do that!"

Dan spoke sharply, but Ben was rubbing the sand
between his fingers.

"Still some moisture," he said. "With the heat in

here, this hasn't happened all that long ago. Do you know her?"

"No," I said. "I thought it would be a girl I've been looking for."

"Hey," Dan said angrily to Shiyoma. "You told me you had a witness."

"I said I would bring a private detective who *might* recognize the body."

"Shit," he said. "You're just using me again, just to get a story. Goddamn you anyway. I shouldn't have said yes."

"But we're here," Shiyoma said, turning to me. "You're positive? It's not the girl you were looking for? It's not Judy Pavatea?"

"Who's that?" Dan asked.

"A Hopi girl reported missing a few weeks ago."

"You have *any* idea who this is?"

"No," I said weakly, stumbling backward.

"Dan, what else is here?"

Shiyoma laid her hand on his arm, squeezing, working her fingers up toward his elbow. I could see he took it as a promise, although it was obvious to me that she was doing whatever it took to use him. Dan pointed the flashlight beam around the cave. I followed the beam, wanting to learn *anything* and seeing only rock wall.

"I've been all over, looking for any of the pieces chopped out of her. You can see that all the blood pretty much drained out right here."

I was shivering, but Shiyoma was in her element and reached into her backpack to pull out a Sony Hi-8 videocamera. Dan tried to stop her, but she was too quick for him and had a minute's taping before Dan put his hand over the lens.

"Shiyoma, please. Don't get me into trouble."

Dan wrapped an arm around her shoulder, whispering in her ear, and we all stumbled out into the sunlight. Shiyoma staggered and sat down abruptly to put her head between her legs. I was in shock, my skin clammy, like the flu with no fever, and yet part of my head recorded everything I saw.

Walking away from the cave, just to get *away* from there, we rounded a vertical sandstone cut and walked directly into a litter of soft-drink cans, beer bottles, bits and pieces of broken Anasazi pottery, dried ears of some ancient blue corn, and even the shattered pieces of several skeletons. A precisely carved, waist-high trench ran through the middle of what looked like a sandstone burial site, surrounded by a series of craters dug in a completely random pattern.

"The backhoe sheared this pot in half," Dan said, not wanting to talk about what was in the cave. "As though they didn't even care, only wanted something in one piece. This trench is really something. They kept digging until they found what they wanted, almost as though they knew where to look, and once they dug it out, they stopped, packed up the backhoe, and left. Look. You can see where they were really careful, right at the end of the trench, digging by hand to get something out."

We heard a distant *whopwhop*, and a second chopper came into sight.

"That's the FBI," Dan said. "You'd better leave. I'll have

a hard enough time just trying to explain why you were here."

It hovered while the pilot looked for the best landing zone.

"Laura." Ben tugged at my elbow. "Come on."

I pulled out of his hand, staring back at the entrance to the cave, allowing Ben to lead me to the chopper. We lifted off just as the other one landed on its skids. Once out of the canyon, Shiyoma tapped my headset, indicating I should turn it on.

"Who was that?" she asked me.

"I have no idea."

"Are you ready to give me some more names of girls you think are missing?"

"Talk to the Hopi Rangers. I can't deal with this anymore."

She laughed, her voice brilliant, edgy, proud. She took out the videocamera.

"One minute of videotape," she said. "I could sell it for five figures, maybe even six figures. But I won't sell it. I'll *use* it. I'll do the story myself. Tonight. And by next Monday morning I'll be getting calls for anchor jobs all over the country. Everybody else working in Flagstaff TV news thinks the real story is the manhunt. They'll spend weeks looking in caves and up dead-end canyons, but they'll never find those men. My news director tried to send me over there this morning, but it's a total waste of time."

She pulled out the FBI report on Grody.

"Tell me how this fits in. I'll give you ten thousand dollars. No questions."

"No."

"This is your chance to make real money. Hitch a ride with me on this."

"No thanks," I answered, but she wasn't even listening.

"Everything I've ever been," she said, "that's all over. Every radio ad I taped in Buttfuck, Idaho, every station manager's cock I had to suck for better assignments, everything I had to *endure* to get ahead, that's all over."

Disgusted and horribly depressed, I ripped off my headset; but she wouldn't give up and stuffed the FBI report into my hands. Watching the chopper's shadow far below, I realized how much I'd hoped to find Judy's body, how disappointed I was to see that it wasn't her, how focused I'd become just to find her and end the search. And now feeling constricted inside a cage with no doors, feeling the inability to let go of Judy, wanting to shatter the cage that held me so completely.

27

I'm my own worst enemy.

Taking my morning Ritalin pill, hyped on emotions, I could no longer tell where to draw the line. I shook the remaining Ritalin pills into my right hand and counted them three times, but I fought off the temptation to swallow more than one. I felt incredibly powerful, conquering that temptation. While I still felt weak at not being able to avoid temptation, I at least had mental clarity to deal with my emotional enemy.

I watched Mary sleep, her young face relaxed, mouth open slightly. I had great difficulty keeping her face in focus as I thought of what my own daughter might look like. I pictured Judy's cornmealed face in the Polaroid, and my mind raced and blurred between Mary and Judy and Spider.

And then the dead girl's face popped into my head.

So much had happened in just five days. On Tuesday morning I'd had little ambition beyond watching hummingbirds, and now I was trying to find somebody who'd slaughtered at least one young girl. At *least* one! That realization terrified me. I'd been paid to find Judy

Pavatea, and now I'd started to believe I'd *never* find her alive.

I'm my own worst fear.

Sometimes I can't stop digging, can't leave the past alone. If somebody was killing Hopi girls, who's to say that somebody else wanted to kill my own daughter? Never mind that I haven't seen her in years, never mind that I don't know where she is, never mind *any* of that, because anything's possible to imagine. If I still believed that Spider was alive, then I could also believe that somebody wanted to harm her.

Be smart, I said to myself. Be clever enough to banish my fears.

You can *not* understand the fatal attraction of suicide, I tell you, unless you've opened the bottle of pills, held the razor blade in your hand, put the gun to your head, wanted to yank the steering wheel hard over while doing eighty, or aimed your car straight at concrete walls. I had to make choices. But it was no longer a choice between fight or flight. Leaving is easy, once you decide to do it. I'd left many places, many people. I sat on the bed across from Mary and wanted to touch her, realizing how *much* I wanted to be with her, and in the same moment I realized that although I'd not be able to keep her with me, at least I would find the man who'd raped her.

A car horn beeped repeatedly outside the motel, the insistent noise snapping my memories. I pulled off my T-shirt just as Mary woke up.

"Laura," she said, "what's that scar on your shoulder?"

Reflexively I covered it with my hand and reached for a short-sleeved blouse.

"I once had a butterfly tattoo."

"Oh, cool. I want to get a tattoo. What happened to yours?"

"You ask too many questions. Let's go get some food."

"Why a butterfly?"

"It was my Hopi name. Kauwanyauma. Butterfly Revealing Wings of Beauty."

"That's beautiful. What do butterflies mean to Hopis?"

"You never heard of butterfly maidens?"

"Maybe, not really."

"Here. Look at this."

I found the Curtis picture of the four butterfly maidens and showed it to her.

"That's kinda weird."

"Oh, I don't know. I think it's beautiful. All young Hopi girls get squash blossoms. At least, if you live in a traditional village. I don't know about the other villages. You don't like it?"

"That stuff is old-fashioned. All those ceremonies, all the secret names, the clan relationships, who you can date and who you can't, your mother getting mad if you look at some boy from your own clan. I want to move away from here."

"Oh, can't be all that bad."

"What would you know?" she said, her mood turning suddenly bitter. She turned on the TV and rapidly surfed the channels. She muted the TV and prowled restlessly around the room and began fiddling with the buttons on my answering machine, which I'd set up on the dresser.

What *did* I know about being a teenager? I tried to read her mood, the look in her eyes, anything to get hold of who she was. I wanted to talk with her, but I *didn't* want to talk to her in case she disappointed me, in case I no longer wanted to be with her. Mary. I didn't know what to say to her, what to do with her being with me.

Ben knocked on the door. I opened the door a few inches, and he tried to push inside, his eyes blazing with excitement and words on his lips.

"The fingerprint!" he said.

I'd forgotten about the Spanish bit. I pulled him outside, shut the door.

"NCIC returned a partial match and faxed this to the motel office."

He thrust a fax sheet into my hands.

Mark Jacob Kliendienst, private, U.S. Army. Enlisted in February ten years before, basic training at Fort Leonard Wood, Missouri. AWOL in three weeks. A young, bitter, unsmiling thin face, his hair shaved to his scalp.

"Do they know where he is now?"

"Not a clue. Here. I made a copy for you. We've got to start running searches. He's out there somewhere. Come on, I've got everything loaded back into the pickup and I'll rent an apartment in Flagstaff. We can be up and running in a few hours."

"What about Mary?"

"Send her back to her family. That's where she belongs, anyway."

"Ben, it's just not that simple."

"Look. If you won't help me with the searches, I'll get someone else."

"Please. Don't push on me."

"You're the one that's pushing," he said finally. "This could be our chance for big money. A hundred thousand dollars if we find this guy. Looks like I'll have another fifty thousand from a television interview I agreed on condition I could find this guy. Of course, once they air my face, I'll have to either stop bounty hunting for a while or go someplace else. We could set up business in California, anywhere."

"I can't leave the girl."

"Fine," he said angrily. "You do whatever you want."

Then my whole life changed again as Mary screamed.

I yanked open the door, Ben right behind me, the SIG in his hand.

"What?" I said, stunned by the intensity of her sudden fear.

"It's him," she whimpered. "That voice on your answering machine. Listen."

She rewound the tape, and pressed the play button.

"I want you."

He sat on me like an animal, he said what a great bull I was, and then he started riding me. I'll never forget his voice, never forget him shouting down me, how I was his perfect ride.

"It's really, really him. He knows where I am, he's coming back to get me."

"Mary, Mary, it's okay, he's not here now."

"But that's his voice."

"It's okay. It's okay."

Stroking her hair, I held her tightly until she finally stopped trembling. I heard footsteps running outside, and somebody pushed at the partly opened door. It was the motel manager, but when he saw Ben's gun he stopped quickly.

"It's nothing," Ben said to him. "Our daughter, she had a nightmare."

The manager retreated back to his office.

"He's going to call the Navajo police," Ben said. "Come on, we've got to get out of here. I'll finish putting everything in the pickup, you get all your stuff together. The police can take this girl back to her family."

"I can't leave her, Ben."

"The police substation is only a few blocks away. Come on. Move!"

"Where did you get *this*?" Mary screamed.

I'd dropped Ben's fax photo on the bedspread, and Mary was holding it.

"Laura, that's *him*!"

"You're sure?" I asked.

"What are you saying?" Ben shouted at Mary.

"It's his voice, it's his picture. Does he know where I am?"

"No. Mary, it's just an old photo."

"My God," Ben said in awe. "We're both looking for the same man."

"He knows where I am," Mary whimpered. "He's coming to get me again."

"He doesn't know you're here," Ben said. "Get a grip on things. Let's go."

I grabbed her shoulders and pulled her tight to my chest.

"Ben, she's just a young girl."

"We've got to *move*," Ben said, grabbing the fax and the answering machine. "I can't deal with Yellowhouse right now. Are you coming with me?"

"You're asking too much of her. And of me."

"Then I'm outta here." He immediately got into the pickup and drove off.

"He's coming to kill me," Mary said, throwing her head back and forth wildly.

"No! He doesn't know where you are, he probably doesn't even know *who* you are. But I'm going to take you to a place where nobody will find you. Trust me."

She buried her face against my breasts for a moment and then looked up at me.

"You promise?"

"You can trust me, Mary."

Then Lieutenant Yellowhouse knocked on my door.

"Miss Winslow," he said awkwardly, "is Mary Nataanie really in there?"

Ben and the pickup had disappeared. I didn't know what to do.

"We've been told she came here with you last night. Her parents don't want her with you. Her parents want her to come home. Is she inside?"

"Yes."

"Would you ask her to please come out?"

Shocked that this was happening, I didn't know what to do.

"Give me a few minutes," I said. "Let me try to explain it to her. She's not going to like it."

"Her parents don't like it, either, their daughter not being home."

"She came here by choice. Even her grandparents said it was okay."

"She's a minor. Her parents have the say about what she should do. You can't just butt into people's lives, you can't just do that."

"Have you listened to that tape I gave you?"

"Yes, yes. That's what I really wanted to talk to you about, except I heard about Mary, and then I got a call from the motel manager. I'm a policeman, Miss Winslow. There are things I have to do."

He sucked in his lower lip, held it with his teeth to avoid showing his confusion.

"You're not her mother, Miss Winslow."

In a flash I knew that he was right. I wasn't her mother, I wasn't her keeper, and the more time we spent together, the harder it would be to finally say good-bye.

"Can you just wait a few minutes?" I said.

"Okay. Ten minutes. Then I want to see her."

Mary sat defiantly on the bed. She'd heard most of the conversation and had both arms crossed tightly against her chest, shaking her head.

"I'm not going."

"Mary, you *have* to go home to your parents."

"You're going to let him take me?"

"I don't have any choice. You don't have any choice."

"I'll run away again."

"Mary. Please."

"You don't care about me after all!" she screamed. She stripped off the long T-shirt I'd given her to sleep in and pulled on jeans and a blouse. Trying to lace up her sneakers, she was blinded by her tears for a moment and shouted with rage while she wiped her eyes clear enough to see what she was doing.

"I don't care about you anymore!"

"Mary, we'll work it out. You *have* to believe me."

"Why? None of you people really care about me."

"Mary. *Listen* to me. I'm going down to the Flagstaff rodeo tonight. I'm going to find those cowboys, the ones in the pictures you identified."

She couldn't get a T-shirt into the backpack after two tries, and she ripped off a sleeve and flung aside the pieces. Her whole body shook with anger and fear.

"I trusted you."

"You can *still* trust me."

"Not likely," she said coldly, no longer crying. "Not fucking likely."

She punched me in the chest with the backpack.

"Mary, you're the only person who's seen these men. If they're the same men who did something to Judy, you are the only person who can identify them. Don't you want me to find them?"

"What do you really care about me?" she screamed.

She punched me again and again until I stood aside. Yellowhouse held open the car door for her. Another policeman sat behind the wheel.

"Let me go with you," I said. "I want to show you something."

Yellowhouse hesitated, then nodded reluctantly. I got all the pictures of the rodeo cowboys and locked the motel room door. Mary slumped in the front passenger seat as I got in back. We drove to the station house, where Charley and Leona Nataanie waited impatiently for Mary to get into their pickup, Leona insisting that Mary sit between them. Agonized, I waved good-bye, hoping Mary would wave back; but she didn't. As they drove away I saw her father shouting at her, and they stopped a few hundred yards down Main Street, the three of them getting out of the pickup, Mary and her mother huddled together as her father walked back and forth. I had to look away.

Yellowhouse was plainly uncomfortable. He pulled out a small tape recorder from the glove compartment of his car and showed it to me.

"My real apologies. Benally's locked up, over in Keams Canyon. He admitted nailing that rattlesnake inside your trailer. He thought by frightening you, he'd get back at Yazzie. I been on the police for twenty-five years. I never had anything like this happen."

He put the recorder back into the glove compartment.

"I had a long talk with Billie Tso. She said that all you really wanted was to find the Pavatea girl. I heard you was up to Canyonlands, that you saw the body.

That must have been a tough thing to do. Billie also told me you think there are other girls missing. Do you really believe that?"

"Yes."

"I talked with Captain Seumptewa, the Hopi Ranger. He said he was trying to track down two girls named Minnie and Sophie, but nobody wanted to talk with him. And like me, he doesn't have any evidence that these girls aren't just off visiting family. And we've got other problems. Reporters from all over the state are swarming out on the mesas. They're already talking about 'the Hopi murders.' It's a zoo, so I'm trying to help him out. But between us, we've got absolutely nothing to go on. If you know anything else, if there's anything I can do, I will do it. Please. I owe you a debt. You can trust me to help you with anything."

I've never trusted a policeman. He saw my hesitation.

"Ma'am. Trust me. Please."

"Mary Nataanie was with Judy Pavatea the night Judy disappeared. They were both raped. Mary told me they were rodeo cowboys."

His body straightened with shock. I laid the two photos on the hood of his car.

"I took pictures of every cowboy I saw at the Flagstaff rodeo Friday night. Mary identified these two. I'm going looking for them tonight. Will you come with me?"

He shook his head.

"Rodeo cowboys. They could be anywhere. Better that I get the Flagstaff police to be at tonight's rodeo. Can I keep these?"

"They're my only copies."

"I'll get some enlargements. I know a guy at the chapter house, he's got a whole photo lab set up in his trailer. I can get him to do it right away, and then I'll send copies to the PRCA office in Colorado Springs. I'll also contact the Colorado Springs police, see if they can get somebody at PRCA to help identify the faces."

"Okay," I said reluctantly. "But I want them back this afternoon, so I can show them to other cowboys at the rodeo tonight. Will you go with me?"

"Please, let the Flagstaff police do that."

I saw no use in arguing.

"Just bring the pictures back to my trailer."

"I'll be there by five. Well. Look at this."

Mary walked back toward us, alone. As she got closer she started to run and didn't stop until she threw her arms around me.

"Can I stay with you a while?" she said timidly.

"Oh, Mary. Please don't ask me to go against your parents."

"My dad, he's so angry with me, he doesn't even want me in the house. My mom, she said Kimo Biakeddy told her you were a good woman. My mom, she said I can stay for a week, if you say yes."

Can she stay? I asked myself. What else did I have of any worth?

"Yes," I said. "Yes, you can stay as long as you want."

Yellowhouse dropped us at the motel. The manager wasn't sure he wanted to see me again, but I paid him for another night with the agreement that I wouldn't

stay there beyond the next morning. I collected my laptop but left everything else in the room. I was tired, so
tired, and only wanted to pack up what was left at my
trailer, figuring that Claude would help me find a place
to stay.

Mary and I walked back to the trailer. Somebody
had nailed the door back on, and a battered, rusted-out
Ford step-side had been backed into the driveway. We
heard the locks working, and the door opened. Kimo
stood there, holding the shotgun.

The kitchen had been repaired, and there was a
small note from Claude telling me to come see him
when I returned and that I didn't owe him anything, he
just wanted to be sure nobody stole what was left. Ben
had taken all the computer boxes from the workroom,
leaving monitors and keyboards unconnected.

"Are you sure we can stay here?" Mary asked
timidly, sensing my resignation at finding so much had
changed. "Will anybody come back?"

"Nobody's going to bother us," Kimo said. "I guarantee it."

28

"Ariocarpus!" he shouted.

"Means nothing to me," I shouted back.

Jukebox at top volume, we had to shout next to each other's ears just to be understood. Mike's Flag 66 Bar was packed solid with rodeo cowboys, including a large contingent of bull riders, all of them drinkers and shouters. One table seemed to be the center of a lot of raw jokes about riders who were thrown or had drawn mediocre bulls.

"Ariocarpus are these slow-growing little cactuses that pretend they're like rocks. Japanese bonsai collectors go crazy for them."

"So?"

"So about nine thousand dollars."

"People pay nine thousand for a rock?"

"Yeah. Hey, cowboy. Stop off here a minute."

We'd left Mary with Claude. Yellowhouse brought me half a dozen eight-by-ten enlargements of both pictures, and Kimo insisted on going with me to the rodeo. We'd shown the pictures to at least a hundred cowboys, but nobody recognized them. When the rodeo ended, Kimo suggested we go to the bar, where

he knew we'd see most of the bull riders still in con-
tention. We continued to show the pictures, and Kimo
had just hauled down a half-drunk calf roper, who
stared blurrily at the pictures and nodded.

"This Indian's name is Jack. Bullrider, I think."

"Jack who?"

"No idea."

"How do you know he's an Indian?" Kimo said.

"Guy says he's Indian, what do I know. But I never
seen this white kid."

"This Indian, Jack. Was he here tonight?"

"I doubt he's here. I know he didn't place last night,
so he's probably already driving to the next rodeo."

"Where's that?"

"Lady, there's six rodeos next week. Me, I'm driving
to Mesquite."

"Thanks," I said. "You're sure this Jack is a bull
rider?"

"Rough stock of any kind, I'd guess. But I seen him
only on bulls. Listen, you don't find him, come look me
up later."

The barkeep put down our third Cuervo with a
Corona back. I pulled on the beer slowly, having never
had three shots and beer backs so quick so late at night
and realizing I was just around the corner from getting
heavy-duty drunk. Somebody gave a loud whoop, and
half the men in the bar took it up.

"Those Ariocarpus," I said. "Did you go down to
Mexico to dig them up?"

"I had a supplier from Guadalajara. Except the Fish
and Wildlife Service seized every damn cactus he had,

including a twenty-foot-high crested saguaro, easily worth seven hundred a foot. That's fourteen thousand dollars for one lousy cactus. And half woulda been mine. Can you see me on my hands and knees like some bracero, digging up plants? No way."

He laid his bad hand on the bar. I stroked the two busted fingers, picked up his middle finger, and saw that the outer joint was fused solid.

"Who buys that kind of thing?"

"I told you. The Japanese."

"Where'd you get hooked up with Japanese rock buyers?"

"San Francisco."

"So you'd take them up there and sell them?"

"Mostly."

"Isn't there some law, you can't take plants from one country to another?"

"There are laws against most of what I've ever done."

A large digital sign, advertising Budweiser, flickered over the doorway, and I'd had to deliberately move around on my stool at twelve thirty-two in order to stop watching the minutes go by. The bar was nothing fancy except for a big sign boasting about their fried chicken legs and wings and an incredible jukebox with hundreds of songs you could choose from a glass-paged catalog on the bar. Just flip the pages, the faded instructions said, feed quarters into a slot, play as many as you like without stopping.

Another group of cowboys surged into the bar.

"You gonna be centered tomorrow night, Neil?"

"Centered, hell," Neil shouted. "I dominate whatever bull I draw."

It was Neil Blackgoat. I studied all the other faces,
but none looked remotely familiar. The pack surrounding him started clapping, and he stood up on the table.

"Give us the sermon, Neil, about your motivating
spirit."

"Listen to this," Kimo said. "They've all got a special
brag about their talent."

"When I get near the chute," Neil shouted, "I've
already thought of myself on top of the bull. I don't care
how rank he is, the ranker the better, 'cause I own him as
long as I'm riding him, I'm staying on the eight seconds
until the horn, and I've got a ride at least up into the eighties."

Kimo turned his back on the table as Neil climbed
down between two of the young women who had been
circling through the bar all night, sitting with men
who'd had a good ride or surrounding a few who had
national ranking. A teenager with purple dyed hair
laughed hysterically when Neil whispered in her ear.

"She's wearing jeans so tight," I said, "you can see
everything she's got."

"Just another buckle bunny," he said.

Neil's table seemed to draw most of the people in
the bar, but Neil was the center of attention, and at that
moment our eyes met and he recognized me in an
instant and came to our table.

"Jane Fonda," he said with his big smile, his hand
sliding from my shoulder down to pull lightly on my
bra strap. "Never thought I'd see you again."

Kimo actually looked surly, and I knuckled him in the chest.

"Kimo Biakeddy. Neil Blackgoat."

Neither of them offered to shake hands.

"I didn't see your ride tonight," I said.

"Eighty-nine. I'll top ninety in tomorrow's go-round. Be there, Jane. I'll wave while I'm up on top. Hey. What *is* your name?"

"Laura. Laura Winslow. I want to ask you something."

I held up the two photographs.

"Do you know either of these men?"

His eyes cut from one photo to the other, back and forth, up to my face.

"Nope."

"This Indian might be called Jack."

"Jack."

He reached out for the photo, held it in both hands, and breathed deeply.

"What makes you think he's Indian?"

"Another cowboy told me that."

"I'm Indian," he said. "And I've never seen this guy. Lots of fake Indians on the circuit. They think taking an Indian name, it gives them power."

"And this other one?"

"Nope. These are just kids. Might not even have their PRCA card yet. Listen. I've got a lot of pictures back at my trailer. Why don't you come see me later. We'll look through them and maybe you'll see something you like."

"No thanks." I smiled.

A passing waitress rubbed her ass against Neil, and he walked off with her.

"What does he mean," Kimo said with some heat, "calling you Jane?"

"Don't worry about him," I said. "Tell me, why is there a whole other group that rides bulls tomorrow?"

"The five best from tonight and last night, they all ride again on Sunday for top money. Listen, why don't we get out of here?"

I felt so happy with him, I began stroking his arm, smiling at him, swinging with the music. Seeing my fascination with the juke, Kimo got ten dollars' worth of quarters. But before I chose anything the juke started playing "Staying Alive."

"Goddamn it!" a cowboy roared so loudly that the place actually quieted down a bit. "Who's playing that fucking faggot music?"

"Hey," Kimo hollered to the barkeep. "Can you turn that juke up louder?"

"What the hell." The bartender grinned. "It's a fast night anyhow."

He cranked up the music powerfully loud. Two men seated at the bar, regular town people and not with the rodeo, finished their beers and almost ran to escape outside, the noise of the music driving them away, wanting to take control of their bodies.

The juke got blasting so loudly that I couldn't even hear Kimo talking to me; the music took over all conversation, and his lips began to move soundlessly just three inches from my ear like some actor on a television with the sound turned off.

Another local man sitting at the bar turned from his bucket of fried chicken legs and complained to the bartender about the music. Stained work uniform, at least two days' worth of whiskers, probably a steady customer, the man looked angry that this Saturday night was different. The barkeep ignored him for a while, but the man was too drunk to give it up and began to rag everybody seated at the bar about the music. When he saw nobody was going to pay him any attention, he fought his way through the crowd, tossing people left and right, went directly over to the jukebox, and yanked out the power cord.

The entire bar went stone silent.

I watched Kimo's face tighten just underneath the eyes, where nobody would notice without looking for it, about ready to bust over the red line of his anger. The man came back to the bar, smirking.

Kimo stood up and picked four chicken legs out of the man's bucket and started juggling them. He was really good at it, the legs flying halfway toward the ceiling. When a leg came down to the hand with the broken fingers he'd snap at the leg with just the thumb and forefinger, plucking the leg out of the air and sending it flying in a fluid swirl.

"You know," he said to the man, "there's two kinda dogs that bark at night. Them smarter ones, they bark at sounds or moving shadows or whatever they imagine's out there. They chase cats, piss on trees, sniff people's crotches, and keep barking through the night."

His eyes turned blank while he kept the legs whizzing round and round, nearly skimming the fake ceiling panels.

"The stupid dogs, they just make noise to see if there's another dumb dog out there. But their noise don't mean shit to a real barking dog."

He started barking, rising half off the stool to snarl loudly into the man's face, spit flying out all over the chicken legs as he barked and howled until the man stepped back, scared; and just like that Kimo stopped barking and flung the legs one at a time into the bucket. The man fled outside. The barkeep went back to the juke and put the plug back in, and the music started up loud; but the edge had gone out of the fun, and the crowd started drifting out of the bar. Neil Blackgoat tipped his $400 white Resistol hat at me while leaving.

"Come on," Kimo said, "time to go."

"Y'all take care now," the barkeep said. I grinned at the Budweiser clock, now reading three forty-two, thinking that in just four hours my life had come pure awake.

Kimo drove to the first motel with a VACANCY sign, and we tumbled into the creaking bed, ripping off the faded chenille bedspread, pulling at each other's clothes, so eager for each other. . . . And why should I tell you what we did? If you've already done it, you don't need me to talk about it.

The cheap air conditioner barely held out the night air, and we both dripped with sweat. He used the sheet to towel off some of the water and then lay back and moved his hand up across me back up to my right shoulder. His body tensed. He carefully propped himself up high enough to study the ugly red scar.

"You just ain't you without your butterfly tattoo. Why'd you do that?"

I shrugged again, my lips parting to tell him why; but I stopped the words, remembering I had made choices long ago to stop thinking of myself as Butterfly.

"And where have *you* been in the last twenty years?" I asked.

"Nowhere. Everywhere. Anywhere I could make money."

"Kimo," I said, "do you realize how much you talk about money?"

"When I was a kid, money meant nothing. I'd just go live off the land. I've been nearly everywhere on the reservation. Up and down every wash, canyon, arroyo, hollow, across ridges and mesas, paved roads, dirt roads, nonroads, tracks, animal tracks. I know where to find wild onions, different kinds of edible flowers, potatoes, the best nut-bearing piñon trees. I've been everywhere. When I was young, that's all I ever wanted to do. Live on the ground, drink from springs, talk to the birds. Lee and Ella Manybeads, that's how I used to live. Close to Mother Earth."

"And now?"

"I have arthritis so bad, I can't sleep on the ground. I want a house with a solid bed, I want a pickup that's gonna last another hundred thousand miles with no trouble, I want . . . I want money. Most of my life I went where I heard there was money to be made. Except, I got there after it was all gone, or maybe it never existed at all. Then I came back here, thinking money wasn't important. There's so much here that's simple, beautiful, meaningful. But I don't seem to feel that anymore.

There's nothing here for me. Nothing. Except now that I'm here I don't know how I'm going to leave again."

He stroked my shoulder, smiled down into my face.

"Oh my," he said. "I got to tell you this," he said, brushing my cheeks, first the left, then the right. "You've truly got a bloom on you." He nestled against my stomach, interweaving their fingers, and moments later his hands slide off mine, and just that quick he fell asleep.

Holding him, I remembered with sadness the beauty of life with my husband, Jonathan, how'd we'd often lie in this same way, him asleep and me tracing patterns on his skin, our love as sweet and pure as the breath of wooden flutes calling forth sunrise.

I woke up at eleven.

Kimo was already gone, and Garcia sat on the floor, going through my purse.

29

"Surprise, surprise," Garcia said. "You hop in the sack with one guy, you wake up and find somebody else in line."

I pulled the sheet up around my neck.

"Hey, relax. I don't want to jump your bones."

I sat up straight against the headboard, my head so foggy from sleep that I could not comprehend what he was doing in the room. He stood and stretched, his eyes as brown as freshly turned soil. He wore baggy camouflage pants with bulging side pockets, laced black combat boots, and a wrinkled blue Navy SEAL Team shirt, the sleeves rolled tightly in two layers across his biceps. He was heavily tanned, which accentuated the acne pits on his unshaven cheeks.

"Where's Yazzie?" he said.

When I didn't answer immediately he strode quickly to the bed, grabbed my hair by the roots, and slammed my head back against the headboard.

"Where is he?"

"I don't know!"

He ripped the sheet off my naked body, and I curled up in a ball, but he only wanted to see if I had anything under the sheet.

"Oh, come on," he said, "cover yourself up. Doing you would be a waste of time, and extra time I don't have. Your boyfriend, does *he* know where I can find Yazzie?"

"No. Why would he?"

"Because he's working for Marvin's Bail Bonds. He left you a note here, about how he checked in with Marvin and went off to bring a bail skipper back from Sedona."

He shredded a paper napkin, crushed it into a ball, and tossed it at me. I spread it open, but whatever Kimo had written was no longer readable.

"I followed you from the bar last night. I'd've come in here sooner, but I fell asleep in my car. I'm really tired, you know? I've been tracking Yazzie for three days without sleep. I picked the lock on your room, hoping I wasn't too late. Sorry I missed your boyfriend, but you are the one I really want."

I looked around the room for my purse, and he saw it in a corner of the room and emptied it on the floor. He stuffed my wallet into one pocket of his camo pants. After shaking the Ritalin vial, he read the label, smiled, and pocketed it. He swept aside my makeup and lipstick, pawed through the negatives and contact prints of the rodeo cowboy, and finally tossed them onto the bed. He threw my cell phone aside and held up the Bersa, flicking the release catch for the magazine. He thumbed out all the bullets and pocketed them, racking back the slide to make sure there wasn't one in the chamber. He tossed the Bersa on the bed.

"A twenty-two. Woman's gun. Actually, hit men use them, too."

He reached underneath his shirt and pulled out a large revolver.

"Forty-four Magnum. A man's gun. Where's Yazzie?"

"I don't know."

He fished in for a silencer, and after screwing it into the revolver, he fired at the TV set. The picture tube exploded, glass fragments showering onto the bed as the electronic boards sparked and died.

"The Kentucky horse woman, the one who came out here yesterday, did Yazzie talk to her about that Spanish bit? One last time. Where is he?"

He waved the revolver at my head and pulled back the hammer.

"Somewhere on the Navajo reservation. He's looking for the horse killer. But I don't know anything about where he is or what he's doing. The last time I saw him was before you came to my trailer this week."

He chewed his lower lip, sucked it into his mouth, and finally nodded his head. Nodding to some inner dialogue, he flopped the gun back and forth as though he were ticking through a list. He tucked the revolver underneath his belt and pulled the shirt over it.

"Jesus, the sorry part of it is, I believe you."

He picked up the cowboy pictures, sorted through them without interest, and then saw the fax with the photo and information about Kliendienst.

"Who's this guy?"

"A bail skipper," I lied.

"What's the bond?"

"Fifty thousand. I found out he's staying in Las Vegas."

He crumpled the fax and dropped it on the floor, opening the motel room door.

"So that's why your boyfriend went out this morning, to set up collecting your ten percent. Five thousand. I remember days when that kind of money looked good. I'd love to stay here and wait for that dumb fuck to come back from Marvin's so I can work him over. But I don't have time. You tell him, though, you tell him that I was here. And that I'll find him again, after I find Yazzie. And after them, I'll have time for you."

He left the door open and was gone. I got up quickly, trying to see what kind of vehicle he was driving, but he'd disappeared. I closed the door and got dressed. My hands shaking with anger, I collected the Bersa, the pictures and negatives, the Kliendienst fax, my makeup, and my checkbook, cramming all of it into my purse.

I started to call Marvin's Bail Bonds, but I had to get out of the room. I walked back and forth across the motel parking lot, trying to get my anger under control. I angrily smashed my fists against the hood of a Nissan Pathfinder, banging my left thumb. As I sucked it in frustration, I jammed the other hand in my jeans pocket and pulled out the fake driver's license for Elizabeth Jane Henderson and the VISA card.

I called Marvin, who said he'd offered Kimo the chance to bring somebody back from Sedona for $2,000 and that Kimo had left me a message at the motel. I ran back to the room for the napkin, but the maid had already started stripping the bed. I rooted through her plastic trash bag, but she'd dumped half-empty Coke cans inside, and when I found the napkin it was wet, the ink totally faded and smeared. The maid handed me Kimo's straw Resistol hat, saying she'd found it on the closet shelf.

What surprised me most was that I was angry, I was *furious*, but I was not afraid. I wanted only one thing, to return to Tuba City and Mary and wait for Kimo while I used my laptop to start probing the PRCA database. Even though Ben had taken away the computers, I'd stored all my downloads on a separate backup tape, and I knew it wouldn't take me long to set up again.

I had my cell phone, I had a credit card. All I needed was a ride.

Two vehicles over, a young Navajo woman kicked the bumper of a derelict Chevy Monza, the driver's side front fender creased just enough so it almost rested on the tire. I thought if I could help her get it going, she might give me a lift; but she said it wouldn't start. Popping the hood, I motioned for her to get inside and try the key. The starter ground away, but nothing else happened. Choking on the raw gasoline smell, I waved for her to stop. I opened the distributor cap. The rotor had worn down almost completely, and the points were just about fried. Instead of an air cleaner on top of the carburetor, a dirty rag was stuffed partway in the top. I pulled out the rag and held open the choke blade. The woman tried cranking it over, but the engine wouldn't start.

"Even if I get it going," she said, "it still don't run too good. Clutch slips, too."

"Maybe you've just flooded the engine."

"I'll just leave it here. My husband buys these old junk cars, he can damn well come tow it home."

I took off Kimo's hat to wipe sweat from my forehead.

"Trade you for that," she said.

"The car for my hat?"

"Sure. Goat ate my favorite hat yesterday."

"Deal," I said before she could change her mind.

She took the hat without saying a word and gave me the key. She opened the glove compartment and fumbled around. I saw an old pair of handcuffs inside, but the woman ignored them. She pulled out the title, looked for the place to sign, and forged her husband's name with a strong, swift imitation.

The hat was too small for her, but she sat it on top of her hair and walked away. I waited twenty minutes or so, patient, and the Monza started right up. When I started to make a left turn, the fender scraped loudly against the tire. I got out and pulled the fender away from the tire.

The Monza started reluctantly. Driving out of the parking lot, I saw the woman trying to hitch a ride east. I limped east for a few miles, but when the engine coughed and almost died I swerved left across traffic, horns blazing at me, and pulled into a repair shop, where the mechanic clucked with delight as he made out the repair estimate.

"Lordy, Lordy, how'd you even get in here? You ain't gonna get but ten miles out of town before that whole car craps out. You need your new shocks, you need your brakes relined, your points are near fried, we're talking major work here, say, four hundred at bottom, plus you'll have to leave it till tomorrow afternoon."

His eyes gleamed as he totaled up the estimate. "Four ninety-seven and fifty-two cents."

"Sure," I told him. "But I need it in an hour."

"Already got four cars ahead of you."

"You own this station?"

"Yes," he said.

"Here's what you do. Tear up this estimate and write another one for seven hundred dollars and get to work on it right away. You get an extra two hundred."

"I like that idea," he said. "But to get it done in an hour, I'll have to call in some help. Cost you another hundred. And even then I doubt we'll do the brakes."

"Sure. Eight hundred."

He ran the credit card through his machine, and I was afraid it was no go and he'd take the card away. But after a minute the machine beeped, and he ripped off a credit slip for me to sign. Pen over the dotted line, I hesitated about being Elizabeth Henderson, seeing my life transition to something foreign, unpredictable, unpleasant. But there was no choice, and I signed my approval.

I walked across the street to a minimall clothing store and picked out a yellow blouse and blue wrap-around skirt and changed into them. I had to wait at the cash register for a cowboy who had his right ankle in an iridescent purple cast. He heaped up a pile on the counter, new socks and underwear, some armadillo skin boots, a red western shirt with plastic pearl-colored buttons, some khaki slacks. He waited patiently while the clerk rang up the purchases, but an argument started when the clerk wouldn't sell just one of the boots.

"I'll pay full price," the cowboy said, shaking his head. I drifted off to one side of the cowboy, and as he whipped his head back and forth I recognized him as a rough stock rider who'd got his spur hung up in the gate rail the day I was at the rodeo.

"You're saying you'll pay full pair price?" the clerk said.

"Yeah."

"What would I do with an extra right boot?"

"Hell," the cowboy said, "stick it in the display window, put some flowers in it, what the hell do I care?"

As I left the store, a delivery truck pulled up and a man unloaded the afternoon edition of the *Flagstaff Sun*.

CANNIBALISM SUSPECTED IN HOPI GIRL MURDER

I grabbed one of the newspapers from his bundle.

"Hey, lady, you gotta pay for that."

I handed him a dollar bill, amazed to read about Shiyoma Lakon's news story on TV, which included my name as witness. But I was stunned by the paragraphs where Julia Crow Dog discussed potential motives, including the possibility of cannibalism.

When the Monza was ready, I drove quickly to the NAU campus.

30

Students were drifting out of the NAU auditorium, which was curved like a relaxed horseshoe and had seats for several hundred people. Venetian blinds had been closed against the bright afternoon sun, but daggers of light angled in around the edges of the blinds, dimming and distorting the slide on the screen.

Julia stood at the lectern in front, shoving papers into a briefcase. I walked down an aisle from the back of the auditorium, and when she recognized me she put an arm around my shoulders.

"Help me, honey. I need a drink right now. And you can keep me from it."

Her office looked as though it had been thoroughly ransacked by burglars. Books, journals, newspapers, students' projects, everything was sprawled in total disorder, little of it in piles, some of it looking as though it had been thrown on the floor.

"Took me nine months to make this mess. I've got two more weeks of this class, and I figure after I take what I want, they can clean up the rest."

"What are you going to do?"

"Well. That's the best part. I'm gonna work at the

Navajo Community College in the health training program. Gonna get myself detoxed for good."

"What'll you be teaching?"

"Gonna be a volunteer secretary, work on a certificate as an LPN, maybe an AA in nursing. AA. That's
what I need. I've tried the AA around here, can't stand
the meetings. Because I'm a quarter Navajo, Dennis
Hatathlie got me into the college, into the program. He
wants to be a singer. He's already a fantastic herbalist
and diagnostician. I've had him talk to lots of my
classes. Nobody's asleep or bullshitting or groping each
other in the back of the room when he gets telling them
about walking in beauty, about being in harmony with
nature."

My foot was tapping nervously on the floor, and I
stopped, embarrassed.

"Okay." She sighed. "I know you're not here to say
hello. What do you want?"

"I've got some questions about cannibalism."

"Cannibalism?" Julia laughed out loud, barking
and coughing at the same time. "I only see that in the
movies—you know, airplane goes down, lifeboats,
draw lots. Oh, wait a minute, wait a minute, I see where
you're going."

She rooted around on her desk and found the
newspaper.

"What a joke, these reporters. They wanted to
make the headline read 'Hopi Girl Slaughtered, Heart
Stolen,'" but I told them that was a stretch. Just because
her chest cavity has been opened, and probably her
heart taken out, they think it's cannibalism."

"Is it possible?"

"You've seen too many movies," Julia said, "like Hannibal the Cannibal, who liked liver for lunch. Nobody really practices cannibalism anymore, not in the U.S. One time, decades, centuries ago, the Kwakiutl did it. But now it's entirely symbolic. You'd be astonished to know that the last major documented cases of cannibalism were in China, during the Cultural Revolution. In the Guanxi, southern China, where the whole class struggle took on new meaning with the slogan 'Eat your enemies.'"

She pulled a quart of vodka from her desk drawer and broke the seal.

"Last one. I know you don't believe me. But it's my sacred vow to you and Billie. One last bottle, I told her."

I turned my head as she drank several long swallows.

"Okay. In 1968, in just one county, there are public documents about sixty-four people who were eaten. Names, where exactly, and by whom it was done, even what body parts. The leaders, Red Guards, whoever, they'd eat the hearts, livers, and genitals, then leave the rest for anybody to take what they wanted. Some eighteen people were eaten entirely—even, so the report says, the soles of their feet."

"Julia, I don't need a lecture about China."

"Bottom line, you shouldn't be thinking cannibalism. Think sacrifice."

"Why?"

"Because something was taken. Something powerful, like the Aztecs, ripping out hearts. Somebody possibly took that girl's heart as an act of blood sacrifice."

"A ritual killing?"

Her eyes sparkled, and she ducked her head, as though she'd caught herself excited about something and was surprised to discover the feeling.

"If this was, say, Brooklyn, on the east side of Prospect Park, where people find dead chickens and things hanging from trees, then we'd talk about rituals, about ritual sacrifice, for all the primitive reasons that anthropologists observe and categorize and try to explain."

"What's different about this?"

"Where it happened. That's what's different. There simply is no group of people out here who would do such a thing."

"What about a Satanic cult, a serial killer, a psycho?"

"You've seen too many movies."

"Anything is possible, any one person, or group of persons, is capable of doing anything to anybody else."

"First, think gender."

"Meaning?"

"A blood sacrifice is almost always gender specific, identified with men."

"Why?"

"Narcissism. Listen, there's a lot of studies, a lot of literature, all the way back to Freud. You've got people at the FBI who deal only with the psychology of serial killers. Why not just stretch that a bit and say that instead of using the word 'serial,' we say that a man kills because he's driven to the act because of any number of psychodynamic factors that make him feel the need to regain some sense of power he feels he's lost. This kind of man operates on the margin of control, of self-esteem, of being out of balance with life around him, of struggling to overcome a terrible anxiety."

"Everybody gets anxious."

"But men and women deal with it differently. A woman turns to her network of friends, relatives, those people she's connected to. An anxious man usually feels apart from other people, has no emotional network that will help him. He feels helpless, he feels out of control, he feels like he's lost power. Through sacrifice, he regains power."

"But only if he kills women?"

"Right. Sacrifice is all based on man's fear of woman, of being different from woman, who gave birth to him, who nurtured him, who has the power of life. They can symbolically merge with a woman by sacrificing her life, to gain her power."

"What kind of man am I looking for?"

"Probably an Indian. Take the Navajos, for instance. They're afraid that some animals can't be controlled, that some animals are evil and may prey on the people."

"Skinwalkers."

"Evil in the shape of a wolf. Now, put that with what I was telling you about male narcissism, and you might have somebody who's just twisted enough to think he can satisfy his lack of power, his inadequacies, his anxieties and fear, satisfy everything by brutalizing women to the point where he actually mutilates them."

"Do you think this killer is probably a Navajo?"

"With all this new age shit, *anybody* can be an Indian. So maybe you've got some white guy who's a skinwalker in spirit. Everybody out here knows about skinwalkers. A lot of whites snicker at it, even though they might subconsciously avoid walking under a ladder, knocking on wood, whatever. But, it's possible that a white man, lost in his own society, finding no spirituality there, could decide he'd gain back some power by, in some kinky way, imagining and then acting out being a skinwalker."

"That's the strangest thing I've ever heard of."

"But, psychodynamically, it's possible. We assume roles most of our life. Some of them we play out quickly, privately, even subconsciously. But some of them we put on like new clothes. This whole new age phenomenon wouldn't have happened if a lot of white people, both men and women, didn't write books that were based in large part on Indian spirituality. All of them are about what's good about being an Indian, what's pure, being in touch with the land. But what if somebody worked at getting in touch with what's evil in Navajo beliefs?"

"Thank you," I said.

"How'd you get involved with this business?"

I started to explain about finding Judy Pavatea but fell silent and finally shook my head, not wanting to talk about it anymore.

"You had a good thing going with computers," Julia said. "I always thought of you as a very private person who stayed out of trouble."

She lifted the vodka bottle in a salute as I left her office.

In the parking lot my cell phone rang.

"This phone number was passed on to me," a woman said. "I've got these Polaroids. I'm in Sedona. Come tell me what else you've got to sell."

Billie's pot!

"I can be there in an hour," I said. "Where do I go?"

"Look for Begay Rugs. I'm Marilyn Begay. My place is in the big shopping center. And let's get this absolutely straight. Whatever you've got to sell, we're not talking about putting it out on the counter. We're talking only about private buyers."

31

"There's two things about starlings," the old man said. "Noise and shit."

Patterned western shirt, a full head of neatly trimmed white hair, knife-edged polyester slacks, and a turquoise bola tie snugged up tightly against his wattled neck. I gave him a noncommittal nod, which he took to be encouragement. He'd lost track of his wife, wandering somewhere in the crowded aisles lined with Navajo rugs, but instead of being impatient with finding her, he'd started talking to me.

"I remember the time I was ten, apprenticed out to this truck farmer, ran an apple orchard over near Cairo, Illinoise. Farmer started me in picked apples, ten hours a day, but when them starlings arrived he soon switched me to an old tin pot and kept me hollering at the starlings, trying to drive 'em away, you see, 'cause they were shitting all over his apples."

Irritated, I nodded again, trying to find Marilyn Begay somewhere in the crowds of women, most of them temporarily escaped from a five-day Phoenix heat wave with temperatures above 110. After the forty-minute flight up, however, they'd quickly learned that

Sedona was just as hot as Phoenix. Churning in and out of the restaurants and boutiques of a large shopping mall, searching more for cool, dry air than fashions or antiques, many of them descended on Marilyn's gallery.

Three sales clerks struggled to handle the tightly packed crowd of women who expected special attention, avoiding body contact with the others but unwilling to show disdain, like finding yourself with a mouthful of rotten fruit that you want immediately to spit out but cannot because of politeness or some other social habit.

A young clerk turned from a sale. She extended her lower lip, blowing upward at a wayward lock of streaked chestnut hair, at the same time pulling her damp silk blouse away from her chest and blowing down. She handed me a map of the Navajo reservation with nine red circles marked at different points.

"This map shows the nine major styles of Navajo rugs and blankets."

"Marilyn called earlier," I interrupted. "Where can I find her?"

"Try the rare-rug room."

Another flock of women pushed in the front door. I found myself pressed even closer to the old man, who was glad he had my attention back.

"That farmer tried *smoke*," he said. "Then he had these recordings of *hawk* cries, even put hawk *decoys* up in the trees. Finally got so he spent the whole day firing double-aught buckshot, killing more apples than birds, got them starlings so pissed off they started dive-bombing him, just like Jap kamikazes in the Pacific, what a time, I tell you. When did you say my wife was going to meet us here?"

Anxiety and anger in his face.

"I don't know your wife," I said.

"Ethel, Ethel."

He began shouting out loud. All talking stopped, and the only sound came from the stereo system, a piano concerto. A well-dressed woman, well into her seventies, materialized beside him, holding a blanket.

"Ethel," he said happily.

"My chief."

She saw my confused look.

"His short-term memory's going. But we're making the most of it."

"How long have you been married?"

"Oh, we're not married," he chirped.

"Thirty-nine years," she said.

He took her arm and they left the gallery. I pushed angrily through the crowd, but a woman stopped me in the Teec Nos Pos section of the gallery. She'd flipped a pile of rugs back to a particular design.

"Could you help me a moment?"

Fortyish, carefully dyed ash blond hair, the woman had on half-lens close-up glasses and was reading a price tag.

"I don't work here."

"Oh. Sorry. You look, well . . ."

Indian, I realized.

"I've seen Persian carpets with a similar design, just this simple geometric pattern, for a lot less money."

The price tag read #EYY6582, 89 x 140 INCHES. ELLA

BEGAY YABANY, RED MESA. The tagged price was $14,495. The woman made a subtle adjustment to the left shoulder pad of her jacket to distance herself slightly from a Choctaw clerk who appeared suddenly at her elbow.

"I mean, it is an outrageous price, don't you think?"

"A rug this size," the Choctaw said rudely, "roughly seven by twelve feet, probably took Ella the best part of a year to make."

"Turn around," the woman said to me, ignoring the Choctaw.

"What?"

"Just turn, you know"—waving one hand in a circular motion, eyeing me over the top of the close-up glasses—"turn for me."

Astonished, not knowing what else to do, I turned halfway, turned back.

"Have you ever done modeling? High fashion, I mean, not catalogs or print."

"Oh, please," I said, looking away from her, "leave me alone."

"How long have you been using smack?"

"What?"

"Heroin. That strung-out look, they don't much use it in New York anymore, but it's perfect for LA. Here."

I was stunned as she stuffed a business card into my hand. Palming the card, I slapped her cheek, hard, the card falling between us.

"I like that spirit," she said without missing a beat. "If you ever get to Los Angeles, call me. Keep that habit and I can make you a lot of money."

Furious, I pushed past her to the rare-rug room. The Choctaw woman followed me and motioned me to another door. Inside what looked like her office, she locked the door and sat down tiredly on a unopened sofabed.

"I'm Marilyn Begay," she said, rubbing her left elbow. "Always wanted to slug women like that. Never could do it."

She was five feet nine and weighed nearly three hundred pounds, arms and fingers garlanded with turquoise bracelets and rings, around her neck a $5,000 squash blossom necklace; she wore a brownish, pleated calico skirt and a green velveteen blouse with huge half-moons of sweat under her arms. Her face was lined with fatigue, and a nervous tic flickered in her left eyelid.

"You called me?" I asked.

She eyed me for a long time. A red spot bloomed on her elbow from the repeated rubbing. She lit a small black cigar and smiled wearily.

"Let's do a test."

"What?"

My anger bloomed, and she saw it and leaned forward, eyes bright and steady as she rummaged through the papers on her desk and held up the *Flagstaff Sun*. After creasing the front page, she circled my name with a marker pen.

"Moment I saw you my bullshit detector went off, honey. Don't get so offended. I know everybody around here who deals in private material, and I don't know you, I've never heard of you, so I've got to believe you're just starting down this road. But why are you dealing in stolen merchandise? I'm not quite sure what to do about you."

"Are you the buyer for what I have?"

"Honey, beginning today, for me it's just not that simple anymore."

She heaved herself up from the sofa and went to a pile of blankets across the room. She picked up a three-pound blanket and held it partway open for me.

"If you're dealing in private material, maybe you recognize this blanket. It's a Honal-Kladi, what we call a chief's blanket, a Bayeta. This one's old and rare."

She held the blanket fully open. The design was simple. Three main sections of black and red bands ran across the top, bottom, and center, with alternating thick bands of black and white between the top center and bottom center. Each of the three main banded sections ended at left and right in triangles, the tips of which pointed toward the center of the blanket. Each triangle contained successively smaller colored triangles within it, beginning on the outside colored red and moving through black and white to red again at the center. Directly in the center of the top- and bottom-banded sections lay a square within a square, while in the middle of the center section lay a diamond within a diamond, and inside this a Roman cross.

"I've got a signed provenance, dated from the late eighteenth century, that it's made of true Bayeta yarn, probably imported from Turkey to Mexico, where it got unraveled, native dyed, and then twisted into a single strand yarn."

"Beautiful."

"Beautiful? Shit, it's extraordinary. I could get fifty thousand for this. Any one of those Phoenix vampires out there would kill to have it on their wall. But the truth is that this rug's a fake from Mexico. I've been selling fakes for two years. And between the time I called you earlier, and you showing up, I've been doing a lot of thinking."

The clerk with the streaked chestnut hairdo poked her head inside.

"That woman says she'll go fourteen five on the Yabany rug."

"Okay."

The door closed.

"I don't care about fake rugs," I said. "I'm here to find a buyer."

"We're getting to that. I just don't have things worked out yet, I just don't quite know what I want to tell you. That Yabany woman, I've been to her hogan, I know how little money she's got. Do you believe in visions?"

"What?"

She flitted from one thing to another too fast for me to follow.

"I have this bad vision again and again. Two, three nights a week. Or maybe it's just a bad dream, but I can't stop it. I'm almost afraid to go to sleep."

Where was this going?

"A friend took me to her psychic to get a reading. You've heard about all the new age stuff down here. Power spots, psychic energy. All those rich white women, after they shop in here, maybe buy a ten-thousand-dollar blanket for their den, they go off to the power spots. Well, about this psychic. I'm skeptical, but I go along, because I was raised to believe in visions, and while I wouldn't call this dream a vision, I'm not sure, am I, and it's driving me crazy. So there I am, sitting in the psychic's living room. She's so normal looking, she could be a middle-class housewife. She's silent, I'm silent, and then she examined my right palm and the sole of my left foot, felt my temples and other bumps under my hair, all the while humming and bobbing her head, and finally she asked if I was having bad dreams. Astonished, I gave her every detail. For fifty dollars, payable in advance, she'll explain it. I paid. She told me about the time when the ancient Chinese philosopher Chuang-tsu dreamt that he was a butterfly, happily taking life's pleasures without wondering who he was. Then he awoke and wondered if he'd actually dreamt of being a butterfly, or if the butterfly was now dreaming that it was Chuang-tsu."

"Excuse me," I said. "I don't have time for this."

"'Thanks a *lot*!' I tell her."

I don't think she even knew I was there at that moment.

"Fifty dollars for some nonsense about Chinese butterflies, I told her. I'd feel better if you'd offered the usual advice, like how there are no quick solutions to problems and you've just got to persist. Or how life isn't just all great or all terrible, but somewhere in between. Stuff like that, which I'd already heard fifty times over from therapists and friends and read in a hundred self-help books. And she says, 'You don't know what's real anymore. You spend so much time making money, selling things that don't really belong to you, and you no longer know what's a dream world to you and what's reality. And if you really won't pay attention to what I tell you about Chinese butterflies, why don't you go home?' I didn't know what that psychic meant until I got called about you. It's not a dream I'm having. It's a vision. You're looking down at me, and I'm looking up at you, and we both are seeking answers."

"Why are you telling me all this?" I said, thoroughly confused, as though I'd come to talk in one language and was hearing another.

"What you're selling, it's connected with that girl's murder?"

"Yes. I think so."

"I've arranged private sales for pot hunters over the last twenty years, but this has made me confront what I've been doing. And I'm really, really angry at myself for being a part of this. I called you earlier without thinking of what I was doing. So right now I need you to tell me, straight out, are you here to sell me stolen pots, or are you really here because somehow pot hunting is connected to murder?"

Our eyes locked, our lives mirrored and reflected, our anger the same.

"'Cause if you're just selling, once you go down that road, you're never able to go back to who you were. It's like leaving your sheep with somebody while you go away for a year. You think those sheep are going to be okay, you think that person will take care of your sheep, and then you come back and find them with mange and missing ears, your rams killed off by coyotes, your ewes sterile."

Tears gushed unchecked down her plump cheeks.

"Part of me never wants to go back to the Rez. Part of me can't leave my mother's hogan. Part of me has gone long past the point of not having enough money. Part of me can't deal with how I make money by selling these fakes."

"Why are you telling me all this?"

"It's a warning, honey. You're living in Tuba City. Part of you, I don't know how much, but *some* of you still wants to be a reservation Indian. I envy that. I'm one-third Choctaw, the rest Dine. I've got family all over the Rez. I never see them, because they never want to see me. I dream about them, but I'll never go back to that life because I'm not sure if I'd live or die."

She wiped her cheeks dry, her eyes narrowing, her mouth a tight string, her voice hard-edged and toneless. She thrust the newspaper in front of me.

"So what is it? Are you just selling?"

"No. I'm trying to find a missing girl. I'm caught up in a lot of things, but it all just comes down to the girl I'm looking for, and other girls that may also be missing or dead like the one here."

"Okay. There's this woman lives north of town, just off the Oak Creek Canyon Road. Last night she asked if I heard about something new on the market. Something Hopi, something rare, something I'd never see again in my life. I called Tularosa, and the woman up there gave me your number, and I passed it on to a buyer, who said she doesn't want the pot, but will call you herself."

"Thank you. I'll let you know if she calls."

She picked up the cigar, but it had gone out and she flung it aside.

"No. Don't bother calling, don't come here again. In the last two hours, I've found somebody who'll buy my entire stock and take over the lease. Somebody else bought my house up in the hills. In two hours I've sold off twenty years of my life, since I didn't care about the price. After packing up what's in the house and putting everything into storage, I'll go visit my mother's hogan. After that, who knows?"

32

But nothing happened for days.

I'd left Sedona feeling clever, capable, and close to finding answers. But nobody called about Billie's pot. I brought it back to her the next morning. She unpackaged it and put it back on the shelf with all the others. Her contacts at Hopi high schools had no information, other than a list of teenage girls who had dropped out of school.

Yellowhouse faxed the PRCA the two pictures that Mary had identified, and he got police departments in six states to distribute the pictures at rodeos.

Nobody believes you, Yellowhouse told me later that day. There's no evidence.

Nobody on the Hopi mesas, Seumptewa told me, would talk about missing girls.

When Yellowhouse came by and saw Mary in the doorway, I expected him to take her back again to her parents. But he said they'd reluctantly agreed that to bring her home was only to invite her running away again, and at least they knew where she was.

On the second day, as Mary and I grew more comfortable together, I realized I was losing my intense desire for Ritalin. I had to work at it every minute I was awake, my need so powerful that I'd watch TV for hours to avoid leaving the trailer. Barely able to eat, I forced myself to eat. Barely able to sleep, I watched TV talk shows and infomercials. I connected my laptop to the satellite downlink dish but had no enthusiasm to use it. I had put everything emotionally on hold and was waiting for Kimo to call.

But he didn't. I had no idea where he was.

That afternoon Mary and I drove out on the mesas. I turned in at Hotevilla, trying to find where I'd once lived. I even asked at the store, but nobody remembered, or at least they *said* they didn't remember. I almost went to the Tribal Offices in Kykotsmovi, but I knew that Seumptewa had nothing more to tell me.

Although I felt no discomfort at being on the mesas, after the long miles of sparse vegetation, partially built concrete-block houses, and abandoned cars, I felt no desire to stay very long. That's not *fair*, I thought, there are good people here, happy people here. After buying fry bread near the cultural center, we stopped at a small store and watched Hopis buying turtle shells, bundles of herbs and sweet grass, different furs and feathers for dancing costumes and Kachinas. Once back home, tired and relieved to be there, I was happy to realize that it *was* home. But still nothing happened.

By the fourth day I realized that I'd reluctantly settled for not having found Judy by having Mary with me.

That afternoon I went out and bought two boxes of ammunition for the Bersa and shot off an entire box as Claude watched with questions in his eyes that he never put to words.

That night I slept ten hours straight and woke up as though from a five-day hibernation. And that morning Kimo came back, and my life changed forever.

33

An unmufflered pickup turned into the dirt driveway at sunrise and stopped directly outside the trailer. The exhaust racketed off the aluminum siding until the driver cut the engine, which dieseled, knocked, finally died.

I dug my thumbs inside an orange, ready to pop its sections apart. Even though I was enjoying Mary's company, I couldn't shake off wanting something to happen, couldn't avoid watching TV news, couldn't avoid calling Yellowhouse every few hours to see if he'd traced the photographs. And always, in the back of my mind, I waited for a phone call from Marilyn Begay's secret buyer.

The engine finally stopped dieseling. I heard that nasty wrenching sound made when fender sheet metal's been smashed in and the door has to be tortured open. I checked in the bedroom to see if the noise had awakened Mary. As she breathed, she puffed out her cheeks like gumballs, like a five-day-old baby, and blew spit bubbles.

Hand poised to open the screen door, I stopped. Not ten feet from me, facing toward the sunrise, Kimo

sat among the dirt and cottonwood leaves, his back
against the bumper of a half-ton Ford pickup with
Washington license plates.

"Hey," I hollered incredulously. "Hey. Where have
you been?"

He shifted in the dirt, favoring his left leg as his body
swiveled slowly toward me. An old .30-30 lever-action
Winchester slanted across his lap, and I cut my eyes
toward the several rust lines spiderwebbing down the
barrel.

"Hello, Butterfly," he said. He crumpled the empty
paper sack, and a jay flew up into a cottonwood. "Need
a tune-up," he muttered, inspecting his right thigh. The
left leg of his jeans was stained almost black around the
thigh with a puckered hole smack in the middle of the
stain. I knew with certainty it was a bullethole.

Using the .30-30 as a crutch, he levered himself
painfully to his feet.

The early morning sunlight poked between two
cottonwoods and lit his handsome face. Three dark
lines ran vertically between his eyes, making me think
wildly at first of war paint, but then I saw they were
worry lines, shadowed by the sunlight, like three
deeply etched tribal scars. His upper lip was puffy and
still stitched together with the tiny waxen threads. How
long ago was that? I wonder. How long ago did I believe
so much in Kimo that I thought he'd hung the moon?

He wobbled a bit, and beads of sweat popped out
on his forehead. "Not now, leg," he said. I looked down
as he steadied himself. "You son of a bitch," he declared
angrily, glowering down at his leg, "don't you quit me

now." But his knee buckled, and, surprised, he sat down hard. I banged open the screen door and knelt beside him.

"The bullet still in there?"

"No," he answered. "Went right through the fleshy part. Go back inside."

"Listen," I said for the third time to him, then stopped myself, finally hearing an old pattern kicking in.

"Go back inside your trailer," he said quietly. "Right now. Do it."

But I didn't really hear him. In the last years with my husband, both of us said "Listen" because neither of us did. To communicate anything, we had to force our angry words sideways into the gaps between what the other said.

The pickup door creaked and Garcia stepped out, holding a faded red airlines bag. My anxiety and nervousness rose higher than kites with broken strings. Garcia removed waferlike shreds of blue corn piki bread from a paper sack, eating some of the bread, throwing the rest at a scrub jay that stood sentinel in the nearest cottonwood.

"Hello there," he said.

Sweat continued to bead up on Kimo's forehead, and his muscles trembled under my hands. Without warning, my arms scarcely able to hold his weight, he fainted. I pulled him inside the kitchen and let him slump to the linoleum floor. Garcia shut both doors behind him as I tried to pull off Kimo's jeans. Blood had glued everything to his thigh. Using scissors, I sliced through the blackened denim. Underneath, pieces of red flannel were tied around the wounds with a strip of black silk.

"That's really touching," Garcia said. "But finish it up quick."

I daubed hydrogen peroxide on the wound, blotting sweat from Kimo's face and neck as the antiseptic bit into the wounds and the pain brought him back to consciousness.

"Where have you been?" I said to him. "Why didn't you call me?"

"I didn't have your number. It wasn't listed. I went to Sedona, for Marvin, and wound up tracking the guy all over Arizona and finally found him up at Monument Valley yesterday, but before I could do anything this asshole shot me."

"Now, now," Garcia said. "I'm in a really good mood, but it only goes so far."

A footstep scuffed beside me. I looked sideways to find Mary shrinking in fear against the wall, a sheet clutched around her as she stared at Garcia.

"Who's that?" she whispered. Her eyes cut to him, back to me, and she hunkered down on the floor anxiously, settling right up beside me, looking into his face.

"Mary, don't be afraid. Go back in the bedroom, just for a while?"

She skittered through the workroom door.

"Look," Garcia said. "Let's get going."

"Where?" I said.

"Sedona. You got a shower in here? Tell you what I'm going to do. That girl stays back in the bedroom while I take a shower. I've got some clean clothes out in the pickup. You get them for me. This guy, he's in no shape to help out, but he needs some new pants. I'll take a shower, you dress him up, and then we'll all get going."

Kimo pulled himself up by putting one hand on the kitchen counter. I started to help him, but he waved me off. As I stood up my hand brushed against the rifle barrel.

"It's empty." Garcia grinned. "Don't bother."

He put the red airlines bag on the kitchen counter, zipped it open, and took out his pistol. Looking for my purse, he saw it on a chair and took out the Bersa.

"This is getting to be a habit. Get the bag of clothes."

He walked back toward the bedroom without looking back. I went out to get his clothes. The bench seat of the pickup was littered with fast-food bags, crumpled napkins, and a flood of other debris nearly covering the badly faded, torn upholstery. A paper grocery sack held some clothes, and I took them inside the trailer and with some difficulty helped Kimo into a brown-and-yellow camouflage jumpsuit.

I zipped open the faded red TWA flight bag and found a package sealed tightly with gray duct tape, a map of the Coconino National Forest, a red circle inked around a place near the Banjo Bill campground on the Oak Creek Canyon Road to Sedona.

"Don't fool with that," Garcia said, standing in the workroom door totally naked, holding a towel as water ran down his body. I dropped the bag on the floor and didn't know whether to touch it, pick it up, or just keep my hands off it.

"Hey. Don't be scared." He toweled himself dry. "Just zip up the bag."

The zipper was rusted in one spot, and I had to tug at it. I ran the zipper back and forth over the rusted spot, trying not to look inside. It finally closed. He took clean underwear and a shirt out of the bag, taking forever to get the black plastic snapbuttons fastened before he pulled on his camo pants and laced his boots.

"Listen," I said. "Let the girl stay."

He hefted the bag while he thought about what to say. A vein suddenly pulsed on his left temple, and he ran a finger alongside the zipper.

"Call her out here."

"Mary!"

She reluctantly came to the workroom door, gripping the jamb with all her fingers, trembling, tears running down her face.

"Don't cry, Mary. It's going to be all right."

"I want her to cry," Garcia said. "While we're gone, I want her to sit here all alone, crying, while she wonders what I'm going to do with you if she calls anybody."

"I won't tell anybody," Mary whispered. "I won't do anything, I promise."

"Good. You tell, they'll both die. And then I'll come back for you."

"You bastard," I said. "She's just a frightened young girl."

"Hey, we were all young once. Let's go."

He let me help Kimo outside and watched as I locked the trailer door.

"My pickup is shot. We're going to take your car. He goes in the trunk."

He had trouble with the key in the trunk lid but finally got it open. He pulled out two plastic garbage bags, looking quickly inside them.

"Clothing. Put them in the backseat. Biakeddy, crawl in there."

After folding himself carefully into the trunk, Kimo stared at me as Garcia closed the trunk lid and tossed me the keys.

"You drive."

As he was settling himself in the passenger seat, the glove compartment lid banged down on his knee. He pulled out a registration slip.

"Who is Marvin Attakai?" he asked. "From Window Rock?"

"Nobody important."

"You're not driving some stolen car, are you?"

"You can see it's signed over to me."

He dangled the handcuffs in front of me, but after getting no reaction from me, he returned them to the glove compartment. I started the engine, and it banged and wheezed.

"Jesus. Will this piece of shit get as far as Sedona?"

I pulled out onto the street. He looked straight ahead through the windshield, smiling, his hand flexing on the red bag as we drove in silence down through Flagstaff and south to Sedona.

34

We dropped down Oak Creek Canyon Road toward Sedona, dipping and plunging and dropping a hundred feet or so with every switchback.

Fighting the wheel through the curves, I had the feeling I'd jumped onto a carnival ride, the lousy shocks and brakes making the Monza nearly uncontrollable as we skittered around the switchbacks, avoiding traffic coming up and always swinging directly into the sun and feeling blinded and not knowing what was coming up the hill. *Get out of my way!* I found myself screaming. *I'm coming down.*

At the last switchback we could see the road leveling out below us, with several cars stopped at a roadblock. I started to brake, scared I wouldn't be able to stop. Garcia shouted for me to stop. The Monza swung back and forth as I struggled for control, the front wheels wobbling violently for a few seconds on the lip of the concrete. Finally I was able to pull onto the shoulder, and I braked to a stop. Garcia unzipped the flight bag to put his gun inside, his eyes flicking from me to the roadblock.

"Here's the deal," he said finally. "If they get snoopy

at the roadblock and want you to pop the trunk, tell them the key's missing."

He twisted the trunk key off the ring and forced his hand down inside my bra, leaving the key there without touching my breasts. I pulled back on the road. Rounding the next curve, I had to stand on the brake to avoid running into two sheriff's cruisers angled across the road, blocking traffic in both directions. An officer waved me forward until he stood just outside my window.

"Good morning, ma'am."

Tan uniform. Coconino Sheriff's Department. Square face and heavyset torso. A metallic name tag, with the name KAVENA etched into the metal, the indented letters painted as black as his eyes and hair. Behind him stood a man in street clothes.

Above the nonchalant, practiced smile, he had that expressionless gaze that policemen perfect, the policeman's gaze that freezes your blood if you're pretending to be somebody you're not, or if you're lying and it's a weak lie; whatever you're doing, you're not sure the lie is strong enough when that gaze beats against you.

"What's the problem, Officer?"

"Oh, nothing much." Scanning the backseat. "Could I see your driver's license, ma'am?" He smiled, waited patiently with the gaze locked on me for several seconds until I broke eye contact and dug the fake license from my pocket.

He studied it carefully.

"Elizabeth Henderson. That you?"

I nodded. He showed the license to the man

behind him wearing a blue windbreaker with DEA in yellow letters on the back. He flicked his eyes over my license while paging through a sheet of printed names. He shook his head, and Kavena handed me back my license.

"And you, sir?"

Garcia took out his wallet, carefully removed his driver's license, and with a smile handed it past me to the officer.

"Miguel Garcia. That you, sir?"

We waited while the DEA man repeated the check-list procedure, shaking his head again. Kavena passed the license across me to Garcia.

"I believe, you know," he said to me.

"What do you mean?"

"The fish sticker on your front bumper. Christian symbol. I have one on my bumper. Not the sheriff's cruiser. My own pickup. Do you believe?"

"No."

"Well, maybe someday."

A four-wheel-drive vehicle pulled up behind me, a dirt bike strapped on behind and fishing gear bristling like antennas from all open windows.

Kavena leaned in my window.

"Nice talking to you, Miss Henderson."

"Can you tell me where we can find Harlow Canyon Road?" Garcia said.

He smiled so hard, his eyes seemed they'd nearly bust from twinkling.

"You're almost there," he said. "Go about seven miles and turn left at Jesus."

He waved me forward. One of the sheriff's cruisers pulled out to let me pass, and I drove extra careful, hands shaking on the steering wheel, panicky about Kimo hidden in the trunk. Seven miles later I stopped near a red sandstone statue of the Last Supper. Before Garcia could protest I got out of the car, walking away quickly to think things out.

A bird sat on His nose. I caught myself thinking of Him with a capital *H*, something I hadn't done for thirty years, since Father Andrew droned his Christian homilies at the Moencopi Mission School. Surrounded by several shrubs and large rocks, He knelt in front of an enormous chunk of red sandstone, His arms extended, hands clasped on the rock, head turned upward, beard and hair running down toward a robe that covered the rest of His body and flowed on the dirt in layers like a bridal gown. The other disciples were chunky and didn't look as good as Jesus. They all sat belly-up to a draped table, but all figures to the left of Jesus had been beheaded. A small sign asked for contributions. The attached metal cup was empty.

"Let's go," Garcia said, appearing beside me.

"Please," I said, "can't you leave us out of this?"

He grabbed me, ripped open my new yellow blouse, tore off a sleeve, and whipped it back and forth across my face.

"You're hurting me."

"You talk like some stupid fucking kid in a TV show. *You're hurting me.*"

He ripped the blouse off completely and smacked my mouth with the side of his hand, as if he were wip-

ing off chicken grease, but hard. A station wagon
zipped by, and I saw a man and woman bug-eyed,
watching me standing in my bra. The man hit the brake
lights for a second, but the woman said something and
he sped up and drove away.

He rooted through the plastic bags of clothing in
the backseat and found a Dallas Cowboys sweatshirt. I
pulled it on. We got into the Monza, neither of us saying anything, the engine missing so badly that I had to
crawl up the road in low gear for half a mile until we
came to an enormous house nestled into a red-rock
cliff.

Unbleached redwood siding, grayed from the sun,
acres of glassed windows, and a Mercedes in the car-
port. We were waved inside by an old Mexican woman
wearing an apron and holding a bunch of carrots and a
carving knife. She showed us into a three-story living
room and left without saying a word.

I recognized some nineteenth-century Navajo rugs,
pottery that was recognizably Anasazi, some modern
sand paintings, and an amazingly large collection of
Hopi and Zuni Kachina dolls. Moving around an ornate
teak bookcase, I came upon an incredible collection of
pre-Columbian pottery and jewelry, displayed casually
in an unlocked glass-front case.

"Good afternoon."

The woman wore a blouse and slacks made of a
soft, sleek fabric, her hair highlighted with amber
streaks on honey blond. The Mexican maid offered us
cheese and fruit, set out on a fancy silver platter with a
silver fruit knife and an elaborate cheese slicer with an

ivory handle. She set it on a sideboard and left the room. None of us looked at it.

"I'm late for brunch," the woman said. "What have you got?"

Garcia opened his red bag and took out the package wrapped in duct tape. He tried pulling off the tape, then picked up the fruit knife and cut through it. The woman's cool demeanor changed as she bent quickly to look at the package. Sweat suddenly beaded on her neck, and her breathing quickened.

Garcia pulled out a tiny piece of carved wood.

"Talaotsumsime."

My thighs trembled and I planted both feet solidly on the oak floor, feeling as if I were standing on a lake sheeted with the first winter's ice and it was cracking beneath me. I would have tolerated anything else underneath that duct tape, I'd have accepted his stealing anything else for money, so desperately did I want to believe that he wasn't the person at Oraibi who killed two people and stole from the shrine.

"Priceless," she said, holding out her palm, into which Garcia placed the carving. She closed her eyes, fondling the wood, delicately putting a long fingernail against the crude face. She raised it to her lips, stroked it softly against her cheek.

"Not priceless," he said, "but very, very expensive."

"Garcia," I said. "Please tell me you had nothing to do with killing those two people in Oraibi."

His eyes flared open, incredulous.

"What people?"

"How did you get those carvings?"

The woman cleared her throat, and Garcia pushed me aside.

"How many do you have?" she said.

"Two. And two *aloosaka*."

"And you're selling them as a set?"

"Only as a set. A onetime purchase."

"Priceless," she said again.

"Not really," Garcia said.

"How much?"

"Fifty."

She smiled. "Oh, not that priceless."

A vibration in my head, all my nerves stretched to the edge of their elasticity and resilience, everything ready to break. I didn't know how to stop him.

"Fifty."

"Twenty-five."

"Forty."

"Twenty-five."

"Thirty-five. That's it."

She picked up a manila envelope from a magazine stand and casually removed three thin, paper-banded packets of new hundred-dollar bills. Then she pushed aside the cheese tray and lined the packets in a row.

"Thirty."

But Garcia noticed her sweat beads, knew he'd come down far enough.

"Thirty-five. No less."

"Done."

"Garcia," I said quietly. "You can't do this."

He put his face close to mine, his eyes blank, the grin starting and stopping.

"You can't sell those things."

Before I could react to the motion of his fist, he punched me against the right side of my jaw. I dropped to my hands and knees, face almost on the floor, feeling nauseated, hearing myself make a mewing sound. I crawled around on the floor, trying to clear my head. He ignored me, holding two packets of money in one hand and slapping them with the third. I put my free hand inside the flight bag, and he drew a deep breath, trying to get to me, but I pulled out his gun and pointed it at him.

"Don't move."

"I'm not moving."

I'd never held a revolver before. I couldn't figure out the differences between it and the Bersa, had no idea if a revolver had a safety on it. I didn't quite know what to do with each finger, and I saw him eye me, looking for an edge.

The woman moved toward the telephone but saw the look on my face.

"Listen," she finally said, "I've changed my mind."

"Go out to our car," I told her.

"Please. Leave my money, take these things, and get out of my house."

"Get the handcuffs. Out of the glove compartment."

She fidgeted, glanced at the phone, at the envelope of money. I moved the revolver between the two of them. She nodded and went outside.

"Garcia. Just tell me you didn't steal these things from Oraibi."

"I didn't."

He slid his left foot forward about six inches. I put both hands on the checkered hard rubber grip in a shooter's stance. He laughed without humor, almost in tears.

"Why?"

"Money. What else?"

"If you didn't steal them, how did you get them?"

"Albert Grody."

"He stole them?"

"Yes."

"But he's dead."

"He sold them to somebody, who sold them to somebody else, who called me because he didn't know the market."

"Where are the two missing ones?"

He started to lie, then saw the look in my eyes and wet his upper lip with his tongue. He shook his head and started toward me.

"I don't know. I swear. Only the four, that's all I have."

"Lie on the floor."

"What?"

"Do it. Lie down on the fucking floor, lie on your belly."

He put a hand behind him, lowered himself slowly to the floor, and rolled over on his belly. I knelt beside him and put the end of the revolver against his neck. I cocked the gun. The precise mechanical click made him draw a deep breath.

"Did you kill those people at Oraibi?" I asked again.

"No."

"I want to believe you, Garcia. I want to believe more than anything else in the world that you had nothing to do with killing them."

The woman came back inside with the handcuffs, dangling them from two fingers as if they were a dead mouse, something distasteful and unnecessary in her house.

"Jesus God," she said when she saw me with the gun on Garcia's neck.

"Be quiet," I said.

"What's going on here? I have a right to know."

She'd had a bad scare at first, but the trip out to the car had given her some courage. Not that she wasn't still frightened, but she had that look of authority that commands people, the eyes and cheekbones and that wide, curving smile that people accede to without question, and all of it backed by the feeling money gives you after a while, the feeling that with enough money you can control anything.

"Get out of my house."

I swiveled the revolver toward her and she pressed her lips together, shaking her head sideways, unwilling to say anything more but determined to protest even in the way she shook her head, and her hands started to shake.

"Where's the bathroom?"

"I've got three, uh, there are three bathrooms."

"Which one is the closest?"

"Powder room."

"Where?"

"Down there." She pointed down a hallway.

"Throw the cuffs at his feet."

The woman looked confused but finally threw them down. I motioned for Garcia to pick up the cuffs. When he did, I waved the gun down the hallway.

"Down there. Move, dammit."

"What are you going to do?"

"I don't know," I answered shortly. "I really don't know, except that it's not right, stealing that stuff and selling it off. Go down that hallway to the bathroom."

"You can't leave him here." The woman was horrified.

Garcia looked at me, thinking I might waver, but I just motioned him down the hallway tiled with beautiful Mexican tile, patterned with flowers and vines. He moved slowly, still looking for an edge but unable to find one. He stumbled, dropped the cuffs, walked a step, and then tried to reach back and pick them up. I just waved him forward, picking up the cuffs as I passed them. We reached the bathroom. The door was closed, and again he tried to turn back.

"It's locked."

"Don't fuck with me, Garcia. Just open it. Sit down facing the wall."

He turned the knob, pushed open the door, fumbled for the light switch, and flicked it on, his leg really bothering him. He sat on the toilet without putting down the lid. I put the handcuffs on the tile floor and kicked them toward him.

"What am I supposed to do with those?"

"Handcuff your arms around the toilet."

He started to get up, pivoting toward me, finally making his move; but his right foot slipped on the tiled floor. I pointed the gun down the hallway and pulled the trigger. In that confined space, the explosion set my ears ringing, and I heard the bullet smash into something of glass. Garcia sat down immediately and clicked one side of the cuffs closed on his right wrist.

"Put your arms around behind the bowl and do up your left hand."

His shoulders sagged. Struggling, having to slide down a bit on the seat, he finally had the left cuff clicked tight. Shaking, I let the gun fall from my fingers. I slid down the wall, sitting on the floor six feet away from him.

I heard the Mercedes start up and pull out of the driveway. When I got to the kitchen the woman had gone, along with her money. I found a plastic shopping bag under the sink and stuffed the *talaotsumsime* and *aloosaka* back into the red vinyl bag. I ran outside to the Monza, hesitating for a moment as I thought about getting Kimo out of the trunk, but I knew I had to hurry.

The engine sputtered, idled, and died.

I heard Garcia bellowing wildly from the bathroom. I went back inside the house and was headed down the hallway when I heard a rumbling, grating noise and looked into the bathroom just long enough to see that he'd pulled at the top of the toilet tank, grinding the tank against the bowl hard enough to break the rubber seal. Water poured all over the floor. Screaming with rage, he struggled to maneuver the handcuffs between tank and toilet bowl. He slipped on the water, doggedly twisting the handcuffs between the two parts of the toilet, and I could see he'd be free in seconds.

Terrified, legs like rubber, I stumbled outside to the Monza, suddenly remembering I'd left the revolver and frightened that he'd already picked it up and was stumping down the hallway.

The Monza took forever to get started, but yes, it did start, and with the exhaust backfiring and in second gear, I rounded the first bend and saw the Mercedes off the road, its front end around a pine tree. I stopped and looked into the front seat. The woman wasn't there, but I could hear noises in the woods and figured she was going back up to the house. I didn't care what she did.

I got the Monza started again and careened down the dirt canyon road, barely able to keep things under control because halfway down the brake pedal went right to the floorboards. I panicked and jerked up the hand brake, the engine barely alive, it was missing so badly; and I slid off the road and rammed head on against a large oak tree, my head hitting the steering wheel and knocking me unconscious.

35

Blood inside on the front seat, the steering wheel, everywhere.

I couldn't see.

Pulling up the sweatshirt, I wiped blood from my eyes. The driver's-side door hung open, and I slid out of the car, my left shoulder screaming with pain when I bumped it on the doorpost. The hood had popped open, and steam hissed from the radiator.

I looked at my face in the side-view mirror and saw a long gash across my forehead. I dug the trunk key out of my bra and went behind the car to pop the trunk lid. Kimo blinked at the sudden light.

"You all right?"

"Where's Garcia?"

I wiped blood out of my eyes just as I heard two gunshots from up the hill, and I quickly helped Kimo out of the trunk and into the pine trees alongside the road.

"Wait here."

"Laura, what's going on?"

I staggered back up the hill. The front door was wide open, but nothing moved. After five minutes I went inside. Blood was spattered all over the tiled front hall. The kitchen floor was covered with broken dishes, smashed wine bottles on the floor. The door to what looked like a small wine closet was open, and the entire contents of the racks had been emptied. The refrigerator doors were open, food swept off the shelves, everything evidence of rage.

The woman's body lay on the carpeted living room floor, a gaping bullethole in the back of her head, blood and brain matter staining the streaked hair, her right hand clenched tightly on a handgun. I pried her fingers off it and held it with both hands, staring at it absurdly, reading the name Glock, an automatic nine-millimeter, my emotions so battered that my mind wanted to focus on data, on names, on something named, as though I could catalog and save it like computer data.

Blood again filled my eyes, and I couldn't see for a moment, panicking until I could wipe it away. Frantic, I ripped an ornate piece of cloth from the sideboard and tied it across my forehead, then searched the entire house.

Garcia wasn't there.

I tracked the blood spatters outside. I could see he was pumping out a lot of blood and finally found footprints on a trail leading up toward several red-rock outlooks. I followed them, the Glock out in front of me. As I rounded a boulder, a gun went off about thirty feet ahead of me and a bullet banged off a rock near my head. Red chips flew into the air, one striking my cheek. After a moment I peered around the boulder and saw Garcia disappearing around a corner of the chimney. I kept climbing for another ten minutes, following the trail of bright red blotches on the sandstone rocks. I went up another chimney, and then the rocks tabled off and I climbed into the sunlight.

Garcia sat with his back against a rock. He held the revolver with the muzzle in his mouth and was pulling the trigger repeatedly, but there were no more bullets in the revolver, and his hand relaxed, flopping on the ground. He opened his palm, and the revolver fell out of it. I came up beside him.

"Shoot me," Garcia said.

I laid down the Glock, pulled off Garcia's belt, and tied a tourniquet around his leg. As I wound the belt around again and started to tighten it, Garcia reached out easily, picked up the Glock, and put the muzzle against my head; but he had neither the strength nor the will to pull the trigger. His hand fell back again, the Glock dropping free.

"Shoot me."

"I can't do that!"

Garcia was weakening, his face pale from the blood he'd lost.

"Easy to do. Just pull the trigger."

"I can't!"

"Please. I'm asking you. Kill me."

"Why do you want to die?"

"Nothing left. For me."

"You're still alive. Is that nothing?"

He sighed, and his head fell forward. He was motionless for at least a minute. With a great effort, he raised his head again.

"No. I'm dying. Finish this. Shoot me."

Garcia lifted his arm and put a hand on my knee. His eyes washed across me, blurred, and focused on my face. His face paled, the blood draining from his body, and he shook his head, as though to clear his light-headedness and fatigue, as though adrenaline would flow and strength would return. But really all he wanted was enough strength to talk.

"Please."

I put the Glock on the ground beside him and ran and ran and ran until I heard a shot and then ran some more. I collected the red vinyl bag from the Monza and had Kimo throw an arm around my shoulders.

When we got out on Oak Creek Canyon Road, I waved at cars whizzing by in packs until a Havasupai in paint-stained bib overalls pulled over and motioned us into the back of his ancient Ford pickup. I neither knew nor cared where we were headed until I saw a sign to the Flagstaff airport and realized we were safe.

36

I brought the sacred objects to Oraibi but could not deal with Johnson Pongyayanoma's thanks, could not deal with being there. All my movement toward settling with my past seemed wasted energy. As I drove back along the mesas, I knew I'd never be able to live there, never feel any real connection with being on the Rez, being an Indian, being Hopi.

But I knew that wasn't completely true, because I now believed completely and absolutely in Patrick's vision.

In leaving the gun for Garcia, somebody had died by my hand.

It was a revelation in a way.

Having lived with violence all my life, some of it directed at me, I now wanted retribution and was appalled at my desire for it. What happened in Oak Creek Canyon partially resolved the mystery of who stole what and resolved *nothing* about Mary and Judy Pavatea. And I would not let it stop there! If I could not accept being Hopi, I could still dedicate myself to the truth of Patrick's visionary belief that I would learn about the girls.

Determined to find the two cowboys Mary had identified, I started a twelve-hour nonstop computer session. I hacked into the PRCA site and finally located the database containing digitized images of registered rodeo cowboys. Using hacker connections I'd long abandoned, I arranged for help to construct a high-speed download link from the PRCA computer and ultimately through a satellite. I bought a pizza-size dish and the download gear, set it up, got the link operational at two in the morning, and began an incredibly long download of all the images, figuring when I had them I could work out some kind of search string by age, using date of birth, and limit what I'd have to view. I'd connected twenty gigabytes of memory, all I had, hoping it was enough for the most ambitious hacking project I'd ever attempted. I also had no idea if the PRCA system people would discover the hack and stop my download.

It finished at five in the morning.

Unwilling to sort and view all the images just then, I did the one thing I'd left undone. At seven-thirty, badly depressed, I took the answering machine to Karen Melnick's office, and as soon as she came in I played the tape for her:

"I want you. . . ."

"That's *horrible*," Karen said.

I started to play it again, but she waved her hand, no, don't.

"What's weird is that I think I've heard his voice before."

"Laura!"

"I keep playing it over and over, but I can't remember."

"What do you want me to do?" She blew air out of her mouth, a sigh, a protest. "I really wasn't listening when you came in the other day. I heard your words, but godammit I wasn't *listening*. I knew you were in trouble, but I thought it was Ritalin."

"I've stopped taking it. There's something a lot more important to me."

I told her how Mary came into my life.

"I know that I'm pretending she's my daughter. I've wondered so long what it would be like to have a daughter, and now there's this girl staying with me. But I'm really just pretending she's my daughter. So. What should I do about her?"

"Send her back to her family."

"She'd just run away again."

"Like you did?"

"Maybe. I don't know. I don't know much about her. We've spent the last week living together, but things are starting to change, and I don't know what to do. Realizing she's not my daughter has taken me back so far. . . ."

Turning my head to the side, I got lost, I drifted.

"Laura."

"What?" Shaking my head.

"You've been silent for nearly ten minutes."

I'd actually been thinking about my husband.

"His name was Jonathan Begay," I said. "I want to tell you about him. You've heard so much about what my father did, but you've never really heard about Jonathan. And whatever violence I suffered from men, it was more from Jonathan than my father."

"Tell me."

"In the beginning, nothing but happy times."

"When you say 'in the beginning,' how many years was that?"

"Five, seven. We got married after eight years, and the troubles all started then. But in those first years, we thrived as lovers, soulmates, and guerrillas for Red Power, ready at a moment to load our half-ton Jimmy and travel to any Indian nation needing help. We'd had some fantastic times in that old Jimmy. We'd bought it nearly brand new from a Bittersweet Clan woman who couldn't make the payments. Jonathan drove and I learned how to do tune-ups, reline brakes, adjust the carburetor, usually because we had to clear out of some place with no money for mechanics and wouldn't have chanced a regular garage anyway because we skipped out on the bank payments and usually changed license plates depending on what state we were driving through."

"Did you love him?"

"In the beginning, I loved the way Jonathan handed me commitment. Straight out, with no fancy dinner plates underneath. We lived with the constant hope of change, of making things better. Our taps wide open, love flowing for all things Indian, always primed to square off against the entire bahana world. Brights flicked on all the time, no turn signals needed. Roaring arrow straight toward trouble. Hold back the dawn against the whites. Off the BIA, the BLM, the FBI.

"I once hoped I could freeze-dry the best of those moments, storing their essence away for later nourish-

ment. But then we got married, came back here, and
the barbed wire went up on Black Mesa, separating
Hopi and Dine families by fenced boundaries, forcing
some of Jonathan's clan to give up centuries-old family
land and move outside of the fence. Our troubles mari-
nated like spoiling summer meat. Never once believing
that troubles on the Rez could possibly touch *our* partnership, we suddenly found ourselves at war because I
wouldn't support armed resistance of the Dine Second
Big Walk.

"Just like the land dispute partitioned off families,
Jonathan increasingly partitioned his life into different
political activities, shutting me out of most of them.
Our only passion was sex, which somehow got more
and more violent. . . .

"Wow. Did you hear that, about how I used those
words in the same sentence?"

"You mean sex and violence? Are those the words
you mean?"

"It was a terrible life. We couldn't talk to each other
because neither of us wanted to listen. Jonathan took to
supplying guns all over the country, talking up armed
struggle from Montreal to Pyramid Lake, while I took to
speaking out in public. Show me a bullet, I'd tell people, that'll kill drunkenness and unemployment and
such on the Rez. People got tired of listening to me, I
got so preachy and shrill. So I asked him to move out.
He did, but only because he had to go to Wyoming, or
someplace, I never knew where.

"Two months after we'd separated, Jonathan came
back to the house, and even when I told him to leave

he'd come whenever he pleased. One day I came home to find that he'd sold my pickup, a beautifully reconditioned old Chevy step-side, nineteen years old, only thirty-eight thousand miles after the engine rebuild. Even though we showed joint ownership on the title, he'd forged my name for the sale and used the money to buy a Blazer four-wheel-drive plus a twenty-four-foot power cruiser, fully trailered and now parked defiantly in my driveway.

"I spent hours with a hacksaw, sawing through everything metal I could find on the power cruiser. He threatened me so bad that night, I knew that I couldn't stay in the house any longer. When he went out for some beer and groceries, I packed a bag and left for Flagstaff. Jonathan became so enraged that he put on his secondhand police flak vest and camie clothing, loaded the shotgun, grabbed two boxes of shotgun shells, his Fairbairn-Sykes commando knife, his three fifty-seven with the six-inch barrel and four autoloaders, and the thirty-aught-six ten-X scoped hunting rifle with the hundred-eighty-grain handloads, crammed everything into his pickup, and started cruising the streets in Flagstaff, looking for me. I was walking from the bus stop, so he saw me before he'd been out not more than a few minutes. I often wondered what would have happened if I'd walked faster or turned down another street.

"But he found me. He took me home and did whatever pleased him for hours and hours. The next morning he dared me to complain to the police, boasting that nobody'd much care about what a husband and wife did in their own home. To my astonishment and despair, when I went to the police station, he was right.

"Everything ended abruptly one night when he got sloppy drunk in a Flagstaff bar and savagely beat up a Havasupai who kept pulling me to the dance floor. After serving ten days in jail, furious because this time I wouldn't go him bail, he walked out of the cell, came home to pick up our daughter, and they both disappeared from my life. I kept hearing about Jonathan getting in worse and worse trouble, about how there were both state and federal warrants out for him, how some of those warrants named me, too. Finally, I just drove off into Mexico."

Somebody knocked gently on the door. Karen looked at her watch.

"I have to go. There's a woman, her husband and two sons died in a car wreck, and it's taken me two months just to get her in here."

"Thank you," I said after we hugged, but she held me at arm's length, worried.

"The way you said that, I'm feeling like I'll never see you again."

"Nothing's definite," I said, but as always, she was right.

37

Later, I would agonize over what would have happened if I'd used my computers instead of drifting through the week with Mary, of going to Sedona, of giving Garcia the gun.

After setting up a graphics viewer program, I opened the database I'd downloaded and began sorting through thumbnails of rodeo cowboys, the two faces burned so vividly into my memory that I could flick through the thumbnails far faster than I'd imagined.

Incredibly, I found one of them in just twelve minutes.

Jack Vidalia.

28851 Route 14. An hour south of Cheyenne.

I called PRCA and learned that Vidalia was registered for the Cheyenne rodeo, which had already begun. I called the Flagstaff airport and found out I could catch a connecting flight to Cheyenne in two hours. I told Kimo where I was going, and he protested, but his leg wound had gotten infected and he could barely stand.

"Don't do this," he said. "Send the police after this guy."

"The police have done nothing for two weeks. Why would they believe me now? Kimo, I have to do this myself."

"You're a stupid woman," he said bitterly. "You've got two people who love you and want nothing more than to have you stay here."

But he saw I was determined and he could do nothing about it. Mary was furious when I told her I was leaving, but I was ice when I took the Bersa out of the kitchen drawer and put it inside my suitcase with the fax photo of Kliendienst. I said good-bye and went out to the pickup Claude had given me.

"You ruined my life!" Mary screamed at me. "I wish you were dead!"

Kimo held her in the doorway, but Mary broke away and came to hug me, and we rocked back and forth, back and forth, clutching each other tightly.

"I didn't mean that," she sobbed. "I just don't want you to go away. If you go away, I'll never see you again."

We had a long hug, a truly bonding hug. The best kind of hug, promising redemption and truth and resolution, guaranteeing we would hug again someday.

"You will see me again," I said, and kept my tears shut inside, along with the sight of Mary's face turned to me in disbelief through the rear window.

I was cold, impersonal, disconnected, intuitive, and impulsive.

I didn't recognize this new persona. I'd gone through many changes in my life, but this new persona was something I hadn't embraced since I'd burned off my tattoo. Up to now, that was the sole defining moment of my life, more important than leaving my father, even more important than leaving my husband, Jonathan.

In youth I'd become a butterfly maiden. In one drunken evening I'd lain in stupor while somebody tattooed me with a butterfly. On another lucid summer night I'd realized that the tattoo was my past and I desperately needed a future.

That night I'd awakened next to a Plains Indian I'd met two hours before. Stroking my butterfly tattoo, he told me stories about the Butterfly People. Clanless, wild with *ajilee* passion, he said they fluttered chaotically between flowers and flames, until, consumed with the constant intensity of sexual excitement, their destructive incandescence burst into fire. So that morning I decided to start fresh by getting rid of my tattoo. I drank a pint of Jack Daniel's and let that gentle man heat up a piece of pipe and then press that cherry red brass directly onto the tattoo, searing my shoulder in one quick rotation from left to right.

On the way to the airport, my gut started cramping when I thought of leaving Mary and Kimo behind, and my head brightened with the uncertainty of ever seeing them again. But I'd jump-started my life many times. I could do it again.

38

I rented a car at the Cheyenne airport with my Elizabeth Henderson credit card, then stopped to ask directions and gradually worked my way west of 87 until I found Vidalia's ranch along the Big Thompson River.

A mile past the first cattle-guard crossing, I saw two hands working horses in a corral. One stood at a post in the center of the corral, the other swung a wide noose at a young, skittish mare. I pulled up the car and walked over to them.

"I'm trying to find Jack Vidalia."

"You a reporter?" one asked. "Goddamn newspeople are like vultures, picking poor Jack clean."

"I'm from the PRCA," I lied.

"Say what?" the second man said.

"From Colorado City. You know, the newspaper . . ." I'd forgotten the name.

"*ProRodeo Sports News?*"

"Yes. Jack's been doing so well this year on the bulls, we wanted to do a feature story about him."

"Feature story."

Both men laughed, exchanged looks.

"Don't reckon you'll want that anymore."

"Why not?"

Having roped the mare, the man pulled the rope toward the center post, and they both stood there, urging the mare to run around inside the rails of the corral.

"Is Jack here?"

"Not likely."

"Where can I find him?'

"Hey!"

An old man, tottering on two metal canes, came out of a barn and shouted at me. He hobbled toward me as fast as he could.

"Get off this place."

"Sir?"

"No reporters, no news vultures wanted around here."

"Hold it, Sy," one of the hands said. "She's up from the PRCA, wants to do a feature on Jack for the *Pro-Rodeo Sports News*."

The man tripped and dropped to his knees. I ran over to him, knelt beside him, and offered to help him up.

"You really come here to do a feature on my son?"

"Yes." Getting used to lies.

The man sobbed, buried his head in his hands.

"You're too late," he said.

"What do you mean?"

He lurched to his feet, tottered away from me to the ranch house. I tried to follow him, but he just waved me off.

"What's going on?" I asked the hands.

"You mean you really don't know?"

"No."

"Young Jack, he liked the girls. Him and his buddies."

"Who are his buddies?"

"Rodeo bums like Jack. I don't know any of them, they didn't come here."

"I heard that Jack was registered at Cheyenne in tonight's draw for the bulls."

"Young Jack, he won't be there."

"No, ma'am." The other hand chuckled, mostly to himself. "He'll most definitely not be there."

"Where can I find Jack?"

"Loveland Hospital, most likely. Unless they've moved him to the jail."

"What happened?"

"Lucas Reno? He's got this daughter, Janine? About fifteen, likes to go for a ride, they say. Anyhow, Lucas came home from his feed and grain business yesterday afternoon, two hours earlier than usual. Said he had a stomach cramp, had to lie down. When he got into his house, there's young Jack and young Janine, both of them pure naked, with Janine sitting backward on Jack's face and bending over to suck his cock."

He glanced at me as he talked, seeing how I reacted to his language. I kept my face neutral, not giving him what he wanted.

"Lucas, he grabs his twelve-gauge pump, waves off his daughter, and puts some double-aught buckshot right into young Jack's chest and shoulder. His right shoulder at that. Hell, he ain't gonna be riding no bulls for a long time."

I turned immediately to walk back to my car.

"He liked that young stuff, he did," the man called after me, laughing. "Put that in your feature article, about how sporting young Jack really was."

Outside the hospital room, an overweight Loveland policeman slouched against the wall, coming upright as I approached the door. His nose was broken and flowered with broken capillaries, his gut hung three inches over his belt, but his quick eyes cataloged me in seconds and he straightened up and put his arm out.

"What do you want, lady?"

"I'd like to talk to the boy."

"Nobody inside. Chief's orders."

"I just want to talk to him for fifteen minutes."

"Uh-uh. Can't let you in. Only five people allowed inside."

As he looked at a hand-printed list on his clipboard, I tentatively pushed against the door to see if it was locked. It wasn't.

"Whoa whoa whoa whoa. You can't go in there, lady."

"How long have you been on the force?"

"What?"

"How long?"

"Fourteen years."

"How long have you been stuck in grade?"

"Come again?"

"What would you say if I were to help you to a promotion, to get your name in the papers, on TV?"

"Don't shuck me, lady. I've still got another five hours here."

"What if I told you that he's wanted by the FBI as a serial killer?"

"*What?*"

"If you let me talk to that kid in there, in private, just for fifteen minutes, I'll let you take full credit for connecting this boy to the serial killings. You can say you read about it, had a hunch, however you want to play it."

"I've heard lots of wild stories," he said, "but you do win the prize buckle. Why should I believe you?"

"Call the Flagstaff FBI office. Agent Foxburn. Call Channel Thirteen, the Flagstaff TV station, ask for Shiyoma Lakon. They'll both verify what I've said."

"You serious? 'Cause I don't rightly believe what you're telling me."

"I'll let you take full credit."

"Why?"

"Because he's only half the story, and depending on what he tells me, I'll have to go track down the rest. Now. How about it?"

"Lady, if you're right, if that's true, it's . . . terrible. I've known young Jack since he was born, know his father."

"It's all true."

"God a'mighty. I don't know how to take this."

"Just let me see him for fifteen minutes."

"What do you want to talk to him about?"

"Afterward, I'll give you enough details so that you can take credit for finding out the information I'm telling you now."

His eyes narrowed, and he asked the questions I'd been dreading.

"Who are you? I'll need your name, to call the FBI.
Can I see some ID?"

Ah.

Who *was* I?

If I was Elizabeth Jane Henderson, I was unknown
to Foxburn and Lakon. If I was Laura Winslow, knowing what I'd come to the hospital to do, I'd never be her
again. I took out my new wallet and showed him my
Arizona driver's license.

"Okay, Miss Winslow. Uh, I'm going to go on some
trust here, because the nearest phone is down the hall,
and I gotta be outside the door while you're in there."

"That's fine," I said, crossing the bridges of identity
and history.

"This statutory rape business he's charged with,
you know, it's all got blowed up out of proportion. Just
to give you local background for when you talk to him,
'cause he'll not want to deal with something like the
FBI."

"What do you mean?" Letting him believe I *was*
with the FBI.

"Girls like Janine, who told on him. In high school,
they have this sex education stuff, they pass out condoms like lollipops, tell them all about pregnancy.
Jesus, doesn't that tell you something? I mean, it's a
scandal, what girls like Janine hear. Turns them on, I
figure. When I was in high school, the good girls, they'd
save it for marriage, for their husbands. Now, giving
them condoms, they figure it's okay."

I kept smiling at him, giving him a small nod, anything to get into the room.

"Young Jack's career is probably ruined, even if his shoulder heals up, and what for? Girls like Janine, they're nobody you can respect, putting out like that."

"I don't have much time here," I finally said. "Is it a deal? I promise you. Let me inside for fifteen minutes and I'll make you famous. Can I go in?"

He chewed on his ballpoint pen for nearly a minute.

"Okay. Fifteen minutes. But. If I see somebody coming down the hallway, I'll bang on the door and you gotta promise to come out of there like quick."

"Fair enough. He won't like what I've got to tell him, so if you hear him protesting, it's just part of what I've got to do. Leave us alone."

"Okay."

He looked up and down the hall, quickly pushed open the door a foot. I slipped through, and he closed the door behind me. The boy's bed was elevated under his head so that he was sitting up, facing directly toward me. His eyes opened wide, but he said nothing as I approached the bed. One arm was heavily casted, with the elbow bent. His chest was wrapped and bandaged. The other arm was handcuffed to the bedframe, its fingernails bitten down, the fingers flexing continually, the hand never still because it didn't want to be controlled. His eyes flickered on me and immediately to the wall and on again somewhere else. He couldn't keep them quiet, he was so nervous.

I recognized him immediately as one of the Flagstaff bull riders I'd photographed. He was barely twenty, with a clear complexion, sandy hair cut short, good-looking in a teenage way, and a long way from being a man. He was frightened and trying hard not to show it.

"I'm not here about what just happened to you. I don't care about that."

He wet his lips, his pink tongue moving round and round, his nostrils flaring as he breathed quickly. I took out one of the eight-by-tens, showed it to him.

"That's you."

"Yeah. How'd you get a picture of me?"

I punched his bad shoulder just above the cast. He gasped with pain.

"Hey!"

"Nobody will come in here."

"You out there. Get this woman away from me."

"He's knows I'm in here. He won't come in."

"What do you want?"

"Tell me who was with you when you raped two girls in Arizona."

"Rape?"

There was no understanding in his eyes. I held out Judy's picture, the one Abbott had given me.

"You don't recognize her?"

"No. Who is she? Who are *you*?"

"How about this girl?"

I held up a photo of Mary Nataanie. Again he stared but shook his head.

"Think back a few weeks ago. You're on your way from Gallup, going to a rodeo. You're in a pickup with three other cowboys, you're all really drunk, and you're driving through Winslow, Arizona. Late at night."

"Yeah. I remember Gallup. Had a good ride, eighty-three points, won about nine hundred bucks. First time I placed in the money."

"Who were you traveling with?"

His eyes widened suddenly, not from fear but more out of curiosity.

"You picked up two girls in Winslow. These two girls. You and your buddies took them off into the desert and raped them most of the night."

He shook his head hard, flinging it from side to side.

I held the pictures up in front of him again.

"You were one of the four men who raped two teenage girls. Right?"

"Fuck you, lady."

"Wait. Let me be real clear about something. You've got a choice right here. You can blow me off, tell me nothing, and I guarantee you that the FBI will be beside this bed before the day's over."

I looked at my watch.

"That policeman out there is coming inside here in just about five minutes. If you don't tell me the other two names, he'll contact the FBI and connect you with at least one murder."

"Whoa, lady, I never did no murder. Jesus, who are you?"

The policeman knocked on the door for some reason, and the boy jumped so hard that he wrenched his side; the pain was so intense, I thought he was going to pass out. I waited, impatient, still not knowing which way he was going to go.

"Five minutes left," the policeman said through the door.

"All right," Vidalia said when the pain subsided. "What do you want to know?"

"Who was with you?"

"I'd hooked up a ride from Gallup with a calf roper named . . . I don't . . . Billy, Jack, Bobby, hell, I don't *remember*. When you're small-time, you travel with anybody going to the next rodeo you are."

I pulled out the picture of the other cowboy, the Indian.

"Who's this?"

"Some guy we picked up hitching east of town. Don't know his name, either."

"Tell me what happened that night."

"Well, they wanted to party, so we took them up on it."

"Who wanted to party?"

"Those two girls."

"They only asked you for a ride back to the Hopi mesas."

"Hell, they wanted it. They all want it."

"What do you mean?"

"All them buckle bunnies, they want to fuck as many of us as they can. Same as around here, same as high school. We have this scheme of collecting points."

"Points?"

"Sure. We get points when we ride the bulls. Why not points for all the buckle bunnies we screw? Besides, when you're in a rodeo, just before your draw, it's great to score points, makes you feel powerful, in control, ready to ride that bull. We called ourselves a posse. Like those high school guys out in California, a few years ago. The ones arrested for doing it with girls, doing what the girls wanted, except they never admitted that part to the police."

"This girl"—showing him Mary's picture again—"said you put a bull rope around her middle, rode her like a bull, then sodomized her."

"That's extra points. Fucking them in the ass."

"And what about this?" I said, fighting to control my rage, shoving the picture of Judy Pavatea in front of his face. He pushed his head back into the pillow, trying to get away from me. I held the picture closer. He whipped his head sideways.

"How many points for hacking a girl's chest open? How many points for ripping out her heart?"

He blanched. "What?"

"You heard me."

"I never did *anything* like that."

"Somebody did, right after they finished scoring sex points with a girl just like this one. Somebody ripped out her heart and left her in a Utah cave."

He started to whimper. "Oh Jesus, oh Jesus, I never did any of that part."

"Who did?"

"I don't know. I swear, I don't know."

I took out the fax photograph of Kliendienst and held it in front of his face.

"Who's this?"

"Nobody I know."

"Look again."

"Honest to God, lady, I tell you, I don't know who that is."

He suddenly grabbed it with his good hand, looked close, and blanched.

"I'm not sure, but it looks like Neil."

"Neil Blackgoat?"

My whole body trembled, and I had to grab the bedpost to stay on my feet. Suddenly nauseated, I had to sit down a plastic chair, put my head between my legs. I wanted to throw up, had to breath deeply, slowly, fighting down the nausea. I looked at the blurry fax photo, but the face there was younger, thinner, even whiter than I remembered. I blinked my eyes and stared again, but I could see no resemblance.

"Was he with you that night?"

"Yeah. He wouldn't remember. I'm just small-time to him. He was with us drinking in a Gallup bar, then later he came along in his pickup just when we stopped to give those girls a ride. He followed behind us. Hell, we figured it might make us in tight with him, and he might get us rodeo connections."

"Is he at Cheyenne?"

"Yes. Sure. I swear to God, he's there for today's go-round."

The policeman burst into the room, held the door tight behind him.

"My chief just came in downstairs."

"Thanks," I said. "I'm leaving. This boy's wanted for rape and murder. Check with the Navajo Tribal Police in Tuba City, Arizona."

"Hey." The boy didn't understand what was going

on. "You said if I gave you the name, you'd fix things up with the police."

"I lied," I said.

"You fucking bitch!"

Vidalia struggled with the handcuffed arm, wanting to swing on me. He spat toward my face and started screaming.

"Go get some help," I said to the policeman.

"You wait right here. I have to go down the hall."

I went outside with him, and when he disappeared down the hallway I went back into the room and took out the Bersa and grabbed a pillow from the bed.

"Whoa whoa whoa!" he screamed. "Somebody get in here!"

I shot him three times, once in each knee so he'd never ride again and the third high up between his legs so he'd never lie with a woman again. Outside the door I saw two uniformed men coming quickly down the hall, and I walked rapidly the other way.

I thought many times over, as I drove to Cheyenne, why didn't I just tell a policeman something, why I felt I had to do this by myself. But I'd mistrusted policemen for so many years, I couldn't stand the thought that they might not arrest Neil, that they wouldn't have enough evidence to convict him if they did. I wanted to make sure I found him and made him confess, and then the police could have him.

39

Fifteen miles south of Cheyenne on Interstate 25, traffic inched ahead as thousands of people hoped to get parked in time to watch the parade before crowding into Frontier Park arena for the three-hour rodeo.

Even after pulling off onto side roads, at noon I was stuck on one of Cheyenne's main streets only a mile from Frontier Park. Cars moved slower than pedestrian traffic. Anxious, frustrated, I pulled off the street behind a truck selling buckskin vests, multicolored chaps, and other leather goods. I parked the rental car in the middle of what looked like a potato field. A man came running to wave me off, but I handed him a twenty-dollar bill and he decided to let me stay there.

I opened the trunk, took my running shoes from the travel bag, and sat on the rear bumper to put them on. I slid the Bersa out of the travel bag and tried to remember what Ben had told me about it. I flicked what I thought was the safety, content when it rocked back and forth. I flicked another lever, and the magazine dropped into my handbag. I saw that it was full of bullets. Experimenting with the magazine, I slid it into the

Bersa, felt it click home. I dropped the Bersa into my handbag, making sure nobody was watching.

I took out jeans and the western shirt and sat low in the front seat while I changed into them. Locking the car, I started for the street. I had no idea where to look for Neil Blackgoat or what I would do once I saw him up close. The handbag bumped heavily against my side, and I switched the strap over my shoulder so it could ride on my hip. Even so, the Bersa banged against me with each stride, its weight predicting its purpose. I held the purse away from my body and was suddenly surrounded by a flock of Japanese tourists, all of them tottering along in new, toe-pinching cowboy boots and wearing ten-gallon Resistols, Stetsons, or black, flat-brimmed felt Indian hats. Trying to get ahead of them, I had to push through an increasingly thickening crowd. Near the town square, the crowd surged and stalled. The tail end of the parade went by, most of it featuring either costumed riders or horse-drawn carriages. On top of a flatbed parade float two middle-aged men staged quick-draw gunfights, their guns loaded with blanks, the crowd roaring its approval and enjoyment with each shoot-out.

I passed store after store with painted windows. HOWDY, PARDNER!!! YIPPY KY YAY!!!

A children's store had large signs about clothing for LITTLE BRITCHES RODEO COWBOYS & COWGIRLS. I had to step out into the street to get around a line at a restaurant, windows painted with buffalo and beefalo burgers. One pane of glass had an advertisement for deep-fried buffalo and bull testicles. I stopped at a variety store with a rack of sunglasses in the window, thinking Neil might recognize me from a distance, wanting to be up close before he knew who I was, the Bersa jammed into his ribs.

I bought the biggest framed sunglasses I could find and also got a Cheyenne rodeo gimme hat. Back on the street, looking blocks ahead of me, I saw a Ferris wheel and other carnival rides. The crowd thickened even more. A neon digital clock in one of the bar windows read 12:55. At the intersection of two main streets, Eighth Avenue and Carey Avenue, I finally saw Frontier Park.

Crossing Carey, I found myself forced by the crowd up against the edges of a mock Indian village, complete with teepees. A Plains Indian was doing a hoop dance, five black hoops woven around his head, arms, and legs. The crowd applauded wildly as he finished. I had no idea where I was going. I walked up to a policeman.

"Which way's the information booth?"

"Keep going up Eighth Avenue, ma'am. It's just alongside the ticket office."

I found it after fighting my way through the crowd another hundred yards. Long lines flowed through the ticket gates, forcing me to wait half an hour for my turn at the information booth.

"Do you have a list here," I shouted, "of today's contestants?"

"What event?"

"Bullriding."

"Sure. Hold on." The woman sorted through some computer printouts.

"I want to know if Neil Blackgoat is in today's draw."

The woman ran her finger down the list, shook her head.

"Don't see him. But this is yesterday's printout, and I've already found two errors."

"I'm his sister," I lied. "I just wanted to wish him luck."

"Why don't you check the ready room?" the woman said.

"How do I get there?"

"You got a ticket to get in?"

"No."

"All sold out. You're not going to get a seat."

"Is there a general admission?"

"Nope. Good luck. Next!"

I worked my way between the lines of people going into the arena until I reached the ticket booth.

"I know there's no seating," I said to the clerk, an elderly woman with a fabric eyeshade pushed into her graying hair. "I'm just here to wish my brother good luck. He's a bull rider. Neil Blackgoat? You heard of him?"

"Honey, this is will call only. I've got absolutely nothing to sell you."

I took out a fifty-dollar bill. I'd brought a few hundred dollars with me but left everything else at the trailer.

"Here's my calling card," I said.

The clerk looked quickly left and right at the other people in the ticket booth. Seeing that both were distracted, she palmed the fifty and pulled a ticket envelope out of one of her racks. I picked up the envelope. On the outside I read the name DELILAH GATES.

"There you go, Missus Gates. Enjoy the show."

I removed the ticket and crumpled the envelope, dropping it beside me as I joined one of the lines and finally handed the ticket over to a teenager.

"Yes, ma'am. Stand B. Lower level, section LB."

"Where's the ready room?"

"Say what?"

"The ready room. It's supposed to be underneath the stands."

"Ah. That's the fenced area, right underneath Stand B, where you're sitting. Just walk around to your left, you'll find it."

I moved past a stage offering free entertainment, with a woman country singer doing a mediocre imitation of Patsy Cline. I passed First Aid and Lost and Found and saw the ready room. Outside, it had the same sign as the ready room in Flagstaff, with the same warning about dress code. I went up to the door guard, a young good-looking man wearing tight Wrangler jeans, what looked like $500 boots, and a brushed felt black hat. He looked me up and down quickly, and I saw him glance at my left hand, checking for a wedding ring.

"Excuse me," I said. "I'm Neil Blackgoat's sister. Can you tell me if he's inside there, if he's riding today?"

"Surely."

He turned aside, called loudly into the din.

"Anybody know, is Blackgoat riding today?"

Several noes came out at him.

"Not today, I reckon."

"Does anybody in there know if he's on the grounds?"

The guard looked irritated, but after I handed him a twenty he hollered the question inside, cupped a hand to an ear, and nodded.

"Over at the pens."

"Where's that?"

"Keep going ahead, past the tour bus parking. You'll see some barns, the animal pens. Likely he's in there somewhere."

"Thanks."

The man smiled, took off his hat, and bowed.

"Glad to oblige. Say, I've got tickets for the concert tonight. Garth Brooks. What say, pretty lady? You got anything planned you can't get rid of to join me?"

"I'll let you know," I said, already moving away.

Once past the bus park, I pulled the sunglasses and gimme hat out of my handbag and put them on. I pulled the handbag strap over my head and let it ride on my left shoulder, unfastening the clasp so I could raise the flap and get to the Bersa quickly. I had to keep my hand on the handbag to stop it from bumping my thigh. I walked into the first barn, saw it was full of calves. Past the second barn I saw a large penned area, at least four times the size of the pens outside the Flagstaff rodeo. I walked past a lot of horses until I saw the first of the bull pens.

I stopped, caught my breath.

I had no plan at all.

Most of the pens held hay, water, a bull, but no people anywhere.

I kept walking.

At the far corner of the pen area a man sat on the rails, staring at a bull. I walked toward him, pulling back the flap of my purse, fingertips brushing the Bersa.

It was Neil Blackgoat.

He was chanting quietly, staring directly into a bull's eyes. He had a leather glove on his left hand, which he flexed open and shut, rubbing it with the fingers of his right hand as he chanted. He wore an old blue workshirt, its sleeves ripped off to show his darkened arms. His left biceps rose and fell as he flexed the hand.

I waited until he'd finished, uncertain how to approach him, but he made it easy by looking up at me and smiling. He nodded at me, and I moved closer, five feet away, close enough to see his black hair underneath the white hat.

"Howdy," he said, sure of himself.

"Howdy."

"How'd you find me?"

"What?" I said, startled.

"I figure you decided to go looking for the best-looking bull rider at this here rodeo, and what do you know, here I am."

"I did come looking for you," I said.

"Mostly young girls come looking. You seem, say, some years beyond the buckle bunny age."

"Actually, I wanted to see you about a young girl."

"Who might that be?"

"Judy Pavatea."

I took off the gimme cap and skirled it sideways. As

I pulled off the sunglasses and dropped them at my feet, his eyes narrowed. He cocked his head to one side, and his eyes lit up.

"Hey. I know you."

I pulled out Abbott's photo of Judy and laid it on the ground. He looked at it, bent over, and shook his head. Beside it I set the Curtis photo of butterfly maidens.

"Mind if I look at that closer?"

I moved backward. He came down off the rails and stepped two paces forward to pick up the Curtis photo; he smiled and then picked up Judy's photo, and I saw the realization in his eyes as they came up to meet mine. But nothing changed throughout his entire body. He didn't flinch, didn't shake his head, didn't do anything except smile at me as he moved backward and climbed on the rails.

"You left another girl's body in the Canyonlands."

He rocked back on the rails.

"Oh, yeah," he said finally. "Oh, yeah, I remember that one."

"Do you remember what you did to her?"

"Mmmm."

His muscles tensed as he calculated whether I was close enough for him to jump off the rails and catch me.

"What did you do with Judy Pavatea?"

"Don't recall. There were so many of them."

"How many girls, all together?"

"I don't know."

"You don't remember how many girls?"

"No. Ten, maybe. Twenty."

"Where are they?"

"I don't remember. I really don't care."

He looked around, stretching his neck. I looked quickly side to side and saw there was nobody within a hundred feet. He saw my fear and smiled.

"Nobody else is here."

He gestured around the pens. A roar went up from the grandstands.

"And nobody can hear. Anything can happen between you and me."

He started to climb off the rails. I pulled out the Bersa and pointed it at him. One leg already reaching toward the ground, he froze. I had no idea if the safety was on or off, figured he wouldn't know that anyway.

"Don't get down. I know how to shoot this thing."

"Well now. I don't know that."

Again, I was astonished at his poise, his calm way of speaking. Music spurted loud on the grandstand PA system, as though somebody had turned it on without checking the volume, and I fired the Bersa once, the slug spanging off the rail beside him. He looked at the mark with wonder, his eyes narrowing as he reassessed things.

"If you move toward me, I'll put the next one in your balls."

He shrank forward slightly, his left hand covering his groin.

"What's your real name?"

He shrugged. I pulled out the army picture of Kliendienst.

"Take a look."

I got close enough to hand him the picture and then stepped quickly away from him. He frowned at my movement, uncertain what I was doing. After studying me for at least a minute, he brought the picture up to his eyes. His body immediately grew rigid. He dropped the picture, put his hands on the rail, and got ready to jump down.

"That was a long time ago," he said.

"So your name's not really Neil Blackgoat?"

"I am who I want to be. Anybody's got that choice. Give yourself another name, another life. You could have been part of my life."

"Never."

"Who knows? If you'd ever talked with me, all those times I called you, who knows what you might've agreed to do?"

I want you!

"That surprised you. I can see it in your face. I've got this electronic gadget that you hook into the phone to disguise your voice. I can talk like a hundred-year-old man or an eight-year-old teenybopper. Just think, what if you had picked up the phone one of those times I called, and I'd used my real voice."

"Why did you kill the horses?"

"Taking their power. I got better at it, along about the thirtieth horse or so."

There was only one thing left to learn.

"How many girls did you kill?"

He grinned. "I have no idea."

"Do you remember their names?"

His grin widened. "Never cared about their names.

Don't even remember all their faces. Hell, I don't remember how many horses *or* girls."

He said this so casually that I was stunned. He moved again on the rails, and I waved the Bersa at him.

"So. What next?" he said.

"You're coming with me."

"I don't think so. Let me guess. You're the only one who knows, isn't that right?"

"No."

"Lady, you may be many things, good-looking being one of them, sexy being another. You've got a great stomach, real flat, kinda skinny, but you're beautiful. And you surely aren't going to make me believe that some policeman knows who I am."

"They know about Mark Jacob Kliendienst."

I spoke in the calmest, most rational voice I could call up. I was in an amazingly calm and bright zone, everything blurred out but his face and body and the rails, all these things outlined so sharp that I saw his jeans pocket shredded at the top, white threads showing against the blue denim and a two-inch thread hanging off the side. I had no fear, no regret, no anger, no conscious feelings except ending it all.

"What could you possibly understand?" he said.

"I don't understand any of this. Why did you kill those girls?"

The loudspeaker music suddenly quit. The grandstand announcer introduced the first saddle bronc rider.

"I need to know why you killed them."

"I'm walking away now."

"Don't do that."

He stepped backward, arms raised, just about to turn and run. I shot him in the right elbow. He looked at the blood, stunned, holding the elbow with his other hand. Instinctively he moved sideways, again ready to run. I shot him in the other elbow. His arms dangled, pain twisting his forehead.

"You'll never hold a bull rope again," I said.

That stunned him even more. He looked into the pens at the nearest bulls. He climbed back up on the rails and swung his feet over to drop inside the pen.

"Why did you kill them?" I screamed.

He stood with the rails between us, his boots carefully together, toe to toe, watching me as a collective sigh swelled from the grandstands behind us, and then a moment of silence, hundreds of people holding their breath—and then a roar. He reached into his back left pocket and fumbled out a modern cattle prod. It was shaped like a policeman's stun gun, the size of a thick checkbook, with two wire prods sticking out of one end. He starting walking toward the next pen.

"Don't go in there."

Lurching from the pain in his elbows, he nudged the gate with his shoulder and moved inside the next pen, now five feet from one of the bulls. He switched the cattle prod to his right hand, almost dropped it, grasped it in both hands.

"When I take their hearts, when I hold in my hand the power of their lives, then my hand is all-powerful. I can ride any bull I want."

He walked to another gate and threw it open.

"Stop right there."

"I made myself into an Indian. I gave myself an Indian name, because I thought that was enough. Crazy Horse, Sitting Bull, Geronimo, all those old Indians, they had such incredible power. They could kill anybody. But just calling myself by an Indian name wasn't enough. Then I thought if I learned how to take power from horses, that would be enough, that would grant me success. And that didn't work. But I liked cutting them up. And one day I saw one of those Hopi butterfly maidens. I read up on them, I read up on their ceremonies and their clans. I knew they had a special power. Their power was *pure*, and I wanted it, and I took it. And the police . . . Well. If I'd taken white girls, if a dozen or two dozen white girls disappeared, you can imagine the intensity of their investigation, of the press calling for the killer. But Indians? Who cares about Indians?"

He walked through other pens, opened up two more gates.

"Wait," I shouted, climbing over rails to follow him.

One at a time he kicked the bulls, all of them eating, and they got to their feet, snorting, one of them pawing his front feet into the dirt.

"How many girls did you kill?"

"I have no idea. No idea at all."

"Where are they buried?"

"All over. Nobody'll ever find most of them."

"Come out of there. Now!"

"You sit square centered on a bull," he said, "the

chute opens, you hold on with one hand, and your other arm is flying like a windshield wiper. There's no way you're ever going to be stronger than that bull. It's never a question of if you're gonna get hurt, it's only when. So you need a special power. You need to be in control."

He closed the gate behind him.

"How many girls?" I screamed. "What were their names?"

"I never knew their names. Nobody will ever know. They're gone."

"Where are their bodies?"

He held the cattle prod against one of the bulls and pushed a button. The bull roared and moved out of its pen to join another bull. He fired the prod against both bulls, and they snorted at him, wild-eyed, uncertain what to do as he herded them into one small pen. None of the bulls wanted to be with another, and they milled around.

"Why did you kill them?"

"I wanted to take their power," Neil Blackgoat said. "Tell the police that when they ask about the girls. Tell them how all of those girls were surprised when I put a knife on their breasts and told them how I was going to take their power."

"You don't even know where they are? Where I can find them?"

"Life's just one big mysterious ride," he said. "Who cares about answers?"

He started firing the prod against all four bulls, waiting only for the prod to recharge before he stuck it on another bull and pushed the button. I jumped onto the rails, determined to pull him out of there, determined that he'd live and be convicted and tell where the girls' bodies were and tell all of their names. But the bulls surrounded him, knocked him down. A bull raised up on its hind hooves and stomped directly on his chest, and the prod flew out of his hand. The other bulls got more agitated, kicking him in every part of his body. After several kicks to his head his skull broke apart, and still the bulls kept stomping, his blood and brains churning into the dirt.

Several men came running, looked into the pens with astonishment and fear.

Together, all of them got the bulls out of the pen, away from the body.

I started to walk away.

"Ma'am, ma'am."

One of the men came running up to me.

"Ma'am, did you see what happened?"

"Not really. I heard some noise. When I got close, they were on top of him."

"Jesus."

He ran back to the pens.

I kept walking, past the crowds, out of Frontier Park, down past the shops with their painted windows, the tourists, the crowds, back to my car. I slumped in the front seat for a long time and then, wearily, started up the car, worked my way through the traffic, and found a clear road out of town to the airport.

I neared the airport, following the directional signs, and at the last moment I turned hard right, nearly cutting off a large semi. I had to swing wide around him, his horn blaring his anger, but I settled into a straight line and jammed down the accelerator until I was rocketing south at a hundred miles an hour.

Rummaging around in my handbag, I fumbled out my own driver's license and then the driver's license and VISA card for Elizabeth Jane Henderson and all the ID of any kind in my wallet and tossed them one by one to the wind. My cell phone went next, and in the rearview mirror I saw it crunch on the road behind me and splatter into a zillion pieces. Passing over a river, I stopped in the middle of the bridge and stood against the barrier railing, sobbing as I flung the Bersa far out into the river until it sank beyond memory.

So many things remaining forever unknown.

Girls, horses, names, places.

So much life, gone and untraceable.

At this moment, only a few things are certain to me.

I am Kauwanyauma, Butterfly Revealing Wings of Beauty. I have forty-seven dollars in my pocket, a full tank of gas in a rental car I'll abandon somewhere south, an unwrapped packet of cheese-and-peanut-butter crackers, a twenty-ounce bottle of Diet Coke, a change of clothing, the pictures of my father, the memory of Kimo's hand on my face, and a magnificent hug from Mary Nataanie to warm my spirit.

What more do you need?

ABOUT THE AUTHOR

David Cole co-founded NativeWeb, an Internet corpo-
ration for Native Americans and indigenous peoples of
the world. He spent twenty years in theatre as play-
wright, director, and lighting designer, and also
worked as a production/technical editor in business
and education. *Butterfly Lost* is his first novel. He lives
in Syracuse, New York, with his wife and five cats,
where he also teaches online courses about social issues
and is building a harpsichord.